I0657769

# Brotherkeeper

## LAWRENCE WINTERS

Copyright © 2014 Lawrence Winters

All rights reserved.

ISBN-13: 978-0615957357 (Lawrence Winters)
ISBN-10: 0615957358

# DEDICATION

I dedicate this book to Helise Winters. You are my captain in rough seas, a guiding hand when I am lost, my soul companion who has led me from the battlefield and my dearly beloved..

# ACKNOWLEDGMENTS

I have written *Brotherkeeper* to bring attention to the poorly communicated emotional tension in relationships between veterans, military and civilians. If you do not have a family member, neighbor or friend who has been involved in war, you may not know how profoundly war affects kinfolk.

In my professional life I served as a combat Marine in Vietnam and, for many years, as Director of Veterans Treatment at Four Winds Hospital. I also developed a program called *Veteran-Civilian Dialogues* (VCD) for Intersections International, a New York City-based NGO, and have personally facilitated sixty dialogues and trained a group of cohorts who are currently disseminating this work throughout New York and the country.

I am grateful to a large and diverse group of people who have told me their stories. Their honesty has been the healing salve that has helped me heal from my war experiences. The characters in *Brotherkeeper* are not real but their honest storylines, I hope, will offer truth to the many that live in the aftereffects of war.

I would like to acknowledge some of the people who have supported me in the creation of this book with their feedback, editing and loving: Peter Pitzele (best friend and co-facilitator of VCD), Susan Pitzele (friend and editor), Scott Thompson (friend and co-founder of VCD), Doug Thompson (digital media expert), Marty Keltz (caring friend), Dave Deyo (best friend and fellow Marine), Wanda Haskel (editor), Wanda Nicholson (artist and friend), Helen Winters (Mom), John D. Winters (Dad), Jamie Winters (son), Kathy Wilcox (editor), Janet Seagel, Sam Klangsburn, Andrew Tepper (artist and friend from Four Winds Hospital), Tom Davison (friend from childhood and the Marines), Rich Samalin (music man and friend), Fred Johnson, Ed Tick (author of *War and the Soul* and friend, singer and fellow Marine), Jake Cohen (adopted son), all the folks in the Earth Tribe, Will Taegel (President of Wisdom University), Jim Garrison (Ubiquity University), Steve Lewis (true friend and writing teacher), Ed McCan (writing friend), Julie Evans (writing-group friend), Mihai Grunfeld (deep reader and friend), Tom Nolan (writer and breakfast friend), Mike Harelick (breakfast friend and webmaster) and Tim Brennan (writing-group friend).

There hundreds of folks I left out. I extend an arm around each of you in deep appreciation for your trust and your stories.

**Genesis 4:8-10**

**New King James Version (NKJV)**

8 Now Cain talked with Abel his brother;[a] and it came to pass, when they were in the field, that Cain rose up against Abel his brother and killed him.

9 Then the Lord said to Cain, "Where is Abel your brother?"

He said, "I do not know. Am I my brother's keeper?"

10 And He said, "What have you done? The voice of your brother's blood cries out to Me from the ground."

*When a soldier kills*
*He must dig two graves —*
*One in the earth for the dead,*
*One in his soul —*
*Or he will not return.*

Lawrence Winters

# FOREWORD

Brotherkeeper, by Lawrence Winters addresses the complexities of combat, and the reintegration challenges faced by the warrior, the family, and the community. Amongst the many novels that stare the effects of combat in the eye, Brotherkeeper is distinctive in that it addresses the root of combat wounds: moral injury. If it takes a village to raise a child, this novel shows that it takes community, tradition, and ceremony to welcome home a warrior.

Jake Flynn is a Marine, and the main character in the novel. From the tears on his pillow, to his nightmares and flashbacks he has never completely left Vietnam behind. He is the kind of guy who sees a therapist at the behest of his wife, not because he would allow his innermost feelings to be unlocked by someone he has to pay once a week to listen. His wife, Naomi, does not completely understand the source of Jake's distress, partly because he doesn't share it openly, and partly because she wants him to leave it in the past. It isn't a perfect system, but they get by.

Jake has carved out a pretty good life for himself considering all he has been through. He is a high school teacher and is married to a woman he loves and needs, and a woman who has paid the price for his service, and is unfairly burdened with the effects of Jake's combat experience. Through a lock and key system he buries the traumas of combat deep inside, fights through his flashbacks, and together they take life day-by-day delicately managing (and often ignoring) Jake's condition.

A phone call from Pax, one of Jake's students interested in joining the Marines destroys this delicate balance, and rips the lock off of the thirty years of emotion Jake has stored inside. When a meeting between Jake and Marine recruiter, Sargeant Howie Watkins exposes some of the moral injuries Howie has kept bottled up and almost leads to a suicide, Jake immediately transforms into the Marine that has tried to leave in the jungles of Vietnam. He has always been good in a crisis, but as Naomi says, "you can't live your entire life in crisis-mode."

What ensues is a tale of brotherhood, as Jake and Howie attempt heal their damaged souls. A tale of sisterhood as Naomi and Howie's wife Alma attempt to regain what they have lost in support of their husbands, and a tale of forgiveness as Pax comes to terms with growing up, facing his past, and uncovering truths about a father he doesn't know. To read Brotherkeeper is to know how it feels to take another's life, crawl through the jungles of Vietnam, and the burden survivors carried back home with them, as only a Vietnam Veteran could explain.

Lawrence Winter puts the reader inside the struggles of a loving wife and mother, inside the motivations of an impulsive teenager, and into the head of a Vietnam Veteran, all of whom are struggling to find life's balance. This tale shows how moral injury knows every generation, and has long reaching affects. It reminds us that ceremony and forgiveness, once a staple for those returning from combat, still hold a place. He shows that bonds of combat know no boundaries, and the need for civilian understanding, acceptance, and forgiveness are intergenerational.

Combat veterans, civilian caretakers and loved-ones, as well as those blessed enough not to have experienced any of combat's long reaching affects will find common ground in this story of hope.

- Joshua Gaccione

OEF & OIF Veteran, US Army 82nd Airborne Division

## ✦✦ CHAPTER ONE ✦✦

*He felt himself let go, falling backward off what he could have only imagined was a cliff. Only the sky and clouds were in his eyes.*

*His days of living rolled by like waves on a beach. In his solar plexus he felt an awareness of passing years, one after another, just as he'd passed neighbors' houses on his way home as a boy. All he could hear was a ticking sound reminiscent of grass on the cuffs of pants. The ticking sped up: first to a dull cry, akin to the noise of a distant flock of birds taking wing, then to the steady roar of a waterfall, heard from a few feet away. A lifetime of words was being sucked out of his ears, and he kept falling.*

*He was emptying, unraveling, overwhelmed. All knowledge left him. He fell through his lifetime, not sure if he was going backward to his mother's womb or forward to his own grave. It didn't matter.*

Jake's tears darkened the red flannel roses on the pillowcase. His head rocked from side to side, as if he were in the woods, trying to see something coming through trees at the periphery of his vision. Dawn was a growing line of light on the windowsill below the shades. He exhaled, like a scuba diver rising from the depths with a cloud of air bubbles trailing him, as he kicked toward the light. Tears had pooled in the hollows of his eyes.

Snaking his hand beneath the blankets, he reached Naomi's thigh. He navigated carefully, knowing that if too much cold air reached her, she'd groan and pull away. It calmed him to touch her. Her skin could still the vortex of sorrow threatening to pull him back down into sleep. Naomi didn't move. Jake let his fingers rest lightly on her warm leg.

A bar of sunlight now worked its way up Naomi's pillow waking her.

1

"What's the matter?" she yawned.

"Nothing."

Always something the matter, he thought. And the worst part was that she was right: there always *was* something the matter. But still he was tired of it always being her first question.

He squeezed her thigh gently, hoping she wouldn't notice the tear stains on the pillowcase. Lying with his eyes closed, he sorted out the thoughts lingering from his dream. He remembered seeing vague faces as he fell. His insides had been stirred by death or was it his birth?

Ladders of light from the venetian blinds were spreading across the bed, and he knew that if he let Naomi get up first, he wouldn't have to answer as many questions. So he lay with his cheek on her chest, inhaling lavender and bayberry shampoo scents. As her arm enfolded him, her heartbeat was anchoring his day.

# ✧✦ CHAPTER TWO ✧✦

*"Sherm, why are you so pissed? Jake's just a kid." Harlin pushed the sleeves of his coveralls up his thick forearms. "Did anyone get hurt? No! For Christ's sake, give the boy a break; he's only eleven."*

*Running a hand over his flattop haircut, Sherm took in a deep breath, pressed his lips together and pushed his bulldozer face at Harlin's. "To tell you the truth, I simply don't give a shit what you think. Who the hell are you preaching to me, anyway? You don't even have kids."*

*Harlin broke from Sherm's gaze and headed for his truck then quickly turned and said, "So, big daddy, you just wanted to punish him for not killing a snake? For god's sake, man, wasn't it enough to make him watch you snap the head off the damn thing? No. You have to drape it around his neck and watch the kid's swallowing his screams as it twitched."*

*"Harlin, your over-sized frigging proboscis is where it doesn't belong. Stick it in someone else's bullshit."*

*The sound of gravel crunching turned both men's heads. Ernest, the owner of the hardware store, stepped out from around the corner.*

*"Hey, Ernest."*

*"Morning, Harlin. Sherm."*

*Ernest walked past them and said, "If you're looking for reinforcing-rod, be careful! There's an old black snake, about six feet long making a home under the pile. I seen her eating a rat the other day."*

*"Not any more, Ernest," said Harlin, looking into the high weeds where Sherm had thrown the snake after taking it off Jake's neck.*

3

*Ernest grunted, "Sherm, your boy's dancing around like he's gonna pee in his pants. He can use the bathroom in the store, if he wants. Just tell Peggy, at the counter, I said its okay."*

*"He's fine," Sherm said his eyes on the boy. He turned and walked toward the reinforcing-rod pill shaking his head.*

*Harlin started toward his truck but seeing Jake squeezing his legs together, he changed course and approached the boy. Raising his hand to Jake's nose with his thumb and forefinger, he pinched the dripping snot, then snapped his wrist and hand at the ground and wiped his fingers on his coverall leg. In a low voice he said, "Go over there and piss in those high weeds. He'll be back there for a few minutes yet." Then, lowering the bill of his John Deere hat, and climbed into his truck. He tore out of the parking lot, his tires spitting stones.*

That morning when Jake awoke he found Naomi had gone into the spare bedroom. He untangled himself from the knotted sheets and went to her.

Climbing beneath the covers he cupped his body against hers and whispered, "Sorry."

She stroked his cheek. "You woke me up again. You've been dreaming every night this week. Take the melatonin tonight." She stretched her arms over her head.

"You getting up now?" Jake asked.

"I've got to clear off my desk, and I want to make a pot of soup for the week. I thought I'd pick up a few things at the store. We're out of vegetables."

"I'll get up with you."

"Is something the matter?"

"It feels like I've been digging my fingers into dirt all night," Jake said, looking at his nails.

"And a good morning to you, too!"

"Sorry," he said, rubbing the backs of his hands against his eyes. "Another bad dream about my old man. I'll meet you downstairs."

"What was it about?"

"Snakes," he said, knowing she wouldn't want to hear about it.

"Yuck!" Naomi said, rolling to the edge of the bed to stand, as though retreating from an actual snake.

Jake sat on the edge of the bed, wondering why he felt like he'd slept on the floor of a jungle instead of his soft bed. He remembered something his therapist had said: "Every man has enough grief buried in him to cry daily for years, but never will."

He'd been seeing Sam, the therapist, for three years and hadn't told him he was a Vietnam vet with a chest full of medals. All they ever talked about was his father.

At their first session he told Sam that he wanted help with finding his feelings. "What feelings are you looking for?" asked the iconically bearded and bespectacled Sam. Jake called him "young Freud" whenever he mentioned him to Naomi.

"I want to feel fun, pleasure, love, peace. That ought to justify the two hundred and twenty-five dollars I'm paying you every two weeks."

Two sessions ago he mentioned, again, that he wanted to find his emotions. Sam shocked him by saying, "If that's what you want, why don't you find a prostitute?"

Jake said, "Listen, man, I'm just sick of living an emotional flat line."

"I don't see it as my job to fix you. In fact, since we're finally getting real with each other, let me tell you how the situation feels to *me*. I feel as though you've just thrown a big job on my desk and said, "Hey doc, fix it!" The problem is that you own the toolbox and it has this gigantic padlock on it. If you're going to just sit there at every session and ask me why I haven't repaired your life, forget about it. You know how many tools you've given me to help you?" Sam held his hand up, his forefinger and thumb making a zero.

Jake wondered where Sam the nice guy had gone. And who was this guy who looked like him?

"Help me out here," Sam continued. "Tell me about a time when you *did* have fun," he said.

After a moment, Jake smiled, remembering a story he'd heard from a friend. The man had gotten up in the middle of the night, taken two potatoes from the kitchen and placed them in his sleeping lover's shoes. The woman had been shocked in the morning when she went to put on her shoes. Jake told Sam he'd been surprised at how hard he'd laughed while hearing the story.

"What do you think stirred you up so much?" Sam asked.

"It was just silly," he said. "It's been so long since I've done anything silly or fun or stupid. Potatoes in the shoes was just stupid and I loved it."

Naomi wouldn't love it though, he thought. Naomi would faint if he ever put potatoes in her shoes' it was just too out of character.

"This must be the new side of Jake," Sam said. "Between your beard and stern expression, you usually look like a senator waiting to spout an official policy."

By the end of the session Jake sensed that they were finally making progress. He'd even begun thinking that he'd tell Sam about Nam.

On his way home Jake mentally replayed Sam's acknowledgment of his playful side. He considered shaving off his thirty-five year old beard and resisted the impulse to stop and buy potatoes. He ran his fingers through his whiskers as he remembered that Sam would be away on vacation for the next month. He wasn't sure how he felt about this.

Returning to the present, Jake stood up and walked into the master bedroom. He put on khaki pants and a white shirt. His choice wasn't difficult; all his shirts were white, all his pants, khaki. Then he went downstairs to eat the healthy breakfast that Naomi prepared every day: a big bowl of yogurt, blueberries, walnuts and almond milk, topped with two teaspoons of ground flaxseed.

## ✧✦ CHAPTER THREE ✧✦

Jake clicked his mouse on one of the twenty emails he'd gotten overnight. Going through email was his morning routine. He heard Naomi doing dishes in the kitchen.

On the screen flashed a headline in red: "Attacks by Juba!" Jake checked the "Sent by" field and saw that his friend Tom, another ex-Marine, had sent the story. He didn't always open Tom's emails. He could be sure they were about the military and often tragic.

Jake moved the cursor toward the delete button but paused, to read the sub-title: "I have a present for George Bush: nine bullets for nine people. Watch me kill them. Watch me now! God is great! God is great!"

Jake watched his cursor move to the link. A video popped open on the screen and he saw an American GI's head exploding. Then a series of photos began streaming across the screen: portraits of soldiers dead from sniper shots. Jake clicked the play button again and again. He couldn't stop himself.

*In the glow and hum of the computer screen he began hearing the voice of his high-school coach, Mr. Ashur. "When I say hit your man, I'm not talking about tapping him on the shoulder to come to the dinner table. I want him down on the field. I want him to need a dentist because his teeth fall out from chattering in fear of you hitting him."*

*After practice Jake told his dad what the coach had said.*

*"For Christ's sake, football's supposed to be fun! There's a ball involved; it's got to be fun," Sherm said.*

7

"He really wants us to hurt the other team. I think when he says 'Make em bleed,' he means it. He told me if he didn't see blood on my uniform after the third tackle, I'd better cut myself and wipe some blood on my shirt."

"It's all talk. Get used to it; that's how men talk. I don't know if you know this, but Ashur's an ex-Marine. He fought in Korea. He's wrapped a little tight, but he's a good man."

"I thought you'd like him, Dad." Jake paused. "Coach Ashur told Don to stomp on a toad that jumped onto the field. Don said he didn't want to, so the coach grabbed him by the face mask and pulled him to the sidelines. We all heard Ashur screaming, but no one understood what he was saying. Don ran back on the field, looking for the toad. When he found it, he started stomping on it with his football spikes until there was nothing but red mud. In the locker room Don said he hadn't wanted to do it, but the coach told him that when he was in Korea if he'd hesitated to kill the enemy, he would have ended up looking like the toad."

Sherm was quiet for a moment. "Not everything that sounds bad is bad," he finally said.

"What's that supposed to mean?" Jake asked, with a wrinkled brow.

"He didn't ask you to kill someone on the other team. Ashur knows there are going to be times when you'd better know you can do what you have to do. There's a lesson in this, son."

"What are you talking about, Dad? Are you saying coach Ashur's trying to teach us how to kill?"

"Maybe. Let's just drop it."

"Is that why you've always done weird things to me, like wrapping a dead snake around my neck? Is there a lesson in that, too? Just preparing me so I'll know I can do what I have to do? Is that it?

"Shut up! That's enough. Drop it. Now!"

✦✦ CHAPTER FOUR ✦✦

Naomi unpacked the groceries before going to Jake's office. She stood in the doorway watching a moment before softly saying, "How long are you going to stare at that screen?"

Jake shuddered.

"Sorry I startled you, but you were staring at the screen when I left — an hour and a half ago."

"Sorry, sorry. I got lost."

"Your face is white. You okay?"

"Yeah, I'm good. Just got too wrapped up in emails. You hungry? Want me to make you something?" Naomi continued looking at him in silence. "Why are you looking at me like that?"

"What's that on the screen?"

"Tom sent me some war stuff."

"I thought you told me you weren't going to open emails from Tom."

"Give me a frigging break," Jake said, his face tightening. "Just tell me how I'm supposed to hide myself from two goddamn wars! Where's the pile of sand I'm supposed to stick my head in? I don't watch TV. I don't

9

read the newspaper. I don't go to war movies. And I don't tell you about the five billion thoughts clogging my brain every frigging time I smell a dead animal on the road, or hear that one of the kids I've taught has turned up KIA." Jake's jaw locked, his eyes narrowed.

"Stop it! Stop it right now!" Naomi screamed. "I will not go there with you again! Stop it, Jake, before you can't." She swallowed, trying to calm herself. When she spoke again her voice was quiet. "This'll destroy our day, and maybe more than that. Let's start over," she said. She reached toward him as though throwing a life preserver.

He grabbed for her hands, letting his breath out. "Sorrrry," he said softly. "I did it again. It was the goddamn gunshots I heard on that video. I shouldn't have watched it." He paused. "There's this guy named Juba who has himself filmed while he's shooting American soldiers with a sniper rifle, and then turns the videos over to Al Jazeera. He shows our boys being knocked off, one at a time, like cartoons in a fucking video game. I keep seeing the blood auras when the bullets hit their bodies."

Naomi closed her eyes, gathered her hair in her hand behind her head, and said, "We'll get there. I know there will be times when it's impossible to avoid being triggered." She drew Jake to her and put her hand on his heart. "Right here. This is what I love." She laid her cheek on top of his head for a moment and then straightened up. "I'll take you up on that offer of food. Make me an omelet? And let's make plans for this Saturday. It's supposed to be gorgeous."

"Okay. But there's one thing I want to tell you first."

"If it's about war, I'm not interested. I mean it, Jake. War has taken my husband, my weekends, and my sleep. It is not allowed in this house today."

"I promise it's not about war; it's about my childhood. I've started having flashbacks to a very young age. I haven't thought about my folks for a long long while, but recently they've been coming into my mind again and again."

"You said you weren't going to talk about war? Your entire childhood was a war." She shook her head. "That reminds me: have you listened to voice mail today? A kid named Pax called. I didn't catch the whole message, but he said something about the Marines. He wants to talk with you. He's a senior, isn't he? I think I know his mom. She's a nurse at my hospital and a single mom; the father hasn't been around for a long time."

"Yeah, I remember him," said Jake, looking out the window. He was in Eloise Kaiden's class last year. Big kid. Played soccer. Nice young man; keeps his nose clean. I'll call him tomorrow. I don't want to talk about the Marines right now." He turned to Naomi. "Forget the omelet. I say we pack a picnic and go to that park along the Hudson up in Saugerties. What do you think?"

"Aye aye, sir," she whispered into his ear.

"Keep doing that and you ain't never gonna make it to that picnic, miss pretty."

# ✧✦ CHAPTER FIVE ✧✦

"Hello. Is this Pax?"

"Right here."

"This is Mr. Finn. I got your message."

"Oh, hi, Mr. Finn. Thanks for calling. Do you remember me?

"Sure, you live with your mom down on Maple Street, right?"

"That's me. Sorry to call you on the weekend, but I wanted to ask you something that can't wait until school on Monday."

"What's that important?"

"I had Mrs. Kaiden for English last year, but Ned Louis, my best friend, was in your class. He told me you were in the Marines.

"Yes."

"That's why I wanted to talk to you. I'm graduating at the end of this year, and I've been talking to the Marine recruiter at school. My mom doesn't want me to join. She wants me to talk to someone with Marine experience before I sign any papers. So I promised her I'd talk to you." He paused. "You there? Mr. Finn?"

"I'm here. You took me a little by surprise. Haven't you been a good student?"

"Pretty good. I got a B-plus average."

Jake rolled his head from shoulder to shoulder, trying to loosen his neck. "I'll talk with you, but this weekend's out. What I can tell you right now is this: don't sign anything. The Marine recruiter can wait. Anything he tells you about needing to sign now is bullshit. There are two wars to choose from; you won't lose your place in line. So don't sign anything for now. Monday after school I'll meet you at Tilly's. I'm buying."

"But the recruiter said I had to sign up this weekend, or I wouldn't get into infantry school."

"You got to be kidding me. Did you hear me use the word 'bullshit'? I don't use that kind of language with students unless I'm trying to get their attention. You hear me?"

"Yes, sir."

Jake took a breath. "I'll promise you something. If that recruiter refuses to give you infantry school, I'll talk with him myself. I mean Marine to Marine. Can you live with that?"

"If you're sure he'll listen to you."

"Two bronze stars and a silver say he'll listen," Jake thought. Aloud he said, "Meet me at Tilly's then."

"Yes, sir."

## ✦✦ CHAPTER SIX ✦✦

Jake swung his backpack onto his shoulder, kissed Naomi goodbye and began his mile and a half walk to the high school. He loved to walk to work and did so all year round. When Naomi complained about his leaving the house an hour earlier than he would if he drove, he told her the walk cleared his head and he needed it.

Jake took a well-worn trail through a glade of ash and white pines along a small pond to the edge of the school baseball field. The trail was a quarter of a mile longer than the sidewalk route, so it wasn't used by many kids. Jake occasionally saw joggers or dog walkers; otherwise, the trail was his.

Jake had expected to use the time during his walk to prepare himself for the conversation with Pax later that day. But halfway to school he was still thinking, "What *am* I gonna say to this kid?" Stopping beneath the arms of a large white pine, he drew his cell phone out and found Eloise Kaiden's number.

"Good morning Eloise, its Jake. I was wondering if you could look in on my study-hall class for the first half hour this morning. Something's come up, and if you can do it, I'd be grateful. Great. Thanks, I owe you one. See you at lunch."

Reaching the pond he sat down on a large flat rock at the shoreline. He wondered how he could talk to Pax without having him run away. He thought it best if he could just get the kid to slow down and look at what he was about to do.

What was making the situation more difficult was that he knew who Pax's dad was. They'd met in the VFW years ago. His name was Shiloh and he'd only been in town for a few years before his wife left him.

Jake knew Shiloh had been a combat Force Recon Marine in Nam and now spent a lot of time resting his elbows on the mahogany bar at the VFW post. Jake's conversations with him had always been casual. He'd never even mentioned that he had been in the Force Recon in Nam.

What stood out most in his mind about Shiloh was the night the whole town of Reeve had seen him humiliate himself. His neighbors watched the drunken Shiloh throw his belongings out the windows of his small ranch house. Then he took his chain saw and stepladder from the garage, leaned the ladder against the house and climbed to the roof where he sank the roaring blade down into the shingles at the ridge. Backing his way down the roof, the saw screaming in his hands, he stepped down onto the stepladder to finish the job. As he began slicing through the siding, the saw blade cut through electrical wires, spitting out brilliant sparks. Shiloh flinched and fell from the stepladder, landing on the ground on his back.

Jake happened to be walking up Maple Street on his way to Naomi's when he heard the chain saw. He stood across the street, watching the police car pull into the driveway. Shiloh was struggling to get up, the chain saw puttering on the ground next to him. "She wants half the fucking house?" he roared. "She'll get half the fucking house!" Jake noticed a frightened face in the bathroom window: young Pax, watching his father on the front lawn.

Jake shifted as the coolness of the rock reached him through the seat of his pants. That must have been ten years ago, already, he thought.

Jake never could understand why Shiloh and his wife had named their kid Pax. The name meant "peace" and the look on that kid's face had nothing to do with peace. Maybe Pax's father, the recon captain, wanted to protect his kid from what he'd seen.

Jake had once come in contact with Shiloh's unit near Quang Tri Province. None of them were in uniform; they wore black pajamas and Ho Chi Minh sandals, with black scarves pulled tightly over their heads. Two of them wore necklaces of human ears. They carried sawed-off shotguns and Ak-47 rifles, instead of the M-16s issued to them. Shiloh must have been on R&R because he didn't remember seeing him.

When Jake finally stood, the morning sun was eating the fog on the pond. He was still unsure about what to say to Pax, his mind unable to let go of the words he wanted to say: "If war doesn't kill you, it'll go through your guts like a meat grinder. Oh, you can be sure you'll never have another full night's sleep in your life. Don't be surprised, Pax, when you come home and discover you're not comfortable around groups of people and sit with your back to every wall you can find.

"You'll desperately need your girlfriend or wife to make love to you much more than she wants to – just to prove that someone in the world loves you. Oh, and you won't give a shit about yourself after all the killing you've done. And don't be surprised when you start hating your girl or wife, because you put her in charge of all the happiness in your life, and she's overwhelmed with the job you can't do."

He knew that this was not what the kid needed to hear, but it felt good to say it – for his own sake. He knew very well that no one could talk to an eighteen-year old. It was obvious he'd already made up his mind. Eighteen-year olds didn't understand that war heroes never leave their battlefields. If he told Pax his father was still in Vietnam, he'd have to admit he was also. The only reason he was willing to even try speaking with Pax was because of the kid's mother.

All of this thinking reminded him of the anthem recited by Naomi and her social-worker colleagues: "Leave the past behind; there is nothing you can do to change it." Jake had been listening to this advice for years, but he couldn't tell Naomi that there was no way he'd ever be able do that, so he'd learned to just nod his head.

Maybe Naomi was right about Pax. "Pat the kid on the back," she advised Jake. "Wish him a good tour in the Marines." She wasn't recommending this approach because she believed it would be best for Pax. She just wanted Jake to stop dealing with anything that had to do with war. Jake admitted Naomi had a good point. Why would Pax be any different from him or his dad? Jake couldn't answer his own question. No, he thought, Pax isn't any different. He'll stand in his own endless line of young men traveling into the void of war. Fathers may tell their sons they're marching into the mouth of a lifelong nightmare. But they know, in their hearts, that their sons cannot listen.

✧✦ CHAPTER SEVEN ✧✦

Instead of resuming his walk to school, Jake found a place on the large rock that he could lean against and sat back down. He felt as if he was boomeranged back to 1967, the year he'd signed up with a Marine recruiter.

*He saw his 18-year old self walk into the house and heard his mother, from the kitchen, yelling at his sister, "Where the hell's your brother? He's been gone all afternoon. I know you know where he is. You gonna tell me? Or you want me to tan your ass? I'll slap your ass so hard you won't be able to sit down."*

*Jake poked his head into the kitchen and saw his twelve-year-old sister standing defiantly, hands on hips, fingers reaching into her back pockets. "I'm right here. Leave her alone!" he said, amazed by his voice. The conversation with the Marine recruiter had given him courage. Gritting his teeth, he planted himself in front of her. "Eda, I could hear you at the end of the driveway!" This was the first time in his life he'd called his mother by her name. His finger jabbed the air two inches from her nose. "Leave her alone?"*

*"Who the hell do you think you are, talking to me like that? Did someone pin a badge on you?"*

*Not a bad guess, thought Jake. That's exactly how I feel: like someone just pinned a Marine badge on me. He said, "You want this conversation to go where it did last time? If you lay a hand on me or her, I'll punch you."*

*Eda pretended she hadn't heard him. "Where've ya been all afternoon?" she asked.*

*"I signed up for the Marine Corps." He paused enjoying Eda's expression. "Oh, don't look so damned surprised. I've been waiting to get the hell out of here for a long time and you know it. I've had enough of living with you and the snore machine in there," he said, pointing his thumb toward the living room where Sherm was asleep in his easy chair. "I guess you forgot I turned eighteen yesterday. I'll be in the Marines a week after graduation and in Vietnam before the year's out."*

*Eda stopped biting her lip and blinked at him as though she'd just woken up. "You think you're so goddamn smart," she hissed. "But that's the kind of move that's gonna get you killed."*

*"Ma!" That's not what you're supposed to say. You're supposed to say, 'Congratulations, son! Today you've become a man. What a brave thing you've done, volunteering to protect our family from the Communists. Come here, son! Let me hold my baby!'"*

*For a moment she stared at him, her mouth open, speechless, she turned her head. Jake walked out the back door, letting it slam behind him.*

A sudden flash of color caught Jake's eye and he was back on the rock, looking at the pond. The sound of a flat rock knifing into the water turned his head. Ed Duncan stood at the edge of the pond with a handful of stones.

Jake knew the boy had been suspended for posting party pictures on Facebook. He'd thought the pictures were harmless images of kids having fun. But Ed was the principal's son. One picture of Ed was him reclining on a sofa with his head thrown back over its arm, his mouth wide open to receive beer being poured into it by his best friend, Graham. Beer cans were strewn across the floor and stacked on the end table.

When Jake stood up and brushed off his pants, Ed noticed him. Turning quickly Jake walked away.

# ✦✦ CHAPTER EIGHT ✦✦

Outside Tilly's Café kids were gathered in groups of three and four. At the sight of backpacks hanging from their shoulders a thought flashed in Jake's mind: these kids looked like urban soldiers in some Iraqi town he'd seen on TV. The cell phones at their ears could just as well be two-way radios. Hang a backdrop of desert behind these kids and they could be in Iraq or Afghanistan right now.

Jake pushed the windowed oak door open and searched the room for Pax. The place was empty except for a few kids at the counter nursing cans of Red Bull. A middle-aged couple was eating hamburgers and fries in one of the booths. Jake assumed the couple was from out of town; locals wouldn't come to Tilly's as school letting out because in a few minutes the place would be swamped with kids. Local customers didn't bother coming in for dinner until around 6:00. Jake took a booth near a window and sat facing the door, his back to the wall.

He'd barely sat down when the door swung open and a big man entered, his head gleaming under the florescent lighting. He spotted Jake and walked toward him, extending his hand.

"Hey, Mr. Finn. Sorry I'm late."

Jake did a double-take. "Whoa! The haircut threw me," he said, shaking Pax's hand.

"Got it yesterday. What do you think?"

"Looks hygienic," Jake said, squinting under lowered eyebrows. He handed the young man a menu. "You want something to eat?" he asked.

"You gonna have anything?"

"Yeah," said Jake, pulling his backpack off the seat and putting it on the table. "I didn't finish my lunch. Got half a tempeh sandwich on eight-grain bread. You want some?"

"What's tempeh?"

"Fermented soy food from Indonesia."

"I'll pass. I think I'll have one of those 'heavy weapon burgers.'"

"What the hell's a 'heavy weapon burger?'"

"It's just a big burger with a bunch of toppings. The name is sort of a joke that Ned came up with. You know Ned?"

"Don't think so. Should I?"

"Only if you know the owner of Tilly's. He's Ned's father. Anyway, Ned worked here before he joined the Army and went to Afghanistan. He's on his second tour now. In between tours he came back and spent a few months on leave helping his dad in the restaurant. He came up with this new burger. It's a pound of meat, jalapeño peppers, and three slices of American cheese, all packed between two pita breads."

"Can't wait to see it," Jake said. He pushed his glasses up the bridge of his nose. "So. You said you had some questions?"

"I do. I understand you were in the Marines during the Vietnam War. Did you see combat?"

"Yes." Jake looked out the window at the trees across the street, shading the lawn in front of the library. Pax sat twisting his napkin. He could see that Jake was organizing his thoughts. Pax was about to excuse himself and go to the bathroom when Nabi showed up at their table. "Hello, Mr. Finn. I haven't seen you in here in a long time."

"Hi Nabi. My wife's got me on a new diet. Do you mind if I eat the rest of my lunch at the table? Pax here wants the heavy weapon burger."

"That's fine, Mr. Finn. I'll get the burger."

"Thanks, Nabi," said Jake. He watched her walk away. "Nice girl. She was in my class last year."

"Very nice girl," said Pax. His eyes followed her all the way to the kitchen door.

"You asked me if I'd seen combat. To be honest with you Pax, I don't talk about my war experience. It still bothers me." He paused. "I'm afraid if I open the footlocker where I've stored my war kit, bamboo vipers and cobra war ships will come slithering out."

"What's a bamboo viper?"

"It's this little snake about two feet long. In Nam they called it the two-step snake. If it bit you, you'd have only enough time to take two steps before you were dead."

"No shit. Hey, Mr. Finn, if talking about this stuff bothers you, I can give my Uncle Max a call. He was in the Marines, too."

"Why haven't you called him already?"

"My mother didn't want me to. He's my dad's brother."

"Gotcha. Have you signed up yet?"

"Not really. The Marine recruiter, Sergeant Watkins, was waiting for me at the front door of the high school this morning, but I told him I had to speak with you before I signed up.

"I really like Sergeant Watkins. He's very respectful; he shakes my hand every time I see him. He's always asking if there's anything he can help me with, or if I need a ride somewhere. He's given me a ride home a couple of times after school. And he didn't even ask me if I wanted to join the Marines until a few weeks ago. Do you know him?"

"I've met him. He came into my classroom once, after school, and we had a few words."

"Good guy, isn't he?"

"Yeah."

Jake pulled down on his beard and took a deep breath. "I'll talk with you, but first I want to understand if you're really interested in knowing what the Marines are about – what going to war as a Marine truly means. If you don't like what I'm saying or how I'm saying it, just let me know. We can shake hands and you can head out without my two cents in your pocket. That's about how much my input is worth anyway. So what do you think? Interested?"

"So far."

"Okay. First there's something you need to know right up front: I hate war. I didn't always. When I was your age I joined the Marines to become a hero. I really *wanted* to kill the enemy. But now I hate killing; I hate war."

A faint smile came onto Pax's face.

"What's the smile for?"

"Sorry. I wasn't smiling at what you were saying; I was just thinking about my dad. You sound a lot like him. He once told me a soldier's only job is to kill, and anyone who says otherwise is lying or stupid."

"Your old man was right." Jake paused. "It's too bad you can't have this conversation with him instead of me. When was the last time you spoke to him?"

"Maybe third grade. I haven't even seen him since then."

"So when he told you about soldiers and killing you were no more than eight years old?"

"Guess so."

Jake was quiet for a moment. "Is Watkins telling you about the fine education you're going to get? About how real men are Marines? I bet he's not telling you that he needs to find killers. When you're a Marine you're nothing more than a part in a machine, and the primary function of that machine is to take enemy lives. Watkins's job is to keep the Marine killing machine running. If one of the parts of his machine gets hung up in the Iraqi desert, he needs a replacement part right away."

"Mr. Finn, I don't mean to be pissing you off."

"Pissing me off is the least of your problems. Put your arm up on the table."

Pax put his elbow on the table as though ready to arm wrestle. Jake said, "I want you to take hold of my wrist with your right hand, your right handed aren't you?"

"Yeah".

"Good. Now squeeze as hard as you can. Don't be afraid; you can't really hurt me. Okay?"

"Yeah."

As Pax put all the strength in his two-hundred pound frame into squeezing Jake's wrist, Jake stared into the boy's face. He saw the fear rise in him. "Now imagine that my wrist is the neck of an enemy child. You with me?"

Pax's eyebrows squished. "I'm with you."

"Someday you're going to become so enraged from what war has done to you that you'll be walking around like a frigging time bomb. Then some wise-ass kid will mouth off and you'll feel like choking him to death. You'll probably never do it, but you'll be able to. And you'll know it." Pax said nothing. "You think I'm shitting you?"

"I got it," Pax said, letting go of Jake's wrist.

Lowering his voice, Jake said, "I know there's really no way to show you what war is like or what it does to you. In fact most men don't have a clue about how war has affected them until years later. They see their marriages fall apart. They have all kinds of problems in their jobs and with their kids. Then they realize there'd been signs all along, from the moment they stepped off the battlefield. They just never bothered to read any of them."

Pax said nothing. He shifted slightly in his seat and looked down at his plate.

Jake looked at his watch. "My wife's expecting me to make supper tonight, so I got to get moving. So. Let me ask you a question and I expect a truthful answer. Are you here only because your mom wants you to talk with me?"

Pax bit at a cuticle on his thumb. "Here's the truth. My dad was a highly decorated Marine in Vietnam. Mom still has pictures of him in uniform hanging on the walls. She says he used to come home drunk a lot and do some crazy stuff when I was little but I was too young to remember. He left us when I was around eight. I haven't heard from him in years."

"When I told my Mom I wanted to join, I thought she'd blow a gasket. It was pretty tense for a couple of days. Then, after she calmed down, she said she didn't want me to make my mind up until I spoke to someone who'd been in. That's when she told me about you. She said, 'Mr. Finn was a Marine and he's a good man. Why don't you talk to him?'"

"That's very nice of her, but your mom doesn't really know me."

"Better than you might think. She told me about the night you brought Clancy to the emergency room. She said you held him in your arms until the doctor took him. She couldn't believe the way you comforted him. She said you held him like he was a soldier wounded on the battlefield." He paused. "She started crying when she told me the story."

"Clancy was in an auto accident; he was almost killed." Jake looked away, then asked, "You want to meet again?"

Pax followed Jake's gaze and saw nothing. Then, turning back, he asked, "Could I ask you some questions about boot camp and what it was like in Vietnam?"

Jake returned Pax's gaze. "I could use some help at my house; about half a day's worth. If you'd like to make a few bucks, you could come by on Saturday. We could talk some more when you're done. What do you think?"

Pax rubbed his wrist. "Sure. What time?"

"Nine o'clock. And bring some gloves."

# ✧✦ CHAPTER NINE ✧✦

Rain pelted the bedroom windows. Jake watched individual droplets connect into rivulets. It was only 6:00 a.m., but he'd been awake for hours. Naomi turned toward him, her long black hair with fine silver threads spilling across her pillow.

"Morning, sweetheart."

"You look like you've been awake for a while."

"I've been thinking about my meeting with that kid Pax yesterday. I think I might've scared him."

"Why do you think so? Were you trying to?" she asked.

"Not consciously. But I know that fear might be the only thing that could wake him up to what he's about to step into."

"Fear didn't change your mind. Why do you think it would change his? Fear excites young men."

"You're right. I'll ease up on him a little bit," he said pushing the sheets back on the bed.

Naomi was pouring milk onto her granola when she heard a knock on the door. She yelled, "Jake, someone's at the back door."

"I'll get it," he hollered from his office in the front of the house. Stepping into the kitchen he said, "It's got to be Pax." He opened the back door and held it wide for the young man. "Hey Pax, come on in. You know my wife Naomi, don't you?"

"Hello, Mrs. Finn."

"Hi, Pax. How you doing?"

"I'm good," he said, looking at her.

"How's your mom? I see her sometimes; we work in the same hospital. Tell her I said hello."

"She's OK, I will, thanks."

Placing his hand on Pax's shoulder, Jake asked, "You bring gloves?"

"Right here," Pax answered, patting his back pocket.

"Let's go to the backyard and I'll show you what needs doing."

Jake pulled his list from his shirt pocket. Pointing at the center of the lawn, he said, "Those leaves need to be raked and bagged. Then I'd like you to clear the branches off the garage roof. There's a stepladder hanging in the garage that you can use. When you get that done, get the steel rake and pull the stones off the grass along the edge of the driveway where the snow blower threw them, can you handle that?"

"No prob."

"How long you think it'll take?"

Pax looked around, rubbing his head. "About two hours."

"Good. If you were being told to do this in the Marines, the drill instructor would say, "You planning on taking an hour-and-a-half nap?"

"Okay," Pax said patiently. "Where do you want me to put the bagged leaves?"

"Over there," said Jake, pointing to the side of the garage.

"Good. When you finish raking the stones, come get me. I'll be in my office in the front. If we have time, there's one more project I'd like to do, but we'll have to do it together. I want to replace the decking on the stairs to the front porch. I've got lumber for the new decking in the basement and I'll need you to help me bring it up."

"Will do," said Pax.

While Naomi ate her cereal, she watched Pax frantically raking in the yard. She put her bowl in the sink and went to Jake's office. Standing behind his chair, she put her hand on his shoulder. "What a fine young man he is. He looks you right in the eye. And now he's out there working like his pants are on fire."

"He thinks I'm expecting him to work on Marine time. I didn't say anything to talk him out of it."

"I think his mom deserves a lot of credit for the way she's raised him. She seldom takes overtime so she can be home with him. I think they live on her nurse's salary and get nothing from Shiloh, the dad. My boss knows Phyllis pretty well, and apparently Phyllis thinks Shiloh's still drinking."

"Phyllis is his mom?"

"Mm hmm. What's your plan with Pax today? Are you going to talk about the Marines again?"

"He said he has some questions for me."

"Do you think you should get into another conversation like that with him?"

"Yeah, I do."

"Why?"

"Because he asked me to, and no one has ever asked me before. Maybe if I had asked someone about the Marines when I was his age, they could have steered me away from the worst years of my life."

Naomi squeezed his shoulders hard. "Just remember what happened last Sunday. You spent an hour and a half watching war scenes on a computer screen." Scowling, she said, "And as you yourself just pointed out, there's no way to avoid being reminded of yourself when you were his age." Jake felt her hands leave his shoulders and listened to the loud sound of Naomi's shoes on the wood floor as she returned to the kitchen.

Jake heard the back door open and looked at his desk clock. It had been twenty-eight minutes since Pax started working. He jerked around to see the boy standing in the doorway.

"Mr. Finn, I got the leaves raked. The stones are off the lawn, the tree limbs are off the garage roof and I put the stepladder away."

Jake nodded, looking out the window at the results of Pax's work. "Looks like we still have some time. Let's take the lumber out of the basement. I'll get my gloves. Head down and open the basement door. The key hangs on a nail on the right side of the door jam."

"Okay."

After carrying building materials and tools up from the basement, Jake and Pax began pulling up the old stair boards. Jake picked up a crowbar from the sidewalk. "Use this to pull up the edges of the boards," he said, handing it to Pax. He took a breath. "What did you think of our conversation the other day?"

"You gave me a lot to chew on," Pax answered, focusing on the board he'd begun prying.

Jake leaned forward to put a crowbar in the opening Pax had made. "Be honest with me," he said.

Pax bit his lip. "Okay. When you had me squeeze your wrist as tight as I could, I kept thinking, from what you said, that you'd killed a child. I know that kind of thing happens in war, but I didn't know what to say to you. I mean I'm sure you didn't, but —well, I couldn't help wondering. You seemed so upset."

Jake got to his feet, turned slightly and looked up into the maple tree. "I'm sorry I came down on you so hard. I don't really know what to tell you about joining the Marines and going to war. There's just no way to describe what those experiences do to you. When most men come home from war, they try to stay in the role of protector. For example, they become cops and firefighters. They want to protect their families from the truth of what they had to do. Before soldiers go to war, they have a lot of heroic pictures in their heads. Those pictures get thrown in the shit-can the second after a soldier's first kill."

Pax pulled hard on the handle of the crowbar causing it to make a high-pitched squeal as the nail pulled out. At the sound, Jake sucked in a quick breath and stiffened.

"Sorry, Mr. Finn."

"For what?"

"I didn't mean to scare you."

Jake gritted his teeth. "This is what I live with every day, Pax. Ask any of the kids in my class. They all know better than to come up behind me. Loud sounds, smells, almost anything can startle me, big time. All the excitement you feel right now, before you sign up? That's what they use to hold your attention in boot camp. They build on that excitement 'til you're champing at the bit to do your job and then they turn you loose on the battlefield. Once you're in battle, the excitement turns into fear. And once you get that fear, you're never without it again: it enters the marrow of your bones and it stays there for the rest of your life."

Pax stepped back, wiping his nose on his sleeve. "Mr. Finn, I got to go in a few minutes. Can I ask you a couple questions?"

"Of course."

"Staff Sergeant Watkins says boot camp's a place where real men are made. If you get through boot camp, no one messes with you again. He told me his father rode him and his brothers hard to join the Marines. His dad's a World War II Marine and he was at Iwo Jima. He was shot in the arm on the beach and crawled under the corpse of a dead Marine to stay alive. His buddies found him after dark."

Jake drew his thumb and forefinger down his nose, letting his hand hide his mouth. "What else has this guy told you?"

"He told me what it was like when his dad and mom came to his boot camp graduation. He said when he was dismissed from formation, he shook his father's hand, looked him right in the eye and said, 'and, it was because of you that I made PFC.' He told me that only one man in the platoon makes PFC. Is that true, Mr. Finn?"

"Right."

"Did you make PFC?"

"I did."

"No shit! I mean, whoo! What was boot camp like for you?"

"Well, it's not what you think. First off, it's impossible to 'make a man' in thirteen weeks. I don't give a shit what Watkins tells you."

"What do you mean?"

"What the Marines might give you, if they don't break you completely, is balls. That's not the same as becoming a man. You need balls to do dangerous things without asking questions. Don't mistake balls for courage. Having balls is more like a way of blocking your rational thinking so you can do things that your brain's telling you not to."

Jake saw Pax's smile. He knew the boy hadn't heard him speak like this before.

"So what do *you* think I should expect out of boot camp? If I go, that is. Are you telling me I shouldn't believe all the stories I've heard?"

"No, I'm not saying that. The stories are all true. Boot camp is set up to test every system you're made of, starting with your system for managing fear. They'll use every creative idea they can think of to scare the hell out of you, while demanding you don't fall apart." He looked at Pax for a moment. "You were on the soccer team weren't you?"

"Yeah, I played goalkeeper."

"Coach work you pretty hard?"

"Yeah, wind-sprints for forty-five minutes, two-hour practices every day after school, rain or shine. He even had us practice on Saturdays."

"In boot camp the day starts with standing in front of your bunk at attention at 5:00. When you look down the squad bay there are no less than a dozen peckers tenting out their Marine skivvies. After that there's a half hour to forty-five minutes of PT – physical training. You do it right there in the squad bay. Then they march you to the chow hall. Seventy men eat breakfast in less than ten minutes. After breakfast the real exercise begins. You go back to the squad bay, put on all your gear, line up in formation and start a five-mile run." Jake looked at the boy's face, hoping to see some kind of fear. Pax was smiling.

"You know what squat-thrusts are?"

"Yeah."

"Show me."

Pax bent over, kicked out his feet, then tucked them back under himself and stood.

"That's it. Now think of doing that a thousand times. The drill instructor issues orders throughout the day to anyone who screws up. He'll scream out something like, 'Pax stand out in that hallway so we can all see you, and give me and my girls a thousand squat-thrusts.' I had to do it once. The entire floor was wet beneath me before I finished."

"That's awesome, Mr. Finn."

Jake was quiet, his gaze fixed on a point in the distance over Pax's shoulder. "I want to tell you about an animal you'll meet in North Carolina," he said, returning his eyes to the boy. "It's the smallest and meanest thing I've ever run into."

"What is it?"

"The sand flea."

"What's the big deal about a sand flea? It can't be worse than the mosquitoes we've got around here."

"Sure it can," Jake laughed. "The sand flea test was the only one I almost failed in boot camp."

"What happened?

"Our platoon had been standing at attention for about a half hour and the sand fleas were thick. I saw half a dozen eating the exposed neck of the man in front of me. We all waited until the drill instructor turned his back so we could swat the fleas on our faces and blow off the ones on the neck of the man in front of us.

"The drill instructor knew we were doing this, so finally he shouted, 'Okay, girls, for every time you swat a flea we'll stand at attention for another five minutes.' Those fucking sand fleas were crawling in our ears and up our noses.

"Soars oozed on the neck of the man in front of me, which seemed to draw more of them. I watched him tense his neck muscles, trying to scare them off. It didn't work. Eventually he gave up; he just stood there and let them feast. I think that was the first time I saw raw courage.

"Watkins's right about the Marines testing you. But he's wrong when he says they'll make you a man. When my life slowed down I thought about the difference between a man and a soldier. A soldier's someone who's trained to kill. The only equipment he uses is whatever's necessary for killing. He follows orders without questioning them. He often operates on automatic and deals with the consequences of his actions after the fact.

"A man is someone who uses all his equipment, including his mind and his heart. He thinks, he considers, he takes in the larger picture. If he needs to, he has the courage and ability to stand up for himself and others. He does not operate on automatic and deal with the consequences afterward. The Marines spend a lot of money to keep young men confused about real manhood so they can make good soldiers. Believe it or not, real men don't always make good soldiers. Sociopaths and instinctive killers make the best soldiers."

"What's a sociopath?"

"Someone who doesn't experience normal emotions. A sociopath doesn't care if he kills somebody because he doesn't have any feelings; killing does not affect him."

It was Pax's turn to be silent. Then, quietly, "It sounds like you think joining the Marines was the worst thing you did in your life."

"It was. It wasn't the Marines that was the problem, though. It was the job I was asked to do as a Marine. It's not as though I didn't *learn* anything in the Marines. They taught me to work on a team, and I learned the value of sacrificing personal needs and comfort for my teammates. They pushed me beyond anything I ever thought I could endure, so I found out about my limits. Most people don't have a clue about their limits. All of that was terrific; I appreciate it.

"The problem was that all of this learning had one goal, and I didn't realize that at first. It wasn't until I was in country that the goal behind all this training, all this learning, finally sank in on me."

"What was that?"

"To kill the enemy. In boot camp we sang songs about killing 'gooks.' These days' recruits sing about killing 'ragheads.' The real nature of our job dawned on me when I watched one of my fire team, Billy, cut off the ear of a Vietnamese he'd just killed. He was just doing what he'd learned in training. No one ever said to cut off the enemy's ear, but it was implied that such things were done. Little atrocities happened day after day.

"Then one night Billy started screaming in his sleep. We expected to be attacked by him revealing our location; we got lucky the VC left us alone. Everyone knew he'd risked all our lives. The next morning no one would look at him. And Billy knew why; he knew what he'd done.

"A few days later we were getting ready to come out of a trench when a rifle shot went off. We crouched down and tried to spot the sniper. After a long while, when there was no movement, we crawled to the edge of the tree line. That's where we found Billy, his M-16 in his mouth. He couldn't take it. They don't show you that kind of shit on Marine Corps posters."

"Aren't there times when we need to stand up for ourselves or people who can't stand up for themselves?" Pax asked, lifting a rotten board off the stair runners.

"Yes, I think so. That's the very reason I signed up myself: I wanted to provide help to people who needed it. That might be your reason for wanting to join, too.

"At this point, though, I think that wasn't the whole story – for me, anyway. When I'm honest with myself I have to admit that what I really wanted was to be a hero. Or at least to feel like I had some power. Until I joined the Corps, I felt pretty powerless. My mother dictated everything – everything I thought, everything I did. And my old man wasn't any help. All he cared about was training me to act fearless. Throughout my childhood he found ways to scare me and then expected me to swallow my fears. It wasn't until I got out that I realized the real reason I'd joined: I was looking for the quickest possible way to become a man. I thought if I were a man, then my mother and father would finally listen to me."

Pax was motionless, his eyes downcast. "My dad loved the Marines," he said quietly.

"He told you that?"

"No, but my mother says he never stopped talking about it. She says he loved the Marines more than her."

Jake was not surprised. "I knew your dad – a little bit."

"Really?" Pax's gaze rose and met Jake's. "What was he like?"

"I met him at the VFW. He seemed to like his drink. That's really all I knew about him."

"Oh, everybody knows that," he said, looking down at the floor again. "Sergeant Watkins said he could look up my dad's service record for me."

"What did you tell him?"

"I said yeah. Why not? I'd like to know what he did in Nam.'"

"I'm not sure Watkins can legally do that. And even if he can, I'm not sure it would be a good idea. You could find out things you don't want to know."

"Do you have your service record?"

"I've got my DD-214. It's kind of an outline of what I did. I never tried to get the full record."

"Why not?"

"It might be more than I want to remember."

"What do you mean?"

"Hand me some of those galvanized number twelves. And while I'm nailing this, take the tools back down into the basement, will ya?"

"Okay."

Jake passed Naomi in the dining room and nodded as he headed to the bathroom. He closed the door softly and sat on the unopened toilet seat. Blood rushed into his face and head. He was sweating, and his breath had become shallow. Closing his eyes, he saw familiar red flashes.

*The new kid had a red bandana around his neck. Jake told him to take it off. "What the fuck's the matter with you?" the kid said. "My old-lady gave this to me." Jake told him again.*

*"While we're walking patrol, that frigging red thing's a goddamn bull's-eye. Take it off before it gets a bullet hole in it." Jake watched as the kid started untying the bandana.*

*A few hours later, deeper into the jungle, Jake's eye caught a flash of red. The bandana again. This time he stepped off the trail and waited for the kid to walk past him. When he did, Jake smacked the back of his helmet with the barrel of his M-16. "You're gonna get all of us fuckin' killed. Take the fucking thing off! Now!"*

*"Sir, my women said it would keep me alive over here. She made me promise never to take it off."*

*Jake's head started moving from side to side as he scanned the jungle.*

*"What are you looking for, sir?" The new kid asked.*

*"Your fucking woman."*

*"She ain't here, sir."*

*"No shit. If she were here I'd ask her to bring me a body bag — for you. Take the fucking thing off now. I'm gonna stand here and watch you do it."*

*The kid looked like he was going to cry as he held the bandana out to Jake.*

*"Oh, fuck it!" Jake said. "Put the goddamn thing in your pack."*

*An hour later they'd stepped out of a lightly forested area. Big Dick, the point man, got into a low crawl and made his way through shallow elephant grass. He stopped and signaled it was clear. The new kid was next in line; he started crawling toward Big Dick. About ten feet out a rifle shot cracked. Everyone hugged the ground, trying to figure out where the shot came from. Five minutes passed. Another shot, this time much closer. They heard a crashing sound as they watched a man fall from a tree, hitting limbs on the way down. Big Dick stood up. "Got him!"*

*Jake had started crawling toward the new kid, who was lying in front of him. "Get up, man. It's clear." The kid didn't move. Jake rolled him over and saw the bullet hole in his face, the red bandana around his neck. "Bull's-eye, you fuckin' idiot," Jake whispered.*

*The kid had been Jake's responsibility. He'd known the boy was going to put the neckerchief back on, and he hadn't had the balls to hurt his feelings. Now there he was, dead.*

Jake sat on the toilet seat reliving this scene for the ten thousandth time; it played on an automatic loop that wouldn't stop. He had no idea how long he'd been sitting there when he heard the familiar knock on the door. "Jake, you okay? Pax says he's got to go home. You want me to pay him?"

"I'll be right out. I'll take care of it." Jake walked out to the kitchen. "Hey, Pax. Sorry to keep you waiting; I had a little upset stomach. What do I owe you?"

"I don't know, about fifteen bucks."

"You were here for almost four hours, and I'm paying you ten bucks an hour."

"That's way too much. In fact, I really just wanted to speak with you. You don't have to pay me at all."

"Listen, I appreciate your helping me and I do want to pay you. I think ten bucks an hour is fair and that's that." Jake pulled his wallet from his back pocket and took out two twenties for Pax. Then he looked around to see whether Naomi was nearby, listening.

"I know I haven't answered all your questions. It's not because I don't want to; it's because sometimes talking about this stuff stirs me up." He paused. "I want to answer every fucking question you have. You hear me? I mean it. There's nothing more important to me right now." Jake started to reach for the boy's shoulder, but dropped his hand and stepped back.

"I just had a flashback in the bathroom. I was remembering losing a kid in my unit while we were on patrol. He wasn't more than a year older than you are now. And it's my fault he's dead; I could have prevented it." Jake brought himself back to the present. "When are you signing up?"

"I'd like to take a little time to think about it, but Sergeant Watkins is pushing me to make up my mind right away. I'm going over to his house for dinner tomorrow."

"Pax, would you mind if I spoke to Sergeant Watkins?"

"About what?"

"Just so I can get a sense of where he's coming from. I blew him off when he came into my class to speak to my students."

"Go ahead."

"Thanks.  Can we hook up one more time before you sign anything?"

"It's got to be soon."

"I'll give you a call Monday."

"All right," Pax said, taking a deep breath and letting it out his nose.

"Promise me you won't sign anything until we meet again.  Okay?"

"No sweat."  Pax walked away, his head lowered.

# ✦✦ CHAPTER TEN ✦✦

*"Jake! Where are you, son?"*

*"I'm in Thailand, on R&R."*

*"Hold on. Let me put your mother on."*

*"No! I want to speak with you."*

*"You okay?"*

*"Yeah, I'm okay. I've got to ask you something, though."*

*"Go ahead."*

*"I've seen a lot of action. I can't even remember how many fire fights I've been in."* He stopped and waited. Static filled a long, wordless moment.

*"You there, son?"*

*"I'm here. Listen, I've been in Nam six months. I've killed eleven times and one time it was a kid."*

Jake could hear his father swallow. *"That's what Marines do, son. You're only doing your job."*

*"Did you ever kill anyone?"*

"No." He paused. "Once I saw a guy – a black man – being killed, right in front of me. I probably could've stopped it but I didn't do anything." Jake waited. "I was drinking in a bar. There was a black guy on the stool next to me. Apparently he complained to somebody standing behind him – a white guy – about his boss. Said the boss had got his head up his ass. Unfortunately, the white guy was the boss's brother. So he picks up a beer bottle and back-hands the black guy across the face. Next thing I know the guy's on the floor, bleeding from the mouth, and the boss's brother's stomping on his neck. With work boots." Jake heard his dad exhale. "I probably could've pulled him off the guy."

"Shit. Multiply that by a thousand, and you'll get an idea of what I'm trying to tell you. I haven't slept in weeks. Today's the first time I've been sober since I started R&R. And I'm leaving in the morning to go back into the bush. You hear me? I'll be back hunting Charlie and his family by this time tomorrow."

"I heard you."

"Oh, really? I don't think so. You hear me say we're shooting women and children? You get that? We set a hootch on fire with two kids and a mother inside."

"Hang on, son, you're forgetting something. Charlie's the enemy, and it's your job to take him out. Remember what they've been doing to our guys. This war is a terrible thing, but it's the right thing. Me and your mother are behind you."

"You're behind me. Great. What do you know about the fucking right thing? I got to go."


"Jake? Jake! Wake up, sweetheart. Wake up!" Naomi pushed Jake's shoulder with her fingertips, keeping her face out of swinging range of his arms.

Squinting in the morning light, Jake rubbed his eye sockets with forefinger and thumb. "Jesus. I was dreaming about my father again."

"You okay?" Naomi asked, moving closer.

"I'm okay. Just need to wash my face," he said, swinging his legs onto the floor. "I'll be fine. Sorry I woke you."

Naomi sat up in bed, her back against the pillows and her arms folded over her chest, as Jake left the room. "It's Pax, isn't it?" she called after him.

"Yeah," Jake yelled from the bathroom. "The kid kicked up a lot of memories." Naomi listened to the water running and her husband grunting into a towel as he dried his face. He stepped back through the bedroom door.

"This war's been fermenting inside me long enough; it's finally forcing itself out. I know I'm breaking the rules. I'm sorry. But I can't keep this stuff locked up anymore. It's not only Pax, either. He's just the latest reminder. Sam has been pushing me to open the door to the jungle."

He watched her face, wishing he could protect her from his words, even as he spoke. "I'm sorry, Naomi. I know it's hard for you to watch me when I've got this crap spinning around in my head." He looked away and spoke quickly. "Sam says the only way you can come to terms with the fact that you married a sick son-of-a-bitch is to let him loose and stop trying to protect him from himself."

"Sam said that? Why didn't you tell me?"

"I just did." He paused again. "Anyway, I want to help Pax. Not just because he needs guidance but also because I think it might be good for me if I can help him." He saw Naomi's face tightening, sharp lines appearing around her mouth and eyes. "You've been great," Jake said gently. "But let me steer my own life for now."

Naomi closed her eyes and Jake watched her take deep, measured breaths. He knew she was trying to avoid a knee-jerk response. When she finally spoke, her voice was quiet. "Why the hell do you think I've been doing what I do for all these years?"

"But why should you do anything? It's *my* life, *my* nightmares, *my* suicidal thoughts."

"You've gotta be kidding," she said, her voice starting to rise. "Who was waiting for you to come out of the bathroom all those nights when you spent hour after hour in there? Who made up excuses for the black eyes you gave me when I tried to wake you up from one of your nightmares? Me, goddamn it! Me!"

"I know that, Naomi. But that's not all you did. You also laid the groundwork for me to stuff my entire life history into a sea-bag and stow it under the bed. It was *you* who laid out rules about what I could and couldn't watch on TV. So I only watched 'acceptable' TV. It was *you* who asked me to stop going to the VFW. So I stopped going. It was *you* who suggested I avoid discussing war in my classes. So I don't discuss it. It was *you* who told me that connecting with my old Marine buddies would only bring on more flashbacks. So I don't visit my friends.

Your rules are choking the life out of me. For twenty-four years I've been sticking to them, and guess what? Following the rules is *all* I've been doing. I haven't been living; I've been keeping rules for twenty-four fucking years!"

Pulling the sheets up to her chin, Naomi said in a soft voice, "All right, maybe it's time to do things your way. I'll leave you alone. I'll get out of your way."

"Great!" he yelled. "Just fucking abandon me because I won't let you control every fucking breath I take! You and Uncle Sam – same story. 'Stuff it, Jake! Pretend that nothing happened! And remember: if you don't keep your mouth shut, we're out of here!' Oh yeah, they'd abandon me all right. It was too painful for them to hear what I'd done for them. And right now what you've been doing feels like the same thing. I really need you, Naomi. But I don't need you to be the general of the war that's inside me anymore."

For a long while they sat on opposite sides of the bed, Naomi with her knees pulled to her chest, Jake with his feet on the floor, his back to his wife. It might have been a half hour before Jake felt a shift on the mattress, then a hand on his shoulder. "You're right. I *have* made a lot of rules, but for a good reason: I didn't want to lose you." She paused. "But I hear what you're saying, Jake. I'm starting to see that if I keep insisting on the rules, I might lose you anyway."

Putting his hand on top of hers, Jake swiveled his feet off the floor and lay back on the bed. He gently pulled her head onto his chest.

"I'm hearing something new from you, Jake," Naomi murmured. "And I'm actually glad. When you were yelling at me just now I felt you were being real for the first time in a long time. I don't mean you're not a good person or a good husband or that you don't love me but – I don't know how to describe it. Your voice was different somehow. I didn't like the yelling but – but I heard what you were saying and it was new. It was like you wanted to stop protecting me from you."

Jake squeezed her, grateful for her understanding. "All I know is that for the first time in years there's a crack of light where the door's been pried open," he said quietly. "And I have to go through that door."

## ✧✦ CHAPTER ELEVEN ✧✦

Pax knew right where Sergeant Howie Watkins lived. He'd delivered papers to the house for years when the Chatwins lived there. Pax gave up his paper route around the same time that Mr. Chatwin's company transferred him to Arizona. The Watkins moved in just after that.

As Pax approached the house he thought, again, with surprise, about all the adults involved with his decision to join the Marines. He was seeing a new side of his mom; she'd started smoking openly in front of him. She was still prohibiting him from signing anything until he finished speaking with Mr. Finn. Why? She hardly knew Jake Finn. It must have something to do with his dad and her.

Mr. Finn was a nice guy, but the man was always trying to scare him. At times, it felt like Finn wasn't seeing him or listening to him. Pax sensed that Finn needed something from him, but he couldn't figure out what it could be. The strange thing was the more he tried to scare him with his war stories, the more Pax wanted to sign up.

Then there was Sergeant Watkins. The recruiter looked like he wanted to cry every time he spoke to him. He seemed stuck between needing Pax's signature and wanting to be his friend. Watkins told him more about his life than Pax's own father had.

As Pax walked up to the front door, he noticed the newly mowed lawn. Every blade of grass had been swept off the sidewalk. The hedges looked like they'd been pruned and checked with a carpenter's square, their tops as flat as Sergeant Watkins's haircut. Pax knocked. His hand was still in mid-air when the door opened. "Hey, Pax. Welcome to our home."

"Hello, sir. Thank you."

Sergeant Watkins wore a white, short-sleeved shirt, crisply ironed and neatly tucked into pressed khaki pants. The Marine insignia on his belt buckle glinted.

The men shook hands. Pax tried to match the amount of pressure he felt from Watkins's hand.

"Come on in," Watkins said. "I'd like you to meet my wife."

Pax entered the living room. "Alma, please come out here. I want you to meet Pax."

A tall woman came through the kitchen doorway. Her black dress matched the hair that fell in soft waves to her shoulders. Her dark eyes held his for a quick moment and he thought he saw the hint of a tear on her cheeks. She offered him a long-fingered hand. "My name's Alma."

Pax took her hand. "I'm – I'm Pax, he stammered."

"Pax? I've never met anybody with that name."

"It means 'peace' in Latin. My dad chose it."

"Very nice to meet you, Pax. Would you excuse me for a minute? I have some more to do in the kitchen."

Pax nodded.

"So your dad named you after the Latin word for peace," Sergeant Watkins said. "My father's favorite wasn't Latin but a Greek guy named Heraclitus, the guy who said, 'Out of every one hundred men on the battlefield, ten shouldn't even be there and eighty are just targets.' Only nine are real fighters, and we're lucky to have them, for they make the battle. Ah, but one, one of them is a warrior, and he will bring the others back."

"Very cool, you have it memorized," said Pax, walking toward Sergeant Watkins. Leaning in, he asked, "How do you say your wife's name again?"

"Alma," Watkins said distinctly.

"I got it. Alma."

"Our kids are at their friend's house for dinner," said Watkins. "Have a seat, he said, gesturing toward the couch. "I'll be right back." He went into the kitchen. A few moments later Alma came back and set a plate of cheese and crackers on the coffee table in front of Pax. "Help yourself."

"Thanks," Pax said, scanning the living-room walls. A large section of one wall was occupied by photos of the Watkins children. Above the fireplace hung a wooden carving of an eagle, holding an American flag in its claws. On another wall a plaque boasting "Semper Fidelis" hung beside an American Indian rug.

Watkins returned to the room and sat in an armchair, facing Pax. "That rug was woven by Alma's great-grandmother. We saw one like it on *Antiques Roadshow* that was priced over ten thousand dollars."

"Wow! Real cash!"

"We'd never sell it. It's a Hopi rug." Watkins pointed to the center of the weaving. "You see these four mountains? They're considered sacred; they represent the four directions of the compass," he explained.

Then his gaze shifted to the mantel. He got up, walked to the fireplace and lifted the "Semper Fidelis" plaque off the wall. Tapping it with his finger he walked toward Pax, "Hold this for a minute."

Pax reached for the sign. "Semper Fidelis," he read aloud. "That means 'always faithful,' doesn't it?"

"It does. That's the glue that holds the Corps together." He paused. "While we're waiting for dinner I thought this might be a good time for you to ask me any questions you might have. Anything on your mind?"

"Yeah, actually there is. I've been talking with Mr. Finn about his time in the Marines."

"He teaches junior English, doesn't he?"

"Yeah, that's him. He's a nice guy. He saw a lot of action as a Marine in Nam," Pax said.

"Really? I didn't even know he was a Marine. I went into his classroom once and asked if I could introduce myself to his students. He wouldn't let me talk to them."

"Yeah, he told me about that. I was doing some work for him at his house over the weekend. He got a little weird when he was telling me about Nam. I kind of expected it. My mother says Vietnam vets are a breed of their own. She should know; she married one."

"Hey, that reminds me. I found out I can't get your dad's records without his permission. Would you like me to write to him and see if he'd let me get them?"

"I would, but I'm not sure how my mom would feel about me getting in touch with him."

"You wouldn't have to. I'll do it."

"Let me think about it."

"What's Mr. Finn been talking to you about?"

Alma coughed softly from the doorway. "Gentlemen, dinner will be ready in five minutes."

Sergeant Watkins nodded.

"Mr. Finn asked me if it was okay with you if he came and spoke with you. I told him I didn't think you'd mind."

"No, not at all. Now that I know he's a combat Marine, I'd love to speak with him. What's his first name?"

"I think its Jake."

Howie, eyebrows lifted and he said under his breath, "Jake Finn." After bringing his hand to his chin he said, "Pax, please go on in, dinner's on the table." Pax noticed Alma, was looking at her husband a little too long.

"We'll talk about signing the papers after dinner."

Pax nodded. "There's something I need to tell you now. I promised Mr. Finn I wouldn't sign anything until he and I spoke again. I gave him my word."

"You must honor your word," Watkins said, placing his hand on Pax's shoulder and shepherding him towards the dining room.

# ✦✦ CHAPTER TWELVE ✦✦

"Did you see my rucksack anywhere? I thought I hung it in the laundry room," Jake asked raising his arms.

"You did. I moved it to the coat closet with your other gear, Naomi said shrugging her shoulders.

"Thanks. Remember, I'm meeting Duncan tonight at the VFW. If you need anything, you can call me on my cell."

"I may go to the movies if you're going be home late."

"Good idea."

It had been years since Jake had gone to the VFW. His best friend, Duncan, had been trying to get him to join again, but Jake had always given him the same response: "I'm not ready."

Duncan never gave up, though. So Jake wasn't surprised, a few weeks earlier, when he ran into his buddy at the health food store and received another invitation.

"There's a talk coming up at the Post that I thought you might be interested in. The speaker's the author of a book titled *The Soul in War*. His name is Ed Tock."

"The name's familiar. Lives over in Albany, right?"

"That's him. What do you think?"

"I'm ready."

"Excellent, excellent," Duncan said.

"I'll pick you up. We could do dinner first, too. What do you say?" Duncan asked.

"Sounds good," Jake said.

"Tilly's okay with you?"

"Yeah. I want to try one of those 'Heavy Weapons Burgers' that Pax ate in front of me the other day."

"Burgers? What happened to the tofu?" Duncan smiled.

Jake pointed into his shopping cart, "Right there. Pick me up at six."

Jake and Duncan found seats in the back row just before Tock started his talk. The author introduced himself as a Marine who served in Nam from 1969 to 1970, specifically as a door gunner in CH 53 helicopters. Jake was happy that the speaker kept his self-introduction short.

Tock began by reading a poem titled, "Confession." The poem described Tock's confusion when he came home from Nam. He read he was proud to be a Marine and ashamed to be a Marine; ashamed he had killed and ashamed that he may not have killed anyone.

By the time Tock finished the poem, Jake was gripping the empty chair back in front of him. "I'm gonna stay here if it kills me," he told himself. "I will not leave until he's done." He felt as though he'd stuck his finger into an electrical outlet and decided he wouldn't pull it out. Tock wound up his talk describing the loss of trust in country experienced by many returning vets.

Jake hadn't moved. The front of his shirt was damp with tears dropping from his beard. Taking in a deep breath he whispered, "I made it." He had not used his default strategy; escaping to the bathroom. He'd even let Duncan put a hand on his shoulder without making him pull it away.

"Those poems really stir up your shit, don't they?" Duncan said.

"Yeah, they do. Thanks, man. Thanks for being there."

"You want a drink before we go home?"

"Might be a good idea," Jake said, blowing his nose in his handkerchief.

Duncan and Jake had no trouble finding two empty barstools. Duncan waved the bartender over. "Hey, Fowler! How you doing? Could we get a couple of Fish Head Dogs?"

"Sure," Fowler said, grabbing frosted beer glasses from the freezer.

"You know my friend, Jake? He teaches English out at the high school. Ex-Marine."

"Shit! If he's a Marine, the drinks are on me." Fowler looked at Jake closely. "I think we might've met before. But it must've been years ago. Were you a Post member sometime in the seventies?"

"Yeah, I was. And I think I remember you, too. Shiloh was Post Commander then."

"Yeah, right. Shiloh. Now there's a Marine's Marine."

Jake thought he knew what was coming next. Fowler was going to tell the story of Shiloh chain-sawing his house in half.

"God, did that man see action. He was in Forest Recon."

Surprised, Jake took a deep draw on his beer. Putting the glass on the bar he said, "So was I. Did you know Shiloh?"

"Spent many a night with him – right here. Were you overseas with Shiloh?" asked Fowler. Then thumping his palm on the mahogany bar. "Marines buddy up. That's why the beer's on me." Fowler picked up his bar rag and looked at their glasses. "You want another one?"

"Yeah, I was overseas with him but we didn't know each other; we were in different squads. And yes another beer please." said Jake. Then he turned to Duncan. "I got this one."

"It good to see you loosen up Jake," Duncan said patting Jake on the shoulder.

"Thanks for telling me about Tock's talk. I'm glad I came tonight. I can't keep running away from my life. It feels good to be with men again. Seems like all of us are still struggling to understand what the sixties was about. Man, when Tock started reading that poem – how he was proud to be a Marine and ashamed to tell anyone he was a Marine – that nailed it for me."

Duncan lifted his beer glass and Jake raised his. They clicked their glasses together, and took large gulps. "You ain't got to worry about any of that shit here; somebody's always got your back. There's not a man in this place that's not made the same kind of mistakes."

Jake felt the beer relaxing his shoulders, looking around the room, he recognized several men from around town. He had imagined he'd be hearing war stories around the bar but most of the men were speaking about their families or jobs. A few were making comments about feelings stirred up in them by Tock's talk.

He turned to Duncan. "Tock was talking about guilt for taking the life of human beings. I don't know about other vets, but it's taken me years to stop seeing the Vietnamese as monsters. You remember how the commands came down over and over again 'Kill anything that moves.' Don't you?"

Duncan snorted though his nose, "I was good at it," then he looked into his beer and lifted his gaze to behind the bar. "I remember when they decided to put up the Vietnam Memorial. I couldn't believe they'd chosen an Asian design. But I went down to see it a few years ago; somehow it made a lot of sense. That long, long wall, snaking around, looking like it's half in the ground and half out, just like the war, an endless line of soldiers on their way into their graves."

Jake raised his eyebrows and nodded. "You just reminded me of something I've been wanting to ask you. Do you know Shiloh's kid, Pax?"

"Yeah, nice kid. His mom's done a great job with him. He was working at Marshall's Hardware last time I saw him. You have him in your class?"

"No, he's a senior now. But he's been asking me about the Marines because he's thinking of joining."

"No shit. My kid, Justin, wouldn't join the Marines if Osama Bin Ladin were camping in our backyard." Duncan lowered his beer glass. "So Shiloh's been gone for years and his kid's signing up? Who the hell knows what runs through these kids' minds? And you can't tell them anything, either; they won't listen." He paused. "And I guess that's nothing new. I didn't listen to a damn thing *my* old man said." He took another sip of his beer. "I don't want my kid joining, but I've made sure he doesn't know that. I give him a disapproving look every time he makes a negative comment about the Marines in Afghanistan."

"You don't tell him you don't want him to join?"

"Nah. He likes to do the opposite of whatever I say. If I say north, he immediately turns south. I don't want him turning south and joining the Marines."

"Sounds like you've figured him out. Got any advice on how I should handle Pax? He's been talking with the Marine recruiter at the high school. I can't believe they let these guys into the schools where they can pluck the ripest fruit. This Watkins guy's been working on Pax to sign up before he graduates."

Duncan took another gulp of his beer and licked the foam off his lips. "I think they've reached the very bottom of the barrel since there's no draft. Only kids that don't go to college or have good job prospects sign up. My son told me Pax is a good student and a great athlete. He must look like the best fruit on the tree to Watkins."

"Have you seen the internet videos by this Iraqi sniper named Juba? The one who's killing GIs?" Jake asked.

"I heard something about him on TV, but I haven't seen the videos."

"This bastard has himself filmed blowing up GIs with a sniper rifle and then posts the movies to a web site. After watching that kind of shit I can't get the image of this happening to Pax out of my head. No one can protect himself from a suicide bomber or a gutless sniper like Juba."

Fowler flipped his towel over his shoulder and leaned toward Jake. "I heard you telling Duncan about Shiloh's kid, Pax. He used to bring the kid in here when he was a boy," Fowler said, holding his hand out, about three feet off the floor. "I'd sit him up on the bar and feed him peanuts, one at a time. Did I hear you say he's thinking about signing up for the crotch?"

"Yeah," said Jake, shaking his head slightly. "Man, I haven't heard anyone use the word *crotch* for years. Anyway, I've been trying to get the kid to wake up to what war's about."

"That's one impossible job, buddy," said Fowler. "Only a Marine would take that on," he added, nodding. "But listen, you just reminded me. A couple of weeks ago I found something pretty interesting."

"Yeah?" asked Jake.

"A notebook of Shiloh's. We were breaking up an old desk to get it out the door, and I found a notebook wedged behind the bottom drawer. I think he must have been writing a book."

"No kidding."

"Actually, it doesn't surprise me." Fowler gazed at colored liquor bottles behind the bar. "I remember, back in his commander days, I'd sometimes see him in here late at night, working on an old typewriter." Looking at Jake, he said, "I read a few pages. It's heavy stuff, man."

"Is it about Nam?" Jake asked, picking up Duncan's glass and waving it at Fowler to refill it.

"Yeah," he nodded. "I'm not sure what to do with it. I mean, I haven't heard from Shiloh since he left town years ago. I guess I could give it to his wife but it occurred to me that Shiloh might not want her to have it. Might freak her out. You think Pax would want to read it?"

Jake rested his elbow on the bar and leaned his chin on his fist. "I have no idea."

Fowler tilted his head. "Might scare the kid out of the crotch?"

Duncan puckered his lips, considering the possibilities. "I mean, the guy didn't leave it on top of his desk. And he wasn't taking it home to work on it. I bet there's stuff in there that would explain a lot about the guy."

"Who the hell knows?" Jake said.

Duncan turned to Jake. "Look, you're the English teacher. Why don't you take a look at it? If it's worth giving to the kid, give it to him. If its stuff he shouldn't read, deep-six it."

"Good idea," Fowler agreed. "Shiloh was a good man when he wasn't drinking. I'd have been happy to have him at my back when I was over there."

Jake looked at the clock behind the bar. "I've got to get going. Naomi will be home from the movies soon. You want to stay?"

"Nah, I've got to go to work in the morning. I'll drop you off."

Jake swiveled on his barstool and put his feet on the floor. A loud thud on the bar stopped him from standing up. Fowler stood with his hand on a thick manuscript. "Here it is," he said. "Take it!"

Jake looked down at the top page and read the Latin inscription:

*Patris est filius Perfer et obdura; dolor hic tibi proderit olim*
-Ovid

"You know what it means?" asked Duncan.

"The first line means "He is his father's son. The second line means, be patient and tough; someday this pain will be useful to you."

"Woooo-hah! Nice going, Jake," said Fowler, tickled by the display of learning by his fellow Marine. "I think you ought to take it. See what it's about."

Jake closed the cover. "I will."

# ✧✦ CHAPTER THIRTEEN ✧✦

It was a cool, sunny Sunday. Naomi had left early to visit her parents for the day. After doing a few chores around the house, Jake took an hour-long jog on the rail-trail. He was back home and stepping out of the shower just before noon. During his run he'd been thinking about Shiloh's manuscript, shoved under a pile of papers on his desk. He hadn't mentioned it to Naomi.

Reaching for it now, Jake noticed how accurately the Latin inscription described Pax's situation. He pushed his swivel chair back. Putting his feet on the edge of the desk, he opened the draft and started reading.

*A tin cup sat on one of the flat stones surrounding a hand-dug well. Perspiration accumulated on my finger as I drew it across my forehead. Careful to keep the drops from dripping, holding my finger above my mouth I let the salty sweat drip onto my parched tongue. It tasted of mildew and jungle decay. From the protection of the tree line I'd been fixating on the tin cup for over two hours. I must have been hallucinating because when I closed my eyes, the cup was the size of a swimming pool with silvery light shimmering up from its blue bottom. Thirst was becoming an overwhelming power, pushing aside all the danger my mind knew was present.*

*I must have gone blank because I suddenly found myself at the edge of the well without any memory of how I got there. My brain must have stopped screaming: "You're dead, man! You are fucking dead!" I scanned the tree line for shooters, I flattened my back against the stones of the well. A wind gust picked up fine grains of sand that stuck to my damp skin. A short clump of elephant grass that was growing around the well* brushed my trousers, making a ticking sound — the sound of a clock, counting the last seconds of my life. I could feel the protective shadows of the jungle pulling me back. Crouching below the rim of the stone, I realized this was the first time in three days I'd been in sunlight.

It would have been safer to wait until after dark to drink. The green bananas I'd eaten hours before had left a coating like dry cement in my mouth.

Beside the well I found a hemp rope. One end was tied to an iron peg; the other, to a hollow bamboo tube. Keeping my head down, I lowered the tube into the well. I heard it splash. Flicking my wrist, I made a loop that traveled the length of the rope and tilted the bamboo tube so it would fill. I had seen this done in a village by an elderly Vietnamese man. I pulled the rope and felt the heft; it worked! The bamboo clanked against the stone walls of the well, reminding me of the elephant bones I'd knocked together a few days before while picking them for edible meat. A line of holes pierced the animal's hide, evidence of a chopper's door gunner practicing on something that couldn't shoot back.

The rope wet my hands making me pull faster. Lifting the bamboo tube over the well rim, I tucked myself down into a small angle of shadow. Pressing my back against the cool stones, I hurriedly lifted the tube to my mouth, stopping when I saw the rotting rim of the tube. I imagined Vietnamese women with decaying black teeth drinking from it. I lowered the tube between my thighs and reached over my shoulder for the cup resting on the stone rim. With shaking hands, I filled the cup and was bringing it to my mouth, after the first drip of water on my white-coated tongue I stopped. A small green head had risen above the surface of the water: I dropped the cup. The water spilled and I watched a tiny bamboo viper wiggling inside the cup. Marines know this snake as "the two-step snake."

After peering into the tube to make sure it was empty, I drank, sloshing water on the front of my shirt. After I had my fill, I carefully picked up the cup and held it at arm's length. Turning it over I expected the snake to drop out. Instead, a circular cut green leaf floated out of the cup landing on the wet spot. The snake stayed inside, even after I shook the cup hard. Then I noticed two holes in the bottom of the cup, with a fine "thread" running between them. The snake's tail had been tied into the bottom of the cup with just enough room for its head to reach the drinkers face.

I tossed the cup to the side muttering, "Fucking gooks." The cup landed on its side. I watched the snake attempt to dart to freedom with only a few inches of its head protruding. It wiggled relentlessly, trying to escape. With each wiggle, though, it succeeded only in embedding the rim of the cup more deeply in the sand.

The voice in my head was screaming again: "Get your ass back in the jungle!" I low-crawled to the protection of the tree line, taking the bamboo tube of water with me. Parting the thick elephant-eared leaves, I entered the safety of not being seen.

*When my breathing returned to normal I surveyed the clearing. I was in "Oklahoma Territory," the Vietnamese equivalent of the US Calvary term for Indian country. I heard, a week ago, some guy at a recon briefing say: "There are so many gooks in Oklahoma Territory that you can walk on their backs – all the way to Hill 55 never touching the ground." That's the hill I had to get to if I wanted to make it out of this fucking mess alive.*

So this is Pax's old man, thought Jake, putting the manuscript down on his desk. No wonder he needed more than one drink.

## ✦✦ CHAPTER FOURTEEN ✦✦

Alma stretched plastic wrap over a bowl of wilting salad greens, wondering whether it was a waste of time having even made the salad. Saving food for Howie was more of a ritual than a practical action these days, since she usually wound up throwing it out. Howie almost never got home in time to eat.

She'd just put the kids to bed and their voices were still echoing in her ears. "Is Daddy going to war again?" asked Andee as Alma lifted her up to the top bunk. The three-year-old hadn't seen her dad for the first year of her life. Howie had been deployed to Afghanistan before she was born.

Bell sniffled, "Is Daddy mad at us? When he comes home he just stays in his office room." Bell was eight and was heartbroken every time Howie shipped out. Alma remembered Bell crying every night at bedtime for the first month he was gone.

Alma and Howie had been married twelve years and had seen some hard times. The hard times had started with Howie's first deployment in March of 2003. When he left for Iraq, money was tight. As a corporal, Howie had not been eligible for base housing.

By the time he came home he'd been promoted to sergeant and could move his family to base housing. Life got back on track. At least that was the impression of everyone other than Howie and Alma.

The truth was, Howie couldn't sleep without a loaded weapon. They'd argued about keeping a loaded gun in the house with the kids. When Alma reasoned that a loaded gun was dangerous, Howie just turned her argument around, saying, "That's why the weapon's loaded. No one will get through the doors or windows of this house without a 5.56 millimeter hole in them." Alma had thrown up her arms in frustration and retreated into a numb silence. Only after she finally said, "I'm leaving if it's not out of here." The compromise was that Howie bought a gun safe.

Howie liked the work the Marines had given him. He even got to go to school to upgrade his job classification from infantry to Marine recruiter. Once the Marines promised he'd be put into the field as a recruiter, he expected the stress in his life to be reduced. He never imagined it would actually get much worse. He'd somehow overlooked or figured he had already been overseas so he was shocked when he found out that the first requirement was deployment to Afghanistan. It was 2008 and the U.S. was confronting a rising crisis there.

Alma hated that Howie was going, but part of her felt relieved – and ashamed for feeling that way. She hoped that time away from the family would help Howie realize that his recent behavior was deeply affecting those he loved.

Meanwhile, she and the kids would have to move off base to her parents' house in Arizona. In the short term, the move would be disruptive, especially for the girls. But in the long run, she was confident that the new arrangement would work out better for everyone.

Howie returned from Afghanistan in the summer of 2009. Alma was glad to see his tanned face when he knocked on her parents' front door. She felt hopeful. The temporary distance between them had been beneficial. The kids had settled into a loving home with her parents. And now, here was Howie, smiling at the door. Maybe things had worked out, after all.

For several months it seemed she'd been right. When they moved to Reeve the kids re-bonded with their father. He performed so well at his recruiting job, sometimes recruiting as many as four or five Marines a month that he was promoted to staff sergeant. Alma noticed a new smile that made Howie's face shine. And there were no weapons in the bedroom.

A few months after his return, Howie received the Bronze Star at a special ceremony. Both sides of the family had driven down to Camp Lejeune in North Carolina for the pinning. Not much was said at the ceremony as to why he'd gotten the medal other than his outstanding bravery in the face of danger. When Alma asked him what he'd done, he said he couldn't really talk about it.

Life was going so well that the couple decided to take their family back to Arizona for a powwow. Alma's father, Shuman, was a chief. At the beginning of every ceremony he led, he put the tribe's warriors in the center of the gathering. This powwow was no different. As tribe members filled the ceremonial grounds, Shuman invited Howie and the tribe's other soldier and Marine warriors to stand in the center while Shuman paid tribute to their courage and sacrifice for their tribe and country.

Afterward Howie said, "Tonight was the first time I felt like I've been seen as a real soldier. No one in the airport, or back home said any more than, 'Thanks for your service.' This ceremony helped me to feel whole again."

But the feeling of wholeness was fleeting. Back in Reeve, Howie started to slip back into his old ways. Alma had known, since Howie's return, that it was dangerous to think everything was better, but she wanted to trust that it was.

She denied telltale signs. She noticed that Howie got home from work later and later. She smelled alcohol on his breath a few times after he'd come home. His mood with the kids had become edgier; his voice got impatient more often.

Sitting on the couch waiting for him, she began doing some honest reflecting and realized that the good life had definitely ended over a month before. That was when Howie got his orders to visit the local high schools, at least once a week, to recruit students. As he'd told Alma, he hated recruiting.

Howie knew he wasn't the only one who disapproved of such recruiting. He'd already approached several principals of elementary and middle schools for lists of students' names and addresses. The principals weren't happy about providing this information; Howie couldn't get it without citing the federal legislation that authorized his request. Howie half-wished the law was not on his side.

"We have no right to be in these schools planting ideas of war in the minds of these little kids," he said.

Alma replied, "That's what your dad did to you, isn't it?"

"Yeah. That's exactly why I think it's criminal. But I'll lose all I've put into the Corps if I don't do it."

There were five schools in Howie's recruiting catchment area, which meant that he had to visit a different school every day of the week. And, in case this news wasn't bad enough, the new orders included a new quota: three to four recruits a month.

Alma reached up and turned off the lamp. Moonlight filtered through the blinds. She loved Howie and believed in what he'd given his life for.

She'd grown up in a patriotic home. Her father, Shuman, had served in the Marines during the Korean War, and her family was proud of that service.

But she also knew, very well, the damaging ways in which war affects families. For several years her mother fought with her father over his drinking and violence. Alma remembered watching him hold up a bottle of Jack Daniels and scream: "If it weren't for Marine blood, nobody – I mean *nobody*, goddamn it – *nobody* would be enjoying the freedom to drink anything." She also remembered her Uncle Catori and thanked the Great Spirit Massau'u for sending him to her family at that time.

She remembered seeing Uncle Catori sitting out on her family's front porch, waiting for Shuman to wake up. Catori's younger brother had passed out after a long night of yelling in his house. When Shuman finally stepped out onto the porch, Catori put his arm around his shoulders and said, "You're coming with me, Shu. You need a little time away. Some of the men from the tribe will join us, too. We'll be back in a week or so. You don't need to tell Elu. She knows."

Catori and other warriors of the tribe escorted Shuman out into the Arizona desert where they'd dug a hole deep enough to come up to Shuman's chin. They stood Shuman in the hole, tamped the sand down with their feet, and left him. They set up camp for themselves about fifty yards away, keeping him isolated but in clear view.

Four days and nights passed. Bugs bit Shuman's lips and crawled into his ears. He squeezed his eyelids shut so the bugs wouldn't creep over his eyeballs. He blew and twitched, trying to shoo them away. He bitched and screamed. He puked. He begged and threatened. "Please, help me! I'm dying of thirst. Dig me out – now! If I die in this hole you'll all pay! I hate each one of you and most of all you, Catori. You're supposed to be my fucking brother, and you're killing me!"

No one paid any attention to him except for giving him an occasional drink of water, which at first he spit back at the man giving it. Hour after hour passed and they listened to him wail. Not until the wail became like that of a desperate child calling its mother did the men turn their heads towards Shuman.

Finally Catori got to his feet, and then all the men stood and followed him over to Shuman. They seated themselves in a circle around Shuman. Catori started by asking his brother to tell them about what he'd done in the Korean War. Shuman sobbed for what seemed hours but said nothing. Suddenly with a signal from Catori all the men all stood up together. Shuman began to beg them not to leave. Catori replied, "It's time, brother."

Shuman then began telling them what he'd done in the Korean War. How he hated himself for the killing he'd done and how he'd been taking out his anger on his wife and kids. How he didn't believe that the war was just and that he'd unjustly taken life given by the Great Spirit. How he hated himself and needed to drink to relieve the pain that hollowed out his insides. By morning he was spent.

Catori offered Shuman a gourd of water and began digging him out of the hole. Several hands reached in and lifted him from the hole. Men brushed the sand from his skin. Warm water was brought in a bucket and the men bathed him and gave him fresh clothes. They led Shuman to their campfire and sat him in a comfortable lawn chair.

"Thank you, brother, for what you have done for me, for this tribe and for our country." Each man, in turn, stepped up to Shuman and offered a gesture of honor; a hand over the heart, a salute, a kiss on the cheek, a hug.

Alma found herself wishing she'd wake up to someone sitting on her front porch waiting to help her husband in that way – or *any* way.

# ✦✦ CHAPTER FIFTEEN ✦✦

Howie stood before the bedroom mirror inspecting his Blue Dress C uniform. Tapping on the shower door, he said, "Sweetheart, I've got to go."

The shower water stopped, and the door cracked open. Alma stuck her head out. "When you coming home?"

"Not sure. I could be late. I've only got two recruits and it's already near the end of May."

The shower door closed softly and the water came back on.

Running the lint roller up and down his blue and red striped pants, he stopped midway on his left leg to pinch the dark blue cloth between thumb and forefinger, trying to straighten it into a sharper crease. The local dry cleaner didn't know how to press uniforms like the cleaners near military bases. Still, he looked crisp with his bronze star hanging below a triple line of campaign ribbons. Kids loved asking him about them. He was always careful not to boast.

Today he was headed to Corin High School to sit behind a recruiting table at a job fair. It was 6:30 and he had to be there at 7:00 to meet three young men who'd agreed to help him raise the flag before school started.

Flag raising was one of his new ideas that seemed to be helping fill his quota. He was teaching the pre-Marines flag etiquette; how to handle and fold the flag. The details he was teaching were making sure that if the flag is to be flown at half-mast, it's lifted to the top for a moment before being lowering to half-mast. When taking a half-mast flag down, one should first raise it to the top before lowering it. He loved knowing such rules and was angry that most Americans had no idea what any of them meant.

He'd already signed up these young men he was meeting, Bill Keets and Tim Haig. He was hoping they'd persuade Pax to pick up the pen, too. He couldn't count Bill and Tim for this month's quota because he'd signed them up last month and they wouldn't be entering the Corps until after they graduated. The reality was that it was May 23rd and he had only two recruits.

Pulling the Ford Explorer door closed quietly, so as not to wake his neighbors, Howie backed out the driveway and pulled the brim of his uniform hat down to block the rising sun. He noticed his breathing was shallow, his forearms tense beneath his khaki shirt as he motored out of his housing development onto Route 308. Not much movement yet; no kids waiting for buses, a few lights on in the houses he was passing. There wasn't a morning that he got into the Ford that he didn't remember driving the Humvee in Fallujah. He watched himself turn his head in a frenzied movement, his eyes darted from side to side, as though an invisible marionette string was left tied to him from Afghanistan.

Each time he returned home from war he'd attended re-entry classes where they pounded one message into his head; there were no IEDs on American roads. He knew, as he drove the local roads, that passing vehicles weren't driven by suicide bombers. It just didn't matter. All the Marines in those classes had nodded their heads in unison when the instructor spoke, but he knew that not one of them drove any differently than he was right now.

It had occurred to Jake that Bill, Tim and maybe Pax would be driving just as he was – if they made it home alive. This sort of thinking was making it hard to keep putting enlistment papers in front of the kids he'd befriended. They looked at him with such awe and respect. They saw only his medals and the creased uniform, not the loaded 45 in the glove box, or the rage he swallowed every time Alma was watching PBS on TV and the dead faces of men and women scrolled up on the screen and he waited for it to be someone he knew or had enlisted. Recruiters like him had enlisted each of those dead men and women on the screen.

It wasn't that he lied to his recruits; it had more to do with the fact that he used eye contact, posture and his voice to steer every conversation toward the positive benefits the Marines had waiting for them. They stared at him when he spoke of the honor woven into the Marine uniform they'd be putting on every morning. He told them the teamwork they'd learn in boot camp would allow them to do what many saw as impossible. He emphasized the important part of history for - which they'd be personally responsible.  He'd worked these points so often they came off his lips as if he were a smooth-tongued street rapper – in uniform.

Looking at his reflection in the side window, he wished that honor and bravery *were* still woven into his uniform. The truth was that they'd been torn out during his first days in combat.  Now the uniform was more like a handsome cooking pot with nothing left in it but boiling water.

## ✧✦ CHAPTER SIXTEEN ✧✦

Over lunch Jake listened to a discussion, on the radio news, about Stop-loss; an involuntary extension of a soldier's active-duty service. A young soldier had challenged the U.S. government by refusing a second deployment to Iraq.

In response to the newscaster's question, a historian explained that the law had been used most recently; immediately before and during the first Persian Gulf War. He went on to say that after that it had been used during deployments to Somalia, Haiti, Bosnia and Kosovo, as well as after the September 11 attacks and during the subsequent War on Terror.

While listening, Jake felt an ache in the pit of his stomach as he wondered how many kids from his classes would have their active duty extended in a war zone. He knew that at least a third of the kids in his classes weren't going to college and the likelihood of the military was a real possibility.

Returning to Shiloh's manuscript Jake read for a few hours. He tossed book onto the desk, mumbling, "This cat was deep in the guts of it."

Meandering into the kitchen, he opened the refrigerator and stood looking into it for a long time. Empty handed, he turned and went upstairs.

Without remembering why, he found himself in the attic, looking at his military footlocker. He hadn't opened it since coming home from Nam in 1970. Snapping its buckles, and lifting the lid, a faint smell of jungle mold and sweat deepened his trance. Lifting out red, mud-stained camouflage utilities, he fished down past notebooks, medals, and documents that contained his orders. When he reached the bottom, he found his tarnished Marine belt buckle. Sliding the buckle into his pants pocket, he closed the lid.

In a kitchen closet he found a can of Brasso. Tearing a paper towel off the roll, he poured a small amount of the ammonia-smelling liquid on it and began polishing his brass. Rubbing the buckle bright he imagined Pax doing this chore in boot camp next month.

Why did this kid's life cross his path? Was it really his job to try and keep him out of the Marines? "No" was the answer that floated up. He couldn't stop Pax anymore than his own mother and father could have stopped him.

Jake knew Pax's situation was different, though. The probability that Pax would be killed was greater than it had been for the men of his generation. As he'd told Pax, in his own case he'd been obliged to complete *only one* thirteen-month tour in Nam. Once he completed it, he *never* had to return. Pax had merely smiled at him in response.

"Wake up man!" Jake said. "You might serve four or even *five* tours of duty before you get to come home. That means the odds of being wounded or killed are pushed up – a lot." Pax had just shrugged. "Do you know about the 1990 policy called "Stop Loss and Stop Movement?" Jake, asked.

Pax shook his head. "That's your assignment," said Jake. "Go on line and read it. Basically it says the law allows the military to keep soldiers beyond the terms of their voluntary commitments. And the "Stop Movement" policy keeps soldiers from moving to new assignments, forcing them to stay in combat zones." Pax's expression was dull, as though Jake was reading from a boring textbook. "I got it, old man," his face said. "I'll take care of myself."

Jake knew that the wars in Iraq and Afghanistan were different from Vietnam, no matter how often news commentators compared them.

The gleam off his brass belt buckle stirred Jake from his reflections. Looking at the clock on the kitchen wall, he realized that Naomi would be home soon. Opening the refrigerator door, he considered what he might throw together for dinner.

At dinner Jake showed Naomi his brass belt buckle. She rotated it and said, "What was it you told me about brass when you first got out of the Marines? Something like, the Marine who doesn't shine the back of his brass doesn't whip his ass."

Jake smiled. "You got it," he said, turning the buckle over in her hand so she could see the back.

In the morning he leaned over and was about to kiss Naomi goodbye – carefully, between spoonfuls of oatmeal – when he interrupted himself. "I forgot something," he said, "I'll be right back." He went upstairs and slipped the belt buckle into the pocket of his dress pants. Back downstairs he kissed Naomi, "I'll be a little late. I'm meeting Pax at Tilly's again after school."

"What time should I start dinner?"

"About six would be great."

A mist from last night's rain was rising from the asphalt street as Jake walked to school. He knew that today was his last chance with Pax. His game plan was to first find Sergeant Howie Watkins at the school job fair and ask him to ease up on the boy. He could feel his jaw tighten as he thought of this conversation. It still wasn't easy for him to talk to a Marine in uniform. He wondered how dress blues still had power over him.

Reading Shiloh's story was like having a truck with a winch back up to his past hooking onto it and dragging it out of the jungle mud. He understood all too well why Shiloh disappeared from his family. The action Shiloh saw in Nam rattled him to the bone. Jake knew most Marine snipers cut notches in the stocks of their rifle. He couldn't stop wondering what Shiloh's rifle stock looked like.

Jake noticed he was shaking after he put the manuscript down. He now wondered what would happen if he suggested to Pax to make contact with his dad at this critical moment. It felt like he somehow worked way into the middle of a life force between Shiloh and his son.

# ✧✦ CHAPTER SEVENTEEN ✧✦

Alma was combing Bell's hair when the phone rang. She glanced at the kitchen clock; it was 8:00.

"Hello? Who is this, again?"

"Mrs. Watkins, its Pax."

"Oh, hello Pax. Yes, I remember you."

"Could I speak with Sergeant Watkins?"

"He's not here right now. I think he's at his office."

"Mrs. Watkins, I saw him leave the office. He seemed upset."

"Upset? What did he say?"

"I couldn't understand. He just seemed angry."

Alma was silent for a moment. "Where are you, Pax?"

"Outside Sergeant Watkins's office."

"Okay, stay right there. I'll be there in a few minutes. I need to ask my neighbor to watch the kids. I'll be there as soon as I can."

"Okay," Pax said, folding his cell phone.

Alma hung up, wrapped Bell in a towel and called Betty.

Pax was pacing outside the recruiting office when Alma pulled into the parking lot. She hurriedly walked toward the young man, who stopped when he saw her, his hands in his pockets, shoulders hiked to his ears. "Tell me, again, what he said!"

"He told me he met Mr. Finn this afternoon and, after talking with him, he decided he was done with recruiting. Then I think he said, "I'm done with everything." I asked him what he meant but he didn't answer. He just turned and slowly walked to his SUV. Then he pulled out of the parking lot and headed toward Warren on 308. His face scared me. I ran after him but he sped up."

Alma began shaking. Pax started to move toward her but, uncertain about whether he should touch her shoulder, he stopped and said, "Maybe we should call Mr. Finn."

"Who's this Mr. Finn?" Alma asked, closing her eyes and biting her lip.

"He's a teacher at the high school who's been talking to me about signing up. He's an ex-Marine. A Vietnam vet."

"What do you think Mr. Finn said to Howie?"

"Not sure. But when I met with Mr. Finn he seemed like our talks got him pretty worked up. My mother made me promise I'd talk with him before signing up. I do know he's angry about having recruiters in the schools." He shrugged. "I don't know. Maybe they had a fight."

"Howie respects ex-Marines; his father's one. He sees them as his brothers. I can't imagine that he'd get into a fight with a fellow Marine. I need to find out what happened. Do you know how to get in touch with Mr. Finn?"

"I had dinner with him at Tilly's today before I went to see Mr. Watkins at the office. I told him I was going to see Mr. Watkins to sign up." Pax put his hand into his pocket and pulled out a shiny brass belt buckle. "Mr. Finn gave me this and shook my hand. I know where he lives. I can take you there if you like."

"Get in the car," said Alma.

# ✧✦ CHAPTER EIGHTEEN ✧✦

Jake reached for the Buddha lamp on the end table from his easy chair. Naomi had gone up to bed a half hour earlier. He rested his fingers on Buddha's head, as he did almost every night before going to bed. Taking in a deep breath, he switched the light off.

As he made his way up the stairs, the phone rang. Jake took the stairs three at a time, hoping to reach the phone before it woke up Naomi. But by the time he go to it, she was sitting up in bed.

"Hello?" Jake paused. "Pax! It's after ten. What's going on?" He listened. "What? Slow down; say it again." He listened again. "Okay. We're at number 14. I'll put on the outside light over the front door. Tell me the rest when you get here."

Naomi was already out of bed, putting on her robe and slippers. "What's going on?"

"They're almost here. I'll tell you downstairs," Jake said, rushing out of the bedroom.

Hands on both banisters, he made it midway down the staircase with his first leap and was on the landing within a second.

Naomi's voice trailed him: "Who's almost here?"

Before she could get down the stairs Jake was bounding up them again. "What the hell's going on?" she yelled, pressing herself against the wall so her husband could get by.

"Pax and Mrs. Watkins are on their way here. Mrs. Watkins's husband is the recruiter who's trying to sign Pax up. Sounds like he may be suicidal."

"What's any of this got to do with us?" she strained, fear rising in her voice.

"I'll tell you after I put some clothes on. Do you know where I put my boots?"

"They're on the shoe rack in the pantry."

Jake and Naomi stood by the front window, looking for headlights, as he filled her in on what he knew.

"I tracked Watkins down at the school job fair and introduced myself to him. I told him I'd been in the Marines and mentioned I was in the 1st Force Recon. His eyes bulged when he heard that. Then he told me that was his dad's unit during Korea. He said that one of his obsessions was to follow the history of that Force Recon unit. He started telling me what we did in Nam. When I told him my last name he sucked his lips in like he was going to cry."

"Why?" asked Naomi, surprised. What does he know that I don't?"

"Nothing. I guess he's one of these gung-ho Marines that lives his life through military history. He was able to reel off the names of my men in Nam. I put my hand up and said, 'Can we do this somewhere else?' I took him to my classroom. There was nobody there."

"Hey, look. There's a car, going slowly," Naomi said, balling up the front of her nightgown in her hand. She turned from the window and said, "I'm going upstairs to change."

"I'll let them in."

Jake watched through the door window. Pax was the first to reach the door. He stood shifting his weight from foot to foot and rang the doorbell before Jake could open the door. Mrs. Watkins was in a housedress that billowed as she came up the sidewalk. She ran her hand through her hair trying to get it out of her face.

Jake opened the door, and Pax blurted out, "Mr. Finn this is Mrs. Watkins, Mr. Watkins's wife."

Jake smiled. "I figured." He gestured for Pax to come in and reached his hand out to Mrs. Watkins.

Taking his hand, she said, "I'm so sorry to bother you so late. It's just that I'm worried about my husband and I thought you might be able to help."

"Whatever you need," Jake said, gesturing toward the living room chairs.

Mrs. Watkins sat on the edge of Jake's chair. He reached past her to the Buddha lamp, brushing its head lightly before turning it on. They all heard a sound in the stairway and looked toward it. "That's my wife, Naomi," said Jake. "Let me introduce you."

Naomi reached the landing and stood with her arms at her sides. "Sweetheart, this is Mrs. Watkins. My wife, Naomi. You know Pax."

Naomi extended her hand to Mrs. Watkins and nodded at Pax. "Good to meet you," she said, sitting on the arm of the chair facing Mrs. Watkins. Can I offer you something to drink?"

"No," Mrs. Watkins said weakly, her voice faltering. "I'm sorry. I wish this were a friendly visit. My husband has been having a hard time and when Pax called to tell me that Howie just drove away from him saying he was done with signing recruits and done with everything, I mean, I got scared and that's why we're here. Pax told me that Mr. Finn had spoken to Howie earlier in the day," she said, facing Jake.

Jake placed his hand on his bearded chin and nodded, and said, "Yes. We did speak."

Pax stammered, "Mr. Watkins told me that you were a hard core Marine. He said that after he spoke to you, he knew he'd have to give up recruiting."

"What else did he say?" asked Mrs. Watkins.

"That's pretty much it," Pax said, looking around the room for a place to sit.

Naomi squinted at Jake. "What happened between you and Mr. Watkins?"

"Well, we talked for about fifteen minutes. Mr. Watkins was very excited after he heard I was in the 1st Force Recon in Nam. I guess he's a military historian, yes?" Jake asked, looking at Mrs. Watkins.

"I wouldn't call him a historian, but he's an expert on the history of the 1st Force Recon. His father belonged to it in Korea."

"Where do we go now?" Jake asked.

"Did he say anything strange to you? I mean did he look like he was coming unhinged? He's been trying to hide his depression by not coming home and overworking. I'm worried about him. I smelled alcohol on his breath a few nights ago, and he never used to drink," Mrs. Watkins said, wringing her hands.

"He was very nervous when we spoke," Jake said. "At one point when he was talking about Pax, his voice broke. But I didn't think he was suicidal. Did he see a lot of action?"

"I don't know. He doesn't talk to me about what he saw in Iraq or Afghanistan."

"He served two tours?" Jake asked.

"Yes. He's been back a while now. The Marines wouldn't let him have the recruiting job if he didn't go to Afghanistan, so he went."

"I didn't know he'd been in combat," Jake said, rubbing his fist on the side of face.

Naomi reached for Mrs. Watkins's hand and said, "I know about the not talking. Have you got any idea where he might be?"

"No! We don't really have any friends here yet."

"Who's his commanding officer?" Jake asked.

"Captain Ragnar. He's the head of all the regional recruiters."

"I think we should give him a call. Maybe he can help."

"If we do that, Howie will lose everything." Mrs. Watkins took a deep breath and let go of Naomi's hand.

In a soft voice Pax said, "He used to take me over the Rhinecliff Bridge and tell me that Force Recon had to be able to belay from as high as the bridge. He would say that every time he took me to the recruiting office in Newburgh. He was headed in that direction when he pulled out of the parking lot."

Alma didn't look at Pax or give any sign that she'd heard him. She was still reviewing her own memories. "I could see it in his eyes," she said. "Less shine every time he signed a new boy. The only thing he thinks he can do is serve the Corps. His dad put so much pressure on him – first to join, and then to stay. He told me if he weren't a Marine he wouldn't know who he is. I told him he's a dad, a husband and a good man. But that just made him shut down more. We had this talk a few nights ago when he came home late," Mrs. Watkins said, looking at the floor. "It was the first time I heard him speak about how he really felt about the Marines."

"All right. Let's drive over to the recruiting office first. Maybe he's come back by now," said Jake. "We'll take my car."

# ✦✦ CHAPTER NINETEEN ✦✦

The tires thumped on the seams of the Rhinecliff Bridge. All their necks craned to see if anyone was standing at the rail, preparing to jump. Jake was driving so slowly that the drivers behind him started blowing their horns.

"Nothing!" Jake said, "Let's go to the office. Maybe he's there."

Pax sat back in his seat and noticed Mrs. Watkins had her hands over her eyes. He touched her sleeve. When she looked at him he whispered, "It'll be okay."

She shook her head slowly, and then spoke. "Mr. Finn, do you know where the recruiting office is?"

"I signed up there. If it's in the same place it was forty years ago, I know where it is."

"It is," Pax confirmed.

Naomi sat with her hands folded in her lap, looking into the dark at the sides of the road. Jake reached his hand to her thigh and squeezed lightly. Her face was taut and grim; he knew she was expecting him to fall apart anytime.

But except for his worry about Howie's disappearance, Jake had rarely felt better. He was alert and focused. He was organized. He had a game plan. He felt as though he'd traveled back in time to Vietnam and was embarking on an operation again.

He remembered when leading a platoon in Nam, he was able to reached a state of knowing calm; it was how he'd been able to keep most of his men alive. He was feeling that state of calm coming again. Everyone in the car was part of his body and his job was to keep everyone alive.

Watkins was out there somewhere – most likely in danger. Jake let himself imagine what Watkins had been thinking and where it might make sense for him to go. He'd learned to do this with his enemy in Nam. Based on what he'd heard from both Pax and Mrs. Watkins, and the expression on Howie Watkins's face after Jake's conversation with him at school, there was little question that something was wrong. Jake had seen it in his eyes.

He chose not to share these thoughts with the others. It would only create panic, and at this moment Jake needed, more than anything, to stay composed. He loosened his hands on the steering wheel and breathed to relax his shoulders.

The recruiting office loomed into view and Jake pulled into the parking lot. He saw Watkins's Ford Explorer straddling two parking spaces at an odd angle. All four doors of Jake's car popped open at the same time.

Mrs. Watkins was the first to reach the office door. She grabbed the knob of the storm door with both hands and tried to turn it. The door wouldn't open. She pounded her fists on the glass, yelling, "Howie, open this door!"

Jake walked up and stood beside her. "I don't think he's in there."

Alma turned and looked at him. "I know." She looked away. "I guess I want him to be in there."

Jake nodded. "Pax, go around to the back of the building," he said. "Check the windows and look for a way we can break in. Naomi, there are still lights on in that house on the other side of the parking lot. Go ask the neighbors whether they saw Mr. Watkins going into the office or walking away."

"It's 11:30 at night.  You know I'm gonna wake them up, don't you?"

"Yeah, that's why I want *you* to do it. Instead of me or Pax. You won't scare them."

Mrs. Watkins was sobbing helplessly, her face in her hands.  Jake gently put his hands on her shoulders and shook her lightly.  "Look at me," he said.  "We don't know that anything has happened.  Time is the most important factor right now."  He took a breath.  "Please stop crying," he added.  He pulled his cell phone from his pocket and handed it to her. "Call him!"

Her fingers trembled as she pressed the keys.  Jake could hear the phone ringing at the other end.  The fourth ring was interrupted by a screaming voice. "Finn! What do you want?" Howie demanded.

Mrs. Watkins's words froze in her mouth.  Her shoulders rose. Holding her breath, she started to hold the phone out to Jake, then suddenly pulled it back and pressed it against her chest. "It's his caller ID," she said quietly.  "He thinks it's you.  Please speak to him.  I know he wouldn't have picked up if he'd known it was me.  I've already called him ten times from our home phone."

Jake brought the cell to his ear.  His chest expanding with air, he screamed, "Where the hell are you, sergeant?"

There was no answer, but no hang-up either.  Jake closed his eyes. After a short silence, he yelled into the phone once more.  "I'm going to ask you again: where the hell are you?"

"Three clicks behind the recruiting office, on a hill above the river."

"Listen to me carefully.  I'm at the recruiting office and I am coming out.  Look at the river can you see the lights on the Newburgh side?"

"Yes, sir."

"There's a red tower light blinking every two and a half seconds.  Can you see it?"

"Yes, sir."

"I want you to stand at attention with your eyes on that light, sergeant," Jake barked, like a drill instructor. I will be at your side before you count to two hundred."

"Aye, aye, sir. Sir, are you alone?"

Jake looked at Mrs. Watkins, still trembling in front of him. "I'm coming alone, sergeant," he said. "Ten-hut! I want you to start counting off now. Keep going until I get to you. You with me Sergeant?

"Yes sir."

"Good!"

Jake clicked the phone shut and yelled to Pax to come back around the building. Then he looked into Mrs. Watkins's face. "I'm going to find him, When Naomi comes back from that house, borrow her cell phone. I'll need an hour. I want all of you to wait in the car. At some point I'll call you on Naomi's phone. Answer it as soon as it rings. "If you don't hear my voice or your husband's, call the police and tell them we're on the knoll fifteen hundred yards behind the building, overlooking the river. If you hear your husband's voice, tell him where you are and that you're waiting for him." Jake reached for her shoulders and centered her in front of him firmly. "You with me?"

"Yes. Yes, sir."

"Tell Naomi what I'm doing. Don't let her call the police or come after me. Do you understand? Your husband's life may be at stake – and mine." Mrs. Watkins nodded.

Pax came running around the corner of the building. He was about fifty feet away when Jake yelled, "Stop right there." Jake looked at Mrs. Watkins and pointed to his car. "Get in the car." He walked over to Pax.

"Here's the deal. You're going to stay in the car with my wife and Mrs. Watkins, while I go into the woods to find Watkins. We've made phone contact."

"Let me help you."

"Keep your mouth shut, Pax. I'm going to say this once more. You will wait in the car. Mrs. Watkins will have Naomi's phone. If I need you, I'll call. If you want to be some kind of hero and sneak your ass out there, remember that a life is at stake – maybe two. I'm almost sure he's carrying a weapon. You with me on this?"

"Yes, sir."

# ✧✦ CHAPTER TWENTY ✧✦

The first hundred yards were thick with saplings of maple, oak and sumac. As the forest rose into mature trees the going became easier, but the canopy was dense and let in little moonlight. Jake moved as fast as he could, holding his right hand out in front of him to ward off eye-level branches.

It surprised him that Watkins seemed to be obeying him, and he wondered how long the obedience might last. He knew that he needed to stay under cover because he didn't want to let Watkins see him approach. At least not until he'd been able to scope out the surrounding area for a rifle or other weapon.

The skyline was becoming visible as he neared; he saw the moon shining off the channel in the Hudson River. Bending so he'd be able to see Watkins's silhouette, he scanned the crest of the hill in front of him. If Watkins' was telling the truth, he had a pretty good idea of the distance indicated by "three clicks." Jake strained his eyes for some sign of Watkins. Nothing. He checked the luminescent dial of his watch he been out fifteen already.

He felt the ground in search of a hand-sized rock, but the best he could do was a stick that felt thick enough to hold as a club. He started again, this time able to move faster, he headed directly toward the crest of the hill. Suddenly, at what seemed to be about twenty yards ahead, he saw what looked like a man's head. Getting down on his knees and elbows, Jake crawled toward what he hoped was Howie. As he got closer he could see that there was a dip just beyond the top of the hill. Watkins was standing there, at attention, looking out at the river and mumbling.

Jake worked his way closer and could hear Watkins counting off: "One hundred ninety-one, and one hundred ninety-two." Jake saw a large tree right beside Watkins. At first he could barely make out the ground on which Watkins was standing. As Jake's eyes began to adjust he saw that Watkins stood on a narrow ledge of rock that dropped off sharply and he was only a few inches from the edge.

Watkins had reached two hundred and stopped counting. Jake heard his feet shuffling and he stood and heaved the wood off to Watkins's right. The sergeant turned toward the sound. Jake then took three huge steps, jammed his hand into the back of Watkins's trousers and yanked him back from the edge of the rock. A taut rope encircled Watkins's neck.

## ✧✦ CHAPTER TWENTY-ONE ✧✦

Rain pelted the windshield as Jake pulled out of the parking lot. He turned on the wipers and looked in the rearview mirror. Alma was sitting in her husband's lap and Pax was looking out the side window. Howie's arm was wrapped tightly around his wife's waist; his head, buried in her chest.

Jake looked at Naomi and shrugged. "We're going to our house," he said. No reply.

Jake wondered whether he ought to drop Pax off at his own house. He thought it might not be good for Pax to continue witnessing Howie's unfolding story. Before he suggested taking Pax home, however, he had another thought. Why was he trying to protect this kid who was ready to sign up and start killing enemy he did not know?

He turned the wiper knob up a notch. The wind buffeted the car on the bridge and he pulled into the left lane. No one spoke. The car was filled with Howie's whispered apologies to Alma.

"We're here," said Jake, pulling into his driveway. He got out quickly and opened the car door for Howie and Alma. The couple got out, while Jake walked ahead of the others to the front door. Jake turned the lights on in the living room.

"Good, it stopped raining," Naomi said. "I'll put up some coffee. Pax, you can use the phone in the kitchen to call your mom and tell her you're okay."

Jake raised his hand to stop Pax. "Before you do that, though, I'd like to have a few words with you," he said. "Would you please step outside with me for a minute?"

Pax nodded. "All right."

Alma and Howie were sitting together on the couch. Alma was crying. She looked as angry as she was upset. Howie's arm was around her shoulders. Naomi handed her a box of tissues and went to the kitchen.

Jake opened the front door let Pax step past him and eased the door shut. Jake said, turning to the boy. "I thought it might be a good idea if I told you how I'm thinking about what just happened."

"Thanks, Mr. Finn," Pax said, pinching his dripping nose with his thumb and forefinger, not knowing what to do with it he put his hand in his pocket.

"I'll be straight with you. Watkins was trying to kill himself. We had a talk. For now I think he's back on solid ground."

Pax crossed one foot over the other and fidgeted as he listened. "How do you know for sure he won't try again?"

"I don't. But I do know that if this story gets to the wrong people he'll be forced out of the military. And I'm pretty sure that if *that* happened, he'll try again."

"Yeah, before he got into his truck tonight he told me he hated what he had to do for his job. He even apologized for manipulating me into signing up. I told him I would've signed up no matter who the recruiter was, so whatever he'd said to me didn't matter. I told him I'd been planning to do this since I was a kid. I don't think he believed me, though. He just nodded and said 'Sure!' Then he drove away."

"Listen, we can't stay out here all night, so I'll cut to the chase. I need you to do one thing; keep what just happened to yourself. You're going to have to trust me to handle Watkins. He needs help, but it can't come from the military. I can't tell you any more than that right now." He paused, watching Pax's face. "You still with me?"

Pax uncrossed his legs and looked into Jake's eyes. "Yeah," he said. "I'm with you."

In that instant Jake caught a flash of Shiloh in Pax. "Good. Thanks, Pax. I'll be in touch with you in a few days to try and help you sort all this out. Now let's go inside."

"Mr. Finn, would you mind if I just went home? I'm not sure I want to hear all of what's going to happen next."

Jake moved toward the boy and put his hand on his shoulder. "Yeah, I think that would be fine. Just remember, don't tell your mom what happened. You'd scare the hell out of her."

"I know."

"All right, I'll tell everyone inside that you and I talked and you needed to go home."

"Thanks, Mr. Finn," Pax said, with a catch in his breath.

Jake drew the boy into a quick embrace, and then firmly pushed him away. Turning him by the shoulders, he said, "Go home. You're going to make a good Marine I saw that in you tonight."

# ✦✦ CHAPTER TWENTY-TWO ✦✦

Jake opened the front door. Naomi was sitting on a hassock in front of Alma and Howie, holding hands with both of them. Jake sat down in his chair and instinctively began rubbing the Buddha's head. Watching Naomi, he recognized her skill as a social worker.

"Are you two okay alone for a few minutes?" she asked.

They both nodded. "Jake, will you come with me into the kitchen?"

"Sure," he said, getting up.

Naomi closed the door between the dining room and kitchen and took a deep breath. Closing her eyes, she said, "Quite an evening."

He nodded.

"What happened to him out there?"

"He was set up to hang himself. I stopped him and was able to convince him to come back with me. He can't see any hope for a career in the Marine Corps. He said, 'If I quit my old man will have a heart attack, and if I stay I'm not going to make it.'" Jake grinned at her. "This is *your* territory; what do *you* think we should do?"

"He's got to be taken to the hospital. It's the law. We have to report this. If we don't report it and the authorities find out, we'll be in big trouble."

"He doesn't want to go to the hospital. He's already told me that."

"Then we'll have to call the police. And if *that* doesn't work, the next on the list to be called will be his commanding officer."

Jake pulled on his graying brown beard, his eyes fixed on the small pond in the backyard. Turning back to his wife, he said, "I'm not sure that's the best thing to do."

"It's not about choosing the *best* thing; it's about the *right* thing. Under the circumstances, we don't have a choice," said Naomi.

Raising his voice, Jake said, "So you think we should go back in that room and tell the them that the police will be here in a few minutes to take them to the hospital? And, by the way, if you don't want to go we'll call your commanding officer, and he can take care of it!"

Biting her lower lip, Naomi said, "That's pretty close to what we should say."

"Okay. Then let me tell you what I think will happen next. Watkins will tell us he's not going to the hospital. We'll call the police and they'll send a patrol car. At least ten of our neighbors will see the police car from their windows. They'll all see who gets into the car. At the station, the police will call his commanding officer. After all, they're required to investigate why he's there and they do what is right. All of this gets put into his military record and before you know it, he's dismissed from the Corps. How long would you predict this man living after that?"

Naomi turned her palms toward the ceiling in exasperation. "All right!" she said. "What do *you* recommend? Send them home as if nothing happened? Like you just did with Pax? An hour ago this man was going to end his life. What has changed in that time that makes anything different?"

"We spoke for an hour before we came out of the woods. I think I know what's driving him."

"You're willing to risk his life on what you *think* you know?"

"Yes," Jake said. "He stood at attention for almost twenty minutes after I told him to. He was counting the blinking tower light when I got there. I'm a Marine and he's a Marine. What else can I tell you?"

"Marine to Marine. That's all it takes to make you confident that this guy's not going to off himself? That he's not going to leave his lovely wife and two kids to fend for themselves?"

"Yup, that's what I'm telling you. He gave me his word of honor."

"And what happens if we call the police? He retracts his word of honor?"

Jake knocked his fist against his forehead. "Calling the cops wasn't part of the deal!" He thought for a moment. "Listen, I could take a few sick days from school."

"Wait a minute! Where are you going with this?" Naomi asked, puffing out her lips.

"I'm willing to spend time with Howie until you feel he's not going to hurt himself. I think he'd be okay if he spent nights at home with Alma and days with me. I'll make sure all the guns are out of his house and get him to promise he won't leave."

"That all sounds great, but have you thought about how this is going to affect *you*? Remember the man who was staring at the computer for an hour and a half because he couldn't turn it off? The man who knows the location of every bathroom within a hundred-mile radius because, at one time or another, he's hidden in each one of them? Have you thought about how he might be affected by this scheme?"

"That's enough! I thought we had a new agreement about this stuff. Maybe you haven't noticed that I haven't fallen apart over the last few hours."

"It's true; you haven't," Naomi said, cautiously. "I'm just worried about the fallout that's coming."

"Stop," Jake said, holding up his hand.

"Okay," Naomi nodded. Her expression made her look lost.

"If you could spend a little time with Alma and the kids, helping them sort some of this out, while I'm with her husband, that would be great."

Naomi was silent for a few moments, her eyes focused on the kitchen table. Finally she looked up. "I'll do that," she said, "if you promise to check in with me next Saturday. If, by that time, we don't have a good feeling and a great game plan for these folks, I want you to promise me we'll hand over the whole situation to the authorities."

"All right," Jake agreed, sighing with relief. "Now, let's go back in there. I'll speak to Watkins separately and tell him the plan. Can you speak to Alma?"

Naomi nodded and then frowned, as she suddenly remembered another question. "Have you forgotten about the kid?" Jake knew she was referring to Pax.

"No, I've already talked to him. I told him not to tell anyone what he knows. I said I'd be in touch with him in a few days to bring him up to speed and help him with his plans."

Naomi nodded again, reassured about Pax for the moment, but still not completely comfortable.

"We're neck deep in this, my love," Jake said, "but we're going to make it."

Naomi smiled slightly and pushed the dining-room door open.

# ✧✦ CHAPTER TWENTY-THREE ✧✦

Both Alma and Howie agreed to the plan. When Naomi saw Howie's face after she explained that they *should* call the authorities and go to the hospital, she knew Jake was right. It was the Marine authorities who'd given Howie reason to lose hope in the first place.

Howie agreed to call in sick for the rest of the week. Alma said she'd call a close friend who lived a few hours away to take the kids for the week. By the time Jake drove them home, a game plan was in place.

It was 6:00 a.m., the following morning, when Jake knocked softly on the Watkins front door. It opened immediately. Howie stood in sweatpants and a hooded sweatshirt.

"Ready?" asked Jake.

"Ready."

"You okay?"

Howie shrugged. "Isn't that what I'm supposed to say?" Looking at the floor, he added, "Yeah, I'm just fine."

Jake nodded. "Let's go. You drive."

"I was going to leave the car for Alma. You want me to tell her we're taking it?"

"No, I want you to drive *my* car."

"Oh."

The two men closed their car doors softly to avoid waking the kids. Alma would go over to the Finns' house after breakfast and spend the day with Naomi. Jake was extremely grateful that Naomi had taken off the week. She had a lot of unused sick days. "I can't think of a better way to use them," she'd told Jake, smirking.

"Duly noted," Jake had thought, observing his wife's sarcastic expression. "But I can't worry about it now." At that moment the only thing that mattered was that Naomi was actually fulfilling her promise to help Alma Watkins.

"Turn left," Jake said, as Howie pulled out of the driveway.

"Where we going?"

"Out of town," Jake said, without looking at Howie. "Turn left again at the stop sign."

After a few minutes the houses began to thin out as Howie and Jake started climbing the foothills. Preoccupied, Jake almost missed a road they needed to take. "Oh, shit," he muttered. "Turn right!" he suddenly yelled.

Without hitting the brakes, Howie made a sharp right turn. All four wheels slid sideways, catching just before the car reached the shoulder.

Jake had braced his hands on the dashboard. "Sorry, man," he started to say. But Howie wasn't listening. Staring straight ahead, expressionless, he jammed his foot on the gas pedal. The car shot forward.

"Stop!" screamed Jake.

Howie's head snapped toward Jake. He hit the brakes hard.

The instant the car stopped, Jake pulled the keys from the ignition and grabbed a fistful of Howie's sweatshirt. "What the fuck's that all about?"

Howie grabbed Jake's wrist and pushed it away. "I wasn't doing anything, man!"

"Don't give me that shit! This time you were gonna kill both of us!"

"Back off, man!" Howie yelled back in Jake's face. "You scared the shit out of me with your fucking yelling. What the fuck! Sounded like I-E-D time to me!"

Jake released his grip and sat back in his seat. He was breathing heavily. "I'm driving," he said quietly.

They got out and changed places. They avoided eye contact as they passed each other in front of the car. "Sorry, man," Jake said.

Howie let out a deep sigh. His head bobbed quickly in acknowledgment.

They drove another ten minutes before Jake found a pull-off and parked the car. Howie gazed out the window and said nothing.

"We're going to take that trail off to the right," said Jake. Pull up your hood if you don't want to be recognized." He pointed to the top of the mountain. "See that cliff jutting out? It's called Spirit leap its about three miles from here. That's where we're going."

"I'm not in shape."

"Follow me," Jake replied, ignoring Howie.

It was an overcast morning, fog filled the valley; on the lower slopes only the tops of the tallest trees poked through. A wind was picking up and it looked like the front coming in might bring rain.

Howie felt stiff and knew it would take a while for his body to warm up. It wasn't until they hit the second hill that he began to think about how sore he was going to be the next day.

Jake was not moving fast, but his pace was steady and he was only a few feet ahead. The hood of Jake's sweatshirt bobbed up and down. Without warning Jake stepped off the trail, bent down and picked up a round rock about the size of a muskmelon. "Carry this," he said, handing the rock to Howie.

The stone was a little too large to carry with one hand, but using both hands made walking awkward. After a couple of hundred yards, Howie cradled the stone in the crook of his elbow, against his chest. That hold worked better. Howie could see a dark line on the back of Jake's sweatshirt and felt his heart beating against the stone. Glancing at the cliff he thought there's no way he'd make it to the top. There had to be at least half a mile of hill left to go.

As if Jake had read his thoughts he stopped at the side of the trail, breathing heavily. Howie dropped the stone and bent over, his hands on his knees.

"Howie," said Jake.

"What?"

"See the rock behind that fern? Grab it and let's get going. And don't forget the one you just dropped."

Howie picked up the new rock and was struggling to get the two rocks adjusted in the crook of each elbow when he saw Jake step off the trail and pick up a rock that was bigger than either of the two he was carrying. "Let's go, Marine," Jake grunted.

If anyone had been watching them jog up to Spirit Leap with rocks bumping off their chests they would have thought they were college kids being initiated into a fraternity.

Howie hoisted the rocks higher and glanced at his watch. Almost an hour had passed since they'd left the car. His back and arms were humming with pain. Each time he lagged behind, Jake would slow down just enough to let Howie catch up. Then he'd increase his speed again, drawing Howie to the edge.

Howie had expended all the reserves he knew he had, and it was coming down to sheer will to take each step. That's when he remembered the previous day. He could feel that his body was no longer strong enough to contain the rage and shame he felt for what he'd done. Deep sobs swelled his chest, a mangled cry tried to break free between his desperate breaths. He knew Jake was close enough to hear him, but he didn't stop or turn around. He just kept lifting his legs. They were no longer jogging. They were barely moving their legs.

Spirit Leap was now within sight, maybe a hundred yards above them. Not a single inch of Jake's sweatshirt was dry. Howie tried to lower his hood by snapping his head back, but had no success. That was when he heard a sound that reminded him of teeth chattering. He quickly found the source of the noise on the side of the trail: a rattlesnake coiled up only a few feet away. Jumping sideways, he threw one of his stones in front of the snake. Its head and upper body snapped forward and the snake struck at the stone, recognizing it too late. Enraged, the snake sped up the trail toward Jake.

"Behind you!" Howie yelled as he shot-putted the other stone at Jake. Jake turned to see a stone in the air between himself and Howie. His arms shot up reflexively to protect himself. He watched the stone fall short, just ahead of the large snake coming right at him. The snake stopped and slithered off the trail into the thick undergrowth.

The two men's eyes met. "Let's go," said Jake, turning. His legs shook as he moved on toward the cliff.

Howie gathered his two stones and got back on the trail. By now, Jake was far ahead of him. Howie watched him reach the cliff and lie down on his back. He still had a hundred steps or so to go. Jake sat up, hung his legs off the cliff and watched him. Howie noticed Jake's slight nod and began to move like a man at the end of a race who was being cheered by a crowd of thousands.

When he reached the top, he stumbled to the cliff edge and heaved the two stones. He sat beside Jake noticing two backpacks lying on the stones.

"Where'd these come from?" Howie asked.

Jake rolled him a bottle of water. "Hydrate, Marine!"

Howie, took a long drink; he could feel as each swallow began to immediately replenish him.

# ✧✦ CHAPTER TWENTY-FOUR ✧✦

Howie lay on his back for a long time, feeling the coolness of the mountain rock drawing the heat out of his body. Only in boot-camp training had he felt his body so challenged. Looking at the sky over the small town where they lived, he thought of what he'd done to Alma and the kids. Some of that grief came out of him on the trail, but he sensed there was a lot more.

Howie couldn't stop thinking that if he'd been a man he'd have faced his rage against the Marines. The quotas they forced on him – requiring him to recruit young men and women who had no idea what they were getting into – was unbearable. It would have been all right if these young people really knew what soldiering was about. If they knew that it was about one thing and one thing only: killing the enemy. His father had made this clear to him before he signed up. "Don't get any ideas that this is a game," he'd said. "You will find yourself up against highly trained men and women whose one objective in life is to kill a Marine. And the worst of it is that they are at home and never get to leave, like you will."

In addition to his rage toward the Marines, Howie was aware of feeling fear – specifically, of his father. He seriously wondered whether his father would disown him when he found out that Howie had tried to kill himself.

It was hard to believe that these realizations were coming to him. Until now he'd had no idea of what he'd been feeling – other than hopeless.

He was finally beginning to recognize his feelings and even able to put names on them. But he still had no idea of what he could do to make his life better.

Looking over at Jake gazing out over the valley he realized the man was almost twice his age. He must have steel cable for tendons. When his dad was younger he'd seen the same kind of stubborn Recon resolve. His father's tenacity was harder to live with. He'd tell everyone what to do, how to do it and what would happen if they didn't do it. Jake was definitely busting his chops but, for some reason he wasn't able to figure out yet. Howie sensed that Jake wanted to help him so he was able to put up with the Marine game they were playing.

Since he was a young kid Howie wanted to be Marine Recon but he was born with a deformed leg. The family miracle, according to his mother, was that by the time he graduated from high school he walked without a limp. His mother said the progress was due to several corrective operations performed by military doctors, but the real reason was Howie's dedication. He'd worked out every single day of high school. If he wasn't in the pool, he was in the gym or the weight room. By the time he entered the Marines his deformity was undetectable.

It was after the Recon accepted him that his leg let him down. He'd had no trouble with the Level Test: push-ups, sit-ups, pull-ups, flutter kicks, eight-count push-ups and scissors, done as fast as possible for two minutes. It was during the forced march that the four miles per hour for eight miles with full pack that his leg gave out.

The recon captain had been nice about it, acknowledging how much Recon meant to Howie and how hard the boy had been working. "Son," he said, "what you need to understand is this. Just as your leg has betrayed you in becoming a Marine Recon, it also has the potential of betraying the men who are with you in the field. There will be a time when their lives depend on your legs. The Corps has lots of good places for a hard-working Marine like you, but not here."

When he told his dad this story, the old man cleared his throat and said, "It's okay, son. I could never say you didn't work at it hard enough. The fact that you made it into the Marines makes me proud."

This was the kindest thing his dad said to him. But he knew there were other feelings his dad hadn't expressed.

"Grab your pack," Jake suddenly barked, standing and hefting his own.

"I thought they were someone else's, said Howie, looking at the remaining pack. "How did they get up here?"

"I brought them up this morning before I came to get you."

"No shit," Howie said, struggling to his feet. When he grabbed the strap of the pack all his weight shifted to his bad leg and he teetered.

Jake was close enough to grab him under the arm. "You okay? What's with your leg?"

"It's nothing. I just stepped sideways on a rock on the trail."

Jake looked at him for a few moments, and then turned toward the growth at the back of the cliff. As they entered the tree line Jake swung around and said, "I think we need to get something straight right now. If you lie to me again you're going to find yourself at Walter Reed hospital. You must think I'm an idiot?"

Howie looked at the ground. Then he lifted his sweatpants, revealing a long scar from just below his kneecap all the way to his ankle.

Jake shook his head. He was used to dealing with high-school kids; he hadn't worked with another Marine since his days in the bush in 1970. Howie's display of his scar made him feel like maybe they were getting somewhere. He wanted to help this Marine and knew if he kissed his ass or started worrying about hurting his feelings it would be all over. His goal was to get this man to see that there was life after the battlefield. With this thought he remembered Alma's weeping in the living room.

Alma sounded like Naomi had twenty years earlier when she found the vacuum cleaner hose stuffed in the tailpipe of their car. Jake had just gone down to the basement for duct tape when Naomi came home for the lunch she'd left on the kitchen counter. She noticed the side door of the garage had been left open and looked in.

That was the day the rules changed, and Naomi became the life jacket wrapped around his chest. From then on no decisions were made without her approval. As he thought about this he realized it had taken twenty years to start to be in charge of his life again. After fighting for that independence, what he neglected to tell Naomi is that he knew he hadn't left the battlefields yet either.

"Watch your face," Jake said, pushing his way into what looked like a wall of limbs.

"Where the hell we going? It doesn't look like anyone's ever been through here."

"You'll see in a few minutes. Just stay back far enough that these limbs don't poke out your eyes," Jake said.

It seemed to Howie that they spent more than a half-hour on their bellies with the backs of their necks being scratched by low-slung pine limbs before Jake yelled, "We're here." Jake got up on his knees. "Check it out, man."

"Looks like a cave."

"It is. It's not very deep but there's enough room to stay dry if it rains. I found this place when I was a kid. No one ever comes here. There's too much thick brush to crawl through."

Howie pulled off his pack and walked into the cave. Stepping past a stone fire ring, he noticed bits of charcoal. "This looks like it's been used."

"Probably me twenty years ago," said Jake. That was the last time I came up here."

Howie touched the cave wall with his figertips. In the shadows he thought he saw markings. As his eyes adjusted he made out shapes. "Jake, what's this on the wall?"

"Petroglyphs."

"Look close and you'll see a deer with a spear sticking out of it?"

"Yep," said Jake. "This must have been a warrior's hunting cave. You're American Indian, aren't you?"

"Yeah, I am. My family hasn't got much connection with their ancestral roots, but Alma's dad is the chief of a small Zuni tribe in Arizona."

Jake looked up at the sky before stepping into the cave, "Just got hit with a couple of drops. It's going to pour." he said. He'd picked up Howie's pack and carried it with him into the cave.

Sitting it on the cave floor he said, "There's a rain slicker in the pack."

✦✦ CHAPTER TWENTY-FIVE ✦✦

Pax had gotten home from Mr. Finn's house around 1:30. He found a note on the kitchen table saying his mother had been called into work because of a major accident on the freeway outside Reeve. He turned off the kitchen light so she would know he was home. He undressed, tossed his clothes on a chair and crawled into bed. A few minutes after sinking into his pillow, he realized how tense he was. A swirl of faces and feelings moved across his mind. He knew why he'd given Mr. Finn his word not to tell anyone about what had happened tonight he didn't want any trouble to come to Mr. Watkins. He repeated under his breath, "No matter what, I won't tell anyone what happened." It was hard to avoid thinking it was his fault that Mr. Watkins tried to kill himself. If only his mother left him alone, he would have signed up a month ago and none of this would have happened.

Pax had never questioned that joining the Marines was what he wanted. It was his mother's idea that he should speak to Mr. Finn. He was tired of being told what to do by her and now by Finn. He wanted to become a man so he'd be treated with respect – even by his mother. The quickest way he knew how to do that was by becoming a Marine. Everyone knew that soldiers coming home from war were different from the people they'd been before going to war. He wanted to be different.

He'd watched how Mr. Finn responded to pressure: his eyes were clear; his voice, strong. He knew how to act with no hesitation. Pax admired the teacher's directness and coolness. He was sure his father had been confident like that, too – before losing control of his life. Pax yearned for such confidence, and he was willing to do whatever necessary to learn it.

The window shades were glowing slightly when he heard the kitchen door open downstairs. Glancing at the alarm clock he saw it was 5:30, and he still hadn't slept. He rolled over to face away from the door, knowing his mom would look in.

About twenty minutes after she'd opened his door he got up, took a shower and dressed for school. He took a few dollars out of his sock drawer and left a note, on the kitchen table, saying he was going to get breakfast at McDonald's before school.

Devouring an Egg McMuffin, Pax looked out the restaurant window at the gathering clouds. Winds started to kick up last year's dead leaves out of the flowerbeds of the house next door. He debated going to school, or to the Marine recruiter in Abner, the neighboring town. After a large swallow of coffee and seeing his bike blow sideways in the bike rack it would be better to go to school. Maybe tomorrow he would ride the twenty miles to Abner.

When Pax entered the school and didn't see the recruiter in his usual spot, the events of the previous night started to come back. Monday happened to be the day that Mr. Watkins routinely visited Pax's high school. He considered going to Mr. Finn's house but decided against it. His next idea was to go to Mr. Finn's classroom and ask him what was going on. But when he looked through the narrow window beside his classroom door he saw a woman sitting at Mr. Finn's desk.

Mr. Finn had never said he'd be in touch with him, so he'd have to wait. He knew Finn didn't want him signing up. He was sure Mr. Finn would let him know what was going on with Mr. Watkins and what he know about enlisting. After what just happened to Mr. Watkins Pax realized there would be no way Mr. Finn would tell his mom that joining was okay. He still hoped that the two of them might not even speak. He just didn't know how to read what was going on. He'd heard in Mr. Finn's voice that he liked the recruiter and was willing to help him.

Pax knew Mr. Finn was concerned about how he'd been affected by Mr. Watkins's suicide attempt.  On the other hand, he'd known two kids from school who'd "offed" themselves in the past year: one with a drug overdose, the other, by jumping off the Rhinecliff Bridge.  There were news articles almost every day about returning soldiers killing themselves after failing to get the treatment they needed from the VA.  This was not going to happen to him.

Pax made up his mind years ago that he wouldn't kill anyone who wasn't trying to kill him.  He knew abiding by this rule, he wouldn't accumulate the kind of guilt that soldiers who kill themselves bring home.  Killing innocent people was not part of his plan.

# ✦✦ CHAPTER TWENTY-SIX ✦✦

As Naomi came out her front door, a gust of wind pulled the screen door from her hand, slamming it shut. She looked at the sky, opened the car trunk for her umbrella, but it was not there. She considered going back into the house for it, but gave up the idea when a fierce gust of wind shook the maples in the yard, making her realize that no umbrella would stay in her hand for long.

She closed the car door and away from the noise of the wind she thought of Jake and Howie up on the mountain. Jake had been up since 1:30 a.m.; she wondered how he was fairing. She was glad he'd said he'd have his cell phone if she needed to reach him.

Jake had spent most of Sunday afternoon putting gear into backpacks. When she'd asked why he needed two, he'd pursed his lips. "One's for Howie."

"What are your plans?" she'd asked.

He looked at her in surprise, as if she should know exactly what he was doing. "We're gonna do some hiking. Some reflecting."

"Could you be a little more specific?" she asked.

"I thought we could hike up to Spirit Leap," he explained. "Beyond that, we'll see what happens. I'm not writing up a meeting agenda, but there are certain things I'm hoping we can accomplish if we just get some time away, undisturbed."

"Sounds kind of vague."

"I can't really plan this outing; I'll have to see how it unfolds. I don't even know what I'm going to say to Howie. But I'm not worried about it, either, because I don't think I'll have to say much. He's a Marine, which makes this easier."

"Well, I'm not," Naomi said. "What are you talking about?"

"There's an unspoken language only Marines understand. So I won't have to use a lot of words to get him to understand what we're doing."

"Which is?"

"Trying to save his life," Jake said, stuffing a thick pair of socks into one of the packs.

Naomi took a close look at the other articles laid out on the floor to be packed. "Are you spending the night on the mountain?" she asked.

Jake nodded. "That's my guess."

Naomi got into the car. She wasn't even out of the driveway before she needed to turn on the wipers. Heading toward the Watkins' house, she wondered how she could help Alma. She knew that showing up as a social worker would only make Alma feel guilty that no one had called the authorities. Naomi hoped they'd be able to connect as women.

She pulled into the driveway of Alma's house with its hedges trimmed in the style of a traditional Marine flattop haircut. Walking up the sidewalk she saw movement through one of the door windows, and before she reached the front door it opened. Alma was in a yellow dress, a toddler hugging her leg. An older girl stood slightly behind her mother.

"Good morning, Alma."

"Morning, Naomi. Let me introduce our children. This is Andee," she said, tousling the little girl's black hair. She looked over her shoulder at her older daughter. "And this is Bella."

"How do you do," said Bella.

"Nice to meet you, Bella," said Naomi.

"My friend, Hildy, should be here any minute. Would you like some coffee?"

"Love some."

"Come on in. We'll sit in the kitchen so I can keep an eye on the driveway."

As Naomi walked through the living room she noticed the Indian blanket and photographs of Howie in uniform. The neatness of the house was remarkable, considering the presence of two young children.

"Lovely home," she said.

"Thanks," said Alma, reaching for the coffee pot. Just as they sat down there was a knock on the front door. "That's got to be Hildy," Alma said. "I'll be right back." She picked up two bags set out in the hallway and called to the kids, who had gone into their bedrooms. There was a quick hello to Hildy, Alma bent to kiss the kids, and they left with no fuss.

"What good kids you have. They didn't complain at all."

"They're used to traveling. And they love Hildegard."

"Well, here we are with the day before us. Any ideas?" Naomi said, lowering her coffee cup and pulling a strand of hair from her eyes.

Alma held her cup with both hands. Taking a deep breath, "I guess we have to get being nice out of the way first, and then we can talk about yesterday."

"Yeah!" Naomi replied, relieved by Alma's directness. Her shoulders dropped slightly as she relaxed. "Did the guys get out okay this morning?"

Alma nodded. "Howie was up about 2:30 and dressed by 2:45. He waited at the door for almost an hour after he ate his breakfast."

"Jake left the house around 4:00. He told me where they were going. I tried to find out what he was planning to do but all he said was that Howie's a Marine and that was going to make it easier. I have no idea what that means. Do you?"

"Well, it explains why Howie was up at 2:30."

"I don't think I'll ever understand what the Marines did to my husband," Naomi went on. "Until I met Jake, I didn't know a single person who'd been in the military."

"My dad was in the Marines," Alma said. "But that didn't help me to understand what happened to my husband," Alma said, looking out the window toward the mountains.

# ✦✦ CHAPTER TWENTY-SEVEN ✦✦

Thunderheads darkened the sky above the trees. A north wind was turning the leaves to their silvery undersides. Howie was sawing off the limb of a nearby white pine. "How many of these do you think we'll need?" he shouted.

"Half a dozen. Looks like it's really going to come down."

"We'll be okay," Howie said, standing the pine limb against the cave opening. "I'm going to gather some dry wood before the rain starts, in case we want a fire."

"Good idea. Looks like we've got about fifteen minutes before it hits."

The rain slapped the stone in large globs of water. Jake sat with his back against the cave wall, stacking the sticks Howie collected. Howie placed the final pine limb over the entrance. Flecks of gray light winked through the carpet of pine. For a long time the two men listening to the rain, their eyes adjusting to the dark.

Howie noticed an opening in the rocks in the opposite wall. He crawled over to examine it. "Looks like a chimney. There's even a little soot on the rocks. If we start a fire below the opening, I think the smoke will rise up the hole."

"Try it," Jake said. He leaned on his backpack and stretched out his legs. "Feels like we're back in Boy Scouts."

Howie shook his head. "I wasn't in Boy Scouts, but my old man used to take us camping. He called it ITR. At the time I didn't know what that meant."

"Infantry Training Regiment," Jake said, closing his eyes. "Advanced Boy Scouts."

"Yeah, push-ups every morning. One morning he was gone from the camp when my brother and I woke up. He'd left a note on his tent that said, 'Find me! Here's a compass and these are the coordinates.' He'd been quizzing us on compass reading for weeks. That's when we realized why."

"Did you find him?"

"No."

The rain was coming down steadily now, but except for a little mist seeping through the pine, they were dry. Howie had moved the rocks from the fire ring to the chimney opening and gotten a small, bright fire going and, just as he'd guessed, the smoke was going up the chimney hole. Shadows flickered on the stone walls, which were beginning to heat up.

Jake took off his jacket and made a pillow out of it. He pushed his hands down on his thighs, squeezing them to stop the trembling in his legs. He cleared his throat, buckled his legs against his chest and wrapped his arms around his knees. "Time to get real," he said, a slight tremor in his voice.

Howie looked at him and their eyes locked. "All right, what do you want me to do? I carried the stones. What's next?"

"Convince me that you're not going to kill yourself."

Howie lowered his head into his hands.

"You know the saying?" Jake asked. "'No Marine left behind'?"

Howie looked up.

"You're the Marine who almost left himself behind, dead in the foxhole – at home," Jake continued. "You broke the code."

"Come on, man, will you leave me alone about that! I'm okay now! I'm not going to do anything! I'm back! Thanks for your help. I'm grateful. My wife and kids are thankful that you showed up. Can we drop it now and move on?"

"You've got to be shitting me. If you think for a minute that the little bit of blubbering you did on the trail convinced me that this chapter of your life is behind you, think again! You didn't pull that shit yesterday because you woke up with a headache.

You've been pissed at someone or something a long time. And that anger's been building up. My wife's a social worker and she's told me, more than once, what you just said is what everyone says after they make an attempt." Jake's face was red in the firelight and he continued, "Thanks for your help, but go away now," he mimicked. "I'm fine, thanks; no problem here. I promise I won't try again!"

After Jake stopped the two sat in silence and minutes passed. Finally Jake burst out, "What are you so angry about that you want to make yourself a corpse?"

"Enough, already!" Howie yelled, raising his open hand in front of Jake to interrupt him. "I've heard enough of this crap!"

Before Howie could get to his feet, Jake's arm shot out and grabbed him by the wrist. As Howie lost his balance, Jake used his free hand to push against his chest, slamming him against the wall. The back of Howie's head hit the stone. "So you've heard enough!" Jake yelled.

Pulling his cell phone from his pocket he shoved it in Howie's face. "I'm going to call my wife right now. She's with your wife. I'm going to tell her to hand the phone to Alma so you can tell her the same shit you just told me! You with me?"

Howie looked at the dirt floor of the cave.

"I was just telling Naomi last night that you're a real Marine and that's why I'm doing this. Well, I was wrong. You're a frigging wimp! I find it hard to believe you wanted to be a Recon. You must have the balls of a mouse."

Spit hung from the corners of Jake mouth and his hands were karate-chopping the air in front of Howie. "So you were upset because you couldn't make your fucking commanding-officer quota for recruits. What kind of shit is that?"

Howie's jaw tightened and he thrust his face into Jake's face. "You want to know why I wanted to die?" he said, between clenched teeth. "All right, Lieutenant, I'll tell you why. I'm sick and tired of rounding up kids to be killed. I've been on the battlefields of both Iraq and Afghanistan and I know *exactly* what's going to happen to at least half of 'em! And, by the way, one third of my recruits are girls. If they don't buy it on their first tour, they'll buy it on the second or third. And there I am, convincing these kids that their lives are worth some political *bullshit* that's got nothing to do with them! You think I like doing this?"

"Yeah, I do!" said Jake.

"Well you're wrong, Lieutenant! Wrong! Each kid I signed up brought me one step closer to that rope."

"Listen, man," Jake said. "I told you before. If you're not telling me the truth, I'm dragging your ass to the VA or the local hospital."

Howie's nostrils flared. "Let me tell you something Lieutenant, you think I was standing out there at attention counting the red light blinking because you ordered me to? That's bullshit. I was waiting for you come so I could hang myself right in front of you. It would have been a fuck you for shoving my face in it at the school, by telling me how many of your kids I was killing."

Jake looked stunned and began to speak when Howie put up his hand for him to stop. "I'm not done yet Lieutenant, now I understand that you were dumping your own shit on me. Thank you but I've got enough of it in the bag I'm dragging around with me, I don't need yours too."

"Look at me, man," Jake said. "I heard all about your recruiter rap from Pax. You've got that kid wrapped around your finger. He's going in – I'm sure of it. Tell me you didn't work your Marine jargon on him."

"I didn't, Godamn it."

Jake raised his hand. This time Howie grabbed his wrist and squeezed hard. "Cut the shit!" he growled. "You've done that one too many times."

Jake pulled his arm free and looked into the middle distance. Rivulets of sweat were collecting in the creases of his face.

Howie wasn't sure Jake was listening anymore but he spoke anyway. "The kid was going in no matter what anyone said to him. I was just hoping to get him into the air wing or someplace where he wasn't gonna get killed."

"Is that true?" Jake squinted at the younger man.

Howie nodded. "That's what I try to do with *all* the kids that come to me," he said. "My commanding officer's pissed that I never recruit anyone who wants to be 311."

Jake milked his chin with his forefinger and thumb. "Pax told me if he didn't sign up when you wanted him to he couldn't be a 311."

"That's what I told him. And I was hoping he would be able to get to me, so I could send him somewhere safer."

"Did you take any time to think about your own kids having a dead dad? And Alma. Did you think about her and what a bunch of shit you'd be leaving her with?"

Jake could see he finally found the button. Howie put his head into his hands. Jake watched the man's shadow rocking on the cave wall. His shoulders shook, but no sound. Finally, through sheer discipline, Howie raised his head.

"No," he said. "I haven't been thinking of them. I've been miserable for years, and the Marines do nothing to help me out. I paid a lot to get this recruiting job. I never thought it would make me feel like a contract killer but – what did I know? So what do I do for a living? I set up parents to lose their kids. Me. A parent myself."

"So I've been worried about these kids. And that's a problem, too. I've been more worried about other people's kids than my own. Last night Alma told me if I didn't get this figured out, she'd leave and take the kids. I believe her."

A clap of thunder echoed off the cliff's rock face. Both men instinctively hunkered down in the cave. Howie noticed that Jake's eyes had closed and he was hugging his knees and rocking again. The cave was hot. Both men were down to their T-shirts.

Howie looked down and froze. A snake was crawling between them. He did a double-take and realized he was mistaken; it was a line of water flowing over the stone floor.

"I think it might be time for you to tell me the truth," said Howie. "What's your story, Lieutenant?"

Jake opened his eyes but continued rocking. He shrugged. "I've been where you are. Maybe I'm still there. I mean, there was a time I wanted to kill myself. I still have the feeling I'll never get over what I did in Nam. With all the shit that's going on right now with Iraq and Afghanistan, there's not a single night I don't feel my cage being rattled. Either it's a kid from school, like Pax, going off to war, or I catch a list of the dead on TV. I'm grateful that at least one media outlet is acknowledging the lost lives. But I can't stand seeing it, either. It stirs up my shit so deep – I'm affected for days."

Howie whispered, "You've seen some real shit, haven't you?"

"Yeah, but –" Jake paused. "It's not so much what I've seen, as what I've done. I spent the first eighteen years of my life going to Sunday school and Boy Scouts. I went into the Marines believing that I was doing something noble for my country. The real reason I went in is a lot harder to face: I just had to get away from my folks."

Howie nodded. "You and how many other Marines?" he asked. "Same with me."

Jake shifted his legs. "But I was such a fast learner. In only thirteen weeks of boot camp I learned to hate the enemy and want to kill him. I was an expert shot on the rifle range, got PFC out of boot camp and was first pick for Recon training. After I got through that I was sent to Quantico to get the two little gold lieutenant bars.

"Recon was my hope, too. Before I joined, anyway," Howie said, lowering his head.

"The Recon took killing up several notches," Jake went on. "And once I got to Nam, I became real good at it. What I was good at was looking indifferent. I knew if I let my feelings get out of control I'd be signing my own death certificate. So I controlled my emotions. Big time. I did such a good job that everyone told me it looked like nothing ever bothered me. My men even started calling me 'Steel' – short for 'Steel Face.' That's how numb I was." His voice dropped. "After all, what's a man supposed to look like after he flushes his soul down the toilet?"

"Come on, man," Howie objected. "You're a teacher now. That can't be true anymore!" He shoved a stick into the fire.

"Not until years after I came home did my face start to crack. Thank god for Naomi and her social worker's super-glue, holding me together." Jake shifted to face Howie.

"You think I'm blowing smoke up your ass?" he continued. "A few years ago I had a hose hooked up to the exhaust pipe of my car. The only reason Naomi found me was that she'd forgotten her lunch and came home to get it. That was the first time in my marriage that she saw the real me."

Howie covered his mouth with his balled fist. "Is that why you're trying to help me?"

Jake turned to the cave wall and looked at the petroglyph of the deer with the spear sticking out of it. "I don't know," he said. "But trying to help you is easier than helping myself."

## ✦✦ CHAPTER TWENTY-EIGHT ✦✦

Alma stared out the window. Turning towards Naomi she said, "My dad was a Marine in the Korean War."

Naomi put down her coffee cup and took in an audible breath. "As I said, Jake's the only Marine I've ever known. And I've been married to him long enough to know what ex-Marine means. When you tell me your dad was a Marine in Korea, I'm guessing you experienced Korea, too – because he brought the war home with him."

Alma nodded. The ends of her long black hair brushed the table.

"How did your mom handle it?" Naomi asked, lifting her eyes to Alma's.

"Not well. My father drank. He was a quiet man when he wasn't drinking but once he got liquored up he was Mr. Gung-Ho Marine. He'd do one of two things. Either he'd beat my mother for trying to stop him from drinking, or he'd fall onto the floor and stay there, crying, until he fell asleep. My brother and I would hide in our rooms or get out of the house."

"How awful for you guys!" Naomi said. "But you said he stopped when you were five years old, right?"

"Yeah, when I was in kindergarten. Not on his own, though. It took a group of his best friends from the Indian council to help him – not just to

118

stop drinking, but to find a reason to live. Now he's the chief of a small group of Zunis where my parents live in Arizona. He's known as a warrior and is greatly respected.

"He and my mom are still married. They get along really well and have this incredible respect for each other. I get upset every time I go home because watching them forces me to see that Howie and I are light years away from having the sort of marriage my parents have."

Naomi reached across the table and rested her hand on top of Alma's. "I've been trying to fix Jake since before we got married. He's a Recon hero, but he's a fragile man." Alma looked surprised.

"Don't get me wrong," Naomi said quickly. "In an emergency, there's no better man to have next to you. The problem is, it's no fun to live in a perpetual emergency."

"He just saved my husband's life," Alma said, lowering her gaze.

"I know. But a few days ago, he locked himself in the bathroom in a funk and I wasn't sure he was ever going to come out. His demons are being triggered every day by stuff in the media and events at school. I think he lives at least half his waking hours back in Vietnam."

"I know what you mean," said Alma. "I won't let Howie drive with the kids in the car anymore. You never know when he's going to flinch and go all over the road." She shifted in her chair. "Let's go sit in the living room. It's more comfortable."

"Okay," said Naomi, standing up.

Naomi sat down beside a bookshelf and started examining a row of framed photographs; portraits of Indians in their native costumes. Naomi pointed at a man with three feathers rising out of his coiled hair. "Is that your dad?" she asked.

"It is. That was taken a few years ago, after a vision quest he led."

"Do you think vision quests really help people?" Naomi asked.

"Depends. People really don't go on a quest to get help as much as to find a direction for their lives."

Naomi stood up and walked to the Indian blanket hanging on the wall. She fingered the wool, enjoying the texture and colors. "Has Howie ever asked your dad for help?" she asked.

"No. Howie doesn't see himself as a real Indian. I mean, he's a full-blooded Indian but he grew up off the reservation and never had any real contact with his native family."

"So he never learned about his culture?" Alma asked.

"Absolutely not. His parents were determined to leave their heritage behind. His dad grew up on a reservation, but that experience was so painful that he left as soon as he could join the Marines. And later, when his dad and mom had kids, he forbade her to teach them anything about Native American culture."

"How long was he in the Marines?" Naomi asked.

"He did twenty years as a career enlisted man. And as far as I know, he never went back to see his remaining relatives on the reservation. Why do you ask?"

"Just seems like if the vision quest was strong enough medicine to save your father, why not your husband? I think that might be what Jake's thinking. He said he was going to take Howie up the mountain to a place he found when he was a kid. It's an old cave with Indian petroglyphs on the wall. Jake thinks it may have been a sacred place for Indians."

"Did he tell you what he planned to do when they got there?"

"Not really. Just that they needed to speak Marine to Marine." Naomi looked at Alma.

"You know I'm a social worker, don't you?" she asked.

Alma shook her head.

"There are rules that social workers are supposed to follow if they encounter anyone who has attempted suicide," Naomi explained. Howie should be in a hospital right now, not up on a mountain with a fellow Marine."

Alma nodded. "So I'm not the only one with a husband who talked her into letting him do what he wanted."

"Something like that," said Naomi. "Once again, the Marine brotherhood trumps everything else. That's what I hate about Marines. They put the Corps ahead of everything and everyone, including themselves. I've heard enough of that 'blood brother' business. 'No Marine left behind.' I'm sick and tired of that crap." Naomi threw her hands up. "And here we are waiting, while they're hiding in a cave on top of a mountain, trying to figure out how to stay alive."

"You know, I've been thinking about that kid, Pax," said Alma. If it weren't for him we wouldn't be sitting here today. It must have been quite a thing for him to have his recruiter try to take his life." Alma's voice quavered as she reached for a box of tissues. "When do you think they'll be home?"

"Jake didn't tell me exactly. He did say it could be a few days. He's taking sick days for the whole week."

"Howie didn't tell me anything. I don't think he knew anything." She closed her eyes and frowned. "Oh, what the hell can they be doing up there?" Balling tissues up in her hand, Alma stuffed them up the sleeve of her sweater. "I don't know if I can take being alone. I may have my mom fly in for a few days."

"Does she know what happened?"

"No. Howie asked me not to tell anyone."

"Won't you have to let her know – I mean, if you're asking her to stay with you?"

Alma hesitated. "I'm just afraid he'll be angry if I tell anyone. Even my mom."

"You feel trapped."

"Exactly," she said, looking up. "What do you think I ought to do, Naomi?"

"I'm not sure. But if I put my social worker hat on, I'd say call her right now. Tell her what's going on and let her take care of you. If Howie gets mad, he gets mad. You can't control him. But he's sure as hell controlling you." She paused. "But I'm not here as a social worker. I'm really here because I've been in the same boat you're in now."

Alma's eyes widened. "Are you saying Jake tried to kill himself?"

Naomi bit her lower lip. "Yes."

"Oh, my god!" Alma gasped.

The two women looked at each for a long time, then rose and hugged. Over Alma's shoulder Naomi saw sunlight dancing on the glass of the framed Indian photos. "I'm so sorry we dragged you into this," Alma whispered.

"And I'm sorry you have to go through this. But as long as you are, I might as well tell you, it feels good to me to be with someone else who knows what its like." Naomi choked up and reached for the box of tissues.

"You think we should go to the mountain?" Alma asked.

"Not now," said Naomi. "I think we should give them some time. Tell you what. How'd you like to come over to my house, instead? I made a big pot of soup a few days ago and haven't had a chance to eat it. It might be good for you to get out of here."

Alma nodded yes.

When they stepped out the front door, a distant clap of thunder came from the direction of the mountain and they looked at each other and smiled.

They were passing the high school when Alma suddenly pointed to a young man on the sidewalk. "Naomi, look! Pull over!" she said.

Naomi pulled up to the curb in front of them. Pax stood with his bike leaning against his hip while he put on his backpack. He was squinting into the early morning sun and gave no sign of recognition until Naomi lowered her window.

"Hello, Pax! How are you this morning?"

"Oh, hi, Mrs. Finn," he said, smiling. "The glare was too strong I didn't see you there."

"Just wanted to say hello. See how you're doing," Naomi said.

"I'm good," Pax said, nodding and lowering his head, "How's Mr. Watkins?"

"He's doing okay. He's with Mr. Finn right now."

"Good, good," Pax said, shaking his head yes.

"You need to talk with anyone or anything?"

"I'm cool. I'm glad everyone's all right."

"Me too. If you need anything, just let me know. You can call me anytime."

Pax bent lower, curious to see who was sitting in the passenger seat. "Hello, Mrs. Watkins," he said.

Alma leaned toward the driver-side window. "Pax, thank you so much for your help last night."

"You're welcome," he said. They were silent for a moment, looking at each other. "I haven't told anyone," he added. "And I'm not going to."

"Thank you, Pax."

"Uh-huh."

As Naomi pulled away from the curb, Alma said, "He acts so cool. He doesn't need to talk with anyone. He reminds me of Howie."

"Pax's father was a Marine."

"I should've known," Alma said. "I'm glad I've got girls."

They approached Naomi's front door and Alma's face took on a dazed expression. "It seems like weeks since we were here but it was really only a few hours ago, wasn't it?" she said.

"Mm-hmm," Naomi acknowledged. Unlocking the door, she warned, "Watch that the cats don't get out. I need to feed them. That's one of the reasons I wanted to come home."

"I didn't know you had cats. I didn't see them last night."

"I locked them in my bedroom."

They entered the kitchen. "Have a seat," Naomi said, gesturing toward a chair at the counter. "I'll heat up the soup." She bent to pet the large gray cat at her legs.

Several peaceful minutes passed as they ate. Alma felt soothed by her surroundings: the quiet house, shadows from a nearby tree moving on the counter, the sound of the cats' dishes moving as they ate in the nearby laundry room. It felt good to her to be here.

"Good soup," she said, as she stood and reached for Naomi's bowl. "I'll do the dishes."

"Thanks."

The peace that settled between the two women gave Naomi a moment to reflect and she realized how much she was enjoying Alma's company. She thought that if she'd met Alma some other way she would have wanted to be friends with her. Even though Alma was much younger, Naomi found it easy and comforting to speak with her. Naomi had never had anyone to talk to about what it was like to have your husband want to take his life. No one she knew understood what war could do to a marriage. Alma was someone who did.

"Alma," Naomi said to the younger woman's back. "Have you ever thought of asking your dad for help?"

"No," Alma said over her shoulder. "He's another ex-Marine. There's still some unfinished business between him and me. And, like I said, I don't know what Howie would do if the word got out."

"Can I be straight with you?" asked Naomi.

"Of course."

"I think we've all given Howie too much power, and he's controlling us right now. I haven't known you long, but I'd like to hazard some guesses about your relationship with him. I'm guessing that if you say anything that might upset him, you worry for a week. I'm guessing that if he's depressed you do anything – you stand on your head – trying to please him."

"You're right," said Alma, focusing on the bowl in her hands. "I've made things easy for him whenever I could. I've babied him. I've forgiven him when I shouldn't have. I've made excuses for him for almost every problem he's had. And I've been doing it for so long that I'm probably as much of the problem as he is." She looked over her shoulder. "I feel lost."

"I know what you mean," the older woman said. "I've been afraid for years that Jake would do something, and I've done my own version of standing on my head to please him."

Alma put the last dish in the drying rack and picked up a tea towel to wipe her hands, looking at her new friend with curiosity.

"Once," Naomi continued, "I told him how much I admired his willingness to help the kids in his class. Boy, was that a mistake! He screamed at me that he hadn't helped anyone in his life. He said he was just there to teach. He told me a story about a time, in Vietnam, when he ran for his life instead of helping some children. He said that school is only window dressing for a paycheck.

"After that, I stopped praising him for anything. I've become an expert in neutral language. I never laugh too loudly or move too quickly. I always let him know when I'm coming into the room.

"He's convinced that we have an enemy, outside our house, whose only intention in life is to kill us. This enemy can see in the dark and hear things from miles away. Jake tells me he can see and hear and even smell this enemy! I don't experience any of that, but I live with someone who does!"

"Wow," Alma said quietly. "I know exactly what you mean. I've just never thought of it that way." She looked down at her hands. "I keep wondering why the air in the house changes whenever Howie comes home. Why the kids lower their voices. Why I'm careful to keep everything in order so he doesn't get upset. I even get nervous when I'm driving because he's nervous. I'm always afraid he'll blow up." She looked up. "Do you think I might have PTSD?"

Naomi tilted her head. "Probably." She looked out the window and waved toward the distant mountain. "What a crazy mess, huh? Here we are, two people who definitely want to live, being controlled by two people who aren't quite sure."

"You're right," said Alma. "What a mess."

Naomi stretched her arms above her head. "I'm exhausted. How 'bout you?"

"Same as you. Howie and I were up most of the night. I couldn't go to sleep until I had some idea of why he was out there in the woods."

"Was he able to tell you?"

"There were lots of reasons. I guess mostly I wanted to know that it wasn't me. He assured me that it wasn't about me or the kids. Didn't help much but it was a beginning."

"I told him that something had to change radically or the kids and I would leave. He said he'd do anything, even quit the Corps. I think that's why he was willing to go up the mountain with your husband." She paused. "What worries me now is that it seems like both of them are lost."

"The wounded helping the wounded," Naomi replied. She brushed some stray hairs from her face. "That's why I was asking about your dad."

"I see what you mean," Alma said, rubbing her eyes with the backs of her hands.

"You know," Naomi said, "I'm not sure I can talk about this anymore right now. What would you say to a nap? I have a guest room. We could sleep for a few hours and then make dinner. I'm pretty sure the guys won't be coming home tonight. What do you say? We can come back to all this later."

"I'm worried that Hildy might call. I wouldn't want to miss her."

"There is a phone in the guest bedroom," Naomi said.

"Okay, then. I really could use the rest."

Naomi smiled. "If you get up before I do, make yourself at home."

The sun was low in the sky when Naomi rolled over and looked out the window. The alarm clock read 5:30 p.m. She lay listening for Alma but heard only the steady drumming of rain on the roof.

She wondered whether Jake and Howie would come home because of the rain and quickly answered her own question. *No way* would she and Alma see the men this evening. Jake had encountered an emergency and had thrown himself into it. For a while he'd be superman. But at some point, she knew, he'd stop leaping tall buildings and trip going into the bathroom.

Naomi put her feet on the floor and softly went downstairs into the living room. Alma was sitting on the couch with her legs curled up, a patchwork throw over her feet. She looked up, smiling, when the door opened. "Some rain, isn't it?"

"I'll say. You get any rest?"

"I did," said Alma. "I've only been up for a few minutes. I was really tired. It felt good to be alone – no kids, no husband –" Still smiling, she went on, "And someone taking care of me. I'm scared about how things are going to have to change when Howie comes home."

"Let's not worry about that right now. Did you reach Hildy?"

"I called her before I went to sleep. She and the girls are fine. She asked me why it was so important that she take the kids. I didn't explain what was going on when I called her this morning, but she must have picked up something in my voice. She seems to appreciate that the situation is serious, but she's not prying. I just told her Howie and I needed some time alone to work things out."

"Well, that's the truth, isn't it?"

Alma turned both of her hands up. "Yeah."

"Okay, listen. You said earlier that you were considering calling your mom because you didn't want to be alone. Truth is, I'd be happy to have some company this evening and you've already checked out the bed in our guest room. Why don't I make us a nice dinner and you can sleep here tonight? You can let Hildy know to call you here if she needs to. What do you think?"

"I should be home in case Howie comes back."

"Listen, I need to do a little food shopping for dinner. We could drop by your place and leave him a note."

Alma bent her head forward, gathered her hair into a ponytail and secured it with the elastic band she'd been holding between her teeth. She closed her eyes for a long moment. "That would be great, Naomi. I think I'd sleep better if I were here. Thank you so much!"

"Don't thank me. I'm glad to have you here. Do you drink wine? I thought I'd pick up a bottle while we're out shopping."

"I haven't in a while. But why not?"

"If we go now we can stop at the market and your house, and be back here by about 6:30."

"Are you sure you want to go out in this rain?" Alma asked.

"Not a problem. Jake just put new wipers on my car. I'm all set."

"All right," Alma said, putting on her raincoat and pulling up the hood.

Their first stop was the Reeve Market. Alma took the shopping list and bought chicken breasts and fresh broccoli, while Naomi walked to the liquor store next door. They met back at the car.

When Alma opened the back door of the car and placed the bag of groceries on the seat, she noticed four bottles of wine standing up in a cut-down cardboard box. Naomi noticed her looking at the wine.

"Don't worry, I'm not an alcoholic. I just happened to find a wine that Jake and I have been looking for, so I got some extra."

Alma didn't say anything; she just got into the front seat.

The rain remained steady as they pulled into Alma's driveway. "You want me to come in with you?" asked Naomi.

"Yeah, I might be a few minutes. Why don't you?"

Alma sat at the kitchen table and wrote a note to Howie. Then she walked into the kids' rooms to straighten up their beds and pick up a few toys from the floor.

As she was coming back into the kitchen, the phone rang. She rushed to it, hesitated and then picked it up. "Hello? Oh, hi, Mom. Well, I was out shopping. I know. We're going to get an answering machine."

Naomi went out to the living room to give Alma some privacy. About fifteen minutes into the conversation she noticed a long silence, followed by the sound of Alma weeping. She wondered whether to go to her, but stayed in the living room. After another fifteen minutes Naomi heard the bathroom door close. A few minutes later Alma was standing in the living room.

"That was my mom," she said.

"I thought so," Naomi said quietly. "You okay?"

"Not really, huh? You want me to leave you alone?" Naomi asked.

"No. I just told my mother what happened. She asked where the kids were. I told her that they're with Hildy and I'm with you. She was glad to hear that I wasn't alone."

Naomi looked into Alma's eyes and smiled. "Ready? We should get going before we float away in this rain."

They dashed to the car and slammed the doors behind them. Naomi backed the car into the street and the two drove without speaking for a few minutes. Finally Naomi broke the silence.

"You seem a little calmer after speaking with your mom," she said.

"Yeah, we talked about my childhood. She reminded me of a story I haven't thought about for a long time. One night when I was five I stood up to my dad after he'd been drinking. I told him to stop hurting everyone and he backed down. My mom said it was only a few days later that my uncle and his friends visited my dad. I told her what Jake was doing with Howie, and she said that he must be a good man."

"No question we both got good men," Naomi agreed. "It's just that they sometimes act like idiots!" she added, shaking her head. She pulled into her driveway. "We've got a good young man and a good old man out there on the mountain, and their two good women are going to have a very fine meal." She turned off the engine. "Ready for one final drenching?" she said, opening her door.

Rain was still streaking down the kitchen windows as they prepared dinner. Naomi had put the chicken breast on a flat pan, sprayed it with olive oil and sprinkled it with lemon pepper. She was opening the oven door when Alma offered to make the salad. "I feel guilty just sitting here watching you work," she said.

"Sure," Naomi said. "The salad spinner and cutting board are under the sink, and the greens are in the crisper in the fridge."

Outside, the wind blew a garbage can across the driveway. "God, it's terrible out there," Alma said.

"I can't imagine what those guys are doing up on the mountain," said

Naomi as she set the table. "Here we are, warm and dry, and they're up there – up there – hugging wet rocks!"

"Whatever it is they're doing, I hope some sense sinks into Howie's brain," Alma said. "Howie's a stubborn man." She shook her head slightly and then looked directly at Naomi. "Howie's told me a little about Jake. He's sort of a Marine historian and he looked up Jake's unit in Nam. Jake's a hero."

"Howie probably knows more than I do," Naomi said. "Jake has told me almost nothing about the war. And that's okay. I've seen how it affects him so I decided a long time ago I don't really need to know all the details." She was quiet for a moment. "Every once in a while I get curious, though," she finally said. Once we were in San Diego on vacation and we met one of his men on the street. The guy hugged Jake so tightly I thought he wouldn't be able to breathe."

Alma pushed her chair back from the table. "What a delicious meal. Adult conversation. No kids to put to bed. This has been really nice. Thank you," she said, reaching for Naomi's empty plate and carrying it to the sink.

"Let's take our wine into the living room. Leave those dishes. We'll get them later."

Alma reached behind her head and pulled the elastic free of her ponytail. Her hair spread out on her shoulders. Taking her wine glass, she walked into the living room. She waited near the doorway for Naomi to come in. "Where's your chair?" she asked.

"I usually sit there," Naomi said, pointing to a cushioned rocker. "But not tonight!" she smiled.

Naomi put the wine bottle on the coffee table and sat in Jake's reclining chair. Alma sat on the couch, grinning. She nodded at Naomi.

"We might as well be comfortable," Naomi said. "Why not? Anyway, I think the guys running this show *need* to share their chairs," Naomi giggled. She tipped her head back and drained her glass.

"I think you're right," Alma said. "The two of them are where they belong right now. Hugging wet rocks!" It was her turn to giggle. Naomi joined her in a much needed laugh.

When they were quiet again, Alma remembered some news she'd intended to share. "My mother's coming to stay for a few days," she said. "I'd like you to meet her."

"I'd love to," said Naomi.

"She'll be here Friday. Think maybe we could get together over the weekend?"

"All of us? Or just us women?"

"Just us women."

"Sure," Naomi said, pouring more wine into her own glass and then reaching over to re-fill Alma's.

Alma raised her hand. "I've had enough," she said. "I'm actually starting to feel good."

"Uh huh," said Naomi, taking Alma's hand in hers. "Sister, after what you've been through, you deserve to feel good!" She squeezed Alma's hand and filled her glass.

# ✧✦ CHAPTER TWENTY-NINE ✧✦

Pax stood up on the pedals of his bike and coasted, at a good speed, across the smooth blacktop of the school parking lot. He was headed home. The wind pushed at him as he turned the corner of Maple.

He was hoping his mom wasn't home so he could just go to his room, put on his headphones and escape. If she was home, he'd have to have dinner with her, tell her what he was doing in school; the usual drill. He didn't want to hurt her feelings, but he was tired of having to report every move he made. He couldn't wait to get out of there – though he knew his leaving would devastate her.

He wheeled up the driveway and punched the numbers on the garage opener and found no car inside.

Pushing the kickstand down with the toe of his shoe, he let go of the handlebars and turned to go into the house. He was halfway to the door when he heard a crash behind him. He turned to see the bike lying on the floor. Dropping his backpack, he bent to pick up the bike and noticed the kickstand hadn't been extended completely. Taking hold of the handlebars he glimpsed a flash of yellow under the bench.

Instantly he recognized the chain saw his father had used to cut the house in half. His mom must have shoved it far under the bench, because he hadn't seen it since the day his dad used it. He wondered whether his father was still alive and what he was doing. He was pretty sure his mom would have told him if he'd died, but he wasn't sure she knew where he was. If he was alive, he was probably drinking.

Pax had been hoping that Mr. Finn would tell him something about his dad, but the teacher either didn't know his father well or was protecting him by withholding stories he thought Pax shouldn't hear.

The boy toed the kickstand again; making sure it was extended all the way down, and went into the house.

Up in his bedroom he put on his headphones, clicked the bottom of his iPod and laid his head back on the pillow. Darryl Worley's "Have You Forgotten?" poured into his ears. His legs moved to the rhythms of the slide guitar. When the song got to his favorite line, he sang out loud:

> *Some say this country's just out looking for a fight.*
> *Well, after 9/11, man, I'd have to say that's right."*

Pax fell asleep before the sun left his bedroom windows. He woke up in the night, music still pounding in his ears. The red numerals on the clock cut through the darkness. It was 3:03 a.m. He lay on his back, posing questions to himself and then letting answers emerge as though they were coming from the Magic Eight Ball he'd gotten as a kid.

"Should I stop by Mr. Watkins's house to see how he is?"

*"Ask again later."*

"Should I tell Mom I'm going to see the recruiter in Abner?"

*"My reply is no."*

"I want to make contact with my dad before I sign up. Should I try?"

*"Concentrate and ask again."*

Pax went on playing this game for a while, never sure whether the answers he came up with made sense.

An image of the yellow chainsaw popped up in his memory. He got up from his bed, turned on the lamp and slid the closet door open. Grabbing his desk chair, he put it inside the closet and stood on it. Reaching up to a familiar ceiling tile he gently pushed it up off its metal tracking. Groping around, above his head, until his fingers found an envelope he'd put there. He pulled it down and jumped off the chair. Quickly, sliding the envelope under his pillow he locked his bedroom door.

Pax lay on his bed and pulled the envelope out noticing it had left dust streaks on the pillowcase. Trying to brush them away with the palm of his they wouldn't come off so he turned the pillow over.

Pax blew the remaining dust off the envelope into his wastebasket. Opening the envelope he took out a small stack of photographs. The picture on top was of him, as a small child, with his dad. He was sitting on his dad's shoulders with his forearms in his father's hands. His chin rested on his dad's crew cut. They were both smiling.

Behind them in the picture was their house – the one in which he was sitting right now. The house had been gray-blue then; the siding was replaced after his father cut through it. He noticed a plastic M-16 lying in the grass next to them. He closed his eyes and tried to remember whether he'd ever had a plastic M-16. He thought maybe he had. Then it came to him.

After his dad had gotten drunk and cut the house in half, his mom forbid him to ever come near them again. She made sure he stayed away by getting a police order of protection.

She'd taken charge of Pax's toys. He remembered her saying, "We've had enough memories of that war for a lifetime. We're going to start over." She took away every toy his father had given him: the M-16, the plastic grenades, the GI Joe dolls and the wooden 45 pistols he'd carved and painted himself. After wiping out his armory, she'd replaced his guns with toys like the Magic Eight Ball, a little computer that helped him learn spelling and Sesame Street stuff that he'd piled neatly in the corner of his closet and never used.

He turned off the light and lay back down on the bed, no longer hearing the rain on the roof.

In the morning he awoke to soft knocking on his door. "Time to get up," he heard his mother say. "What do you want for breakfast?"

"Nothing, Ma. I'm good."

"I don't want you eating every meal at McDonald's. Tell me what you want and I'll make it," she said, through the door.

"Eggs?"

"Okay," she said. "Toast?"

"Yeah."

Noticing the envelope on the floor, he picked it up and returned it to its hiding place in the closet. Then he headed downstairs, drawn by the smell of coffee. He looked at the glass of orange juice next to his plate and turned to his mother. "Can I have coffee?" he asked.

She smirked. "That's why you go to McDonald's, isn't it?"

He nodded.

"Go ahead. There's milk in the fridge."

She placed her bowl of oatmeal on the table and sat across from him. "I'm not going to be around today; I have to put in some overtime. We're still short-staffed from that big accident a few days ago. My supervisor wants me to work a double-shift. Can you take care of yourself tonight? Maybe pick up a sandwich at the deli on your way home from school? I'll give you some money."

"Sounds good."

She looked at him for a long moment. "Are you okay? You seem distracted."

"I'm good, I'm good. Just trying to get ready for finals. They're next week, you know."

"I know. I also know that final exams have never been a big deal for you."

"Come on, Ma! You always exaggerate. If my hairs messed up you think I need brain surgery. I'm okay."

She got up and took a ten-dollar bill out of her purse. Leaning over to put it on the table, she rested her hand on his shoulder. "I'm sorry. You've become a man right in front of me, and sometimes I still see you as my little boy. It's me, not you. You've been a good boy, I mean young man. It sounds so strange to say it that way." She rumpled his hair. "I love you," she said and turned toward the garage.

"Thanks, Ma," he yelled as she closed the door.

Pax finished his eggs and poured another cup of coffee. He wondered what he was going to say to his mom after he signed up. He wished that the Magic Eight Ball offered a wider choice of answers.

Pushing open the door to the garage, he saw his backpack lying on the floor where he'd left it the day before. Bending to pick it up, he caught another glimpse of the yellow chainsaw.

All these years later, he still overheard people mentioning his dad's rooftop performance. Once he'd been web-surfing and came across several pictures of their house with a cut running down the roof and one side. Below the picture was the infamous caption: "She wants half the house? I'll give her half the house!" As he studied the online photo, he thought he could glimpse his own face looking out the bathroom window.

Pax gripped the bike's handlebars and pushed the button to open the garage door. Then, without warning, he felt himself turning back and leaning the bike against the garage wall. Bending over, he pulled the chain saw out from under the bench. Opening the gas cap he saw that there was still a little gas in it. He knew how to start the saw. The previous summer he'd cleared trails at the local state park.

Flipping on the switch, he took hold of the rubber handle at the end of the rope and pulled. The saw putted. Then he sat it on the floor of the garage, stuck the toe of his shoe into the handle and pulled the cord with both hands. The saw putted again, but didn't start. He moved the sparkplug wire and watched green corrosion dust sprinkle to the floor. Taking a rag off the bench, he pulled off the wire, cleaned the plug and reconnected it. Then he noticed a small lever marked "Choke" and pulled it out.

Pax pushed the saw away from his body with one hand while pulling the cord with the other. This time the saw sputtered and coughed, almost catching. The next pull got it started.

Pulling the trigger, he watched the rusted chain spin. With each pull of the trigger he felt the torque come up his arms. For a minute he imagined what it must have felt like while his dad was cutting. On the verge of sinking the chain into something, Pax hit the kill switch and pushed the saw back under the bench.

Pax closed the garage and went back into the house. He'd made up his mind to wait a few hours at home and then ride the twenty miles to Abner. He'd find the recruiter there and sign up. The rain had stopped but he wanted to wait until some of the puddles dried.

Back in his bedroom, he turned on his computer and checked his email. He found a few messages from Nabi. Pax had been exchanging email with her since the day she'd waited on him and Mr. Finn at Tilly's.

On the side of the screen Pax noticed an advertisement for finding lost relatives for free. He clicked a link to the company's homepage and started reading. He filled out the contact information and then filled in a box provided for the name of the "lost" person, he typed "Shiloh DuBois." He pressed the "Enter" button and, less than five seconds later, a result popped up: "Shiloh DuBois, Black Mesa, AZ 85928."

Pax stared at the address. "He's alive," he said out loud. For a fee he could have the phone number, too. Instead, he just copied the address and looked it up on an online map. Then he called directory assistance and got Shiloh's phone number. His alarm clock read 8:33 a.m. Smirking, he mumbled, "Homeroom's starting."

It had to be at least eleven years since he'd seen his dad. Except for one drunken call around Christmas eight years ago, they hadn't spoken since.

Pax felt torn. He knew he wanted to talk to his dad about signing up for the Marines. But the idea of calling him was nerve-wracking. It occurred to him that he was being ridiculous: if he was willing to face his fear of Marine boot camp, why couldn't he face the fear of speaking with his dad?

He raised the receiver and tapped in the numbers, trying to imagine what Black Mesa must look like. It was in Arizona; must be all desert. It wasn't until the second ring that terror came up into his throat.

"Hello?"

Pax did not respond. He was still sorting out the syllables he'd just heard. He was pretty sure the speaker wasn't drunk.

"Is anyone there?"

"It's Pax."

Now the silence was at his father's end of the phone.

"Son?"

"Yeah, it's me, Dad."

"Give me a minute, will ya? I want to walk outside where the reception's better."

"Go ahead."

Pax could hear his father's muffled voice saying something. Then he heard what he thought was a door opening.

"Son? Are you there?"

"I'm here. How you doing, Dad?"

"Not sure right now. I haven't heard your voice in a long time. I wasn't expecting the voice of a grown man. But I'm happy to hear from you, Pax." He was silent for a moment. "Is there a reason you're calling me?"

"I don't know. I'm signing up for the Marines and I figured maybe you might have some advice for me. I know you loved the Corps."

"Yeah, I did. Saved my life. Helped me leave home. Your grandfather and I didn't get along. Anyway, that's not important right now. Have you signed any papers yet?"

"No. I'm going to do that today."

"You just turned eighteen on May third, didn't you?"

"Yeah," Pax answered, stunned that his dad had remembered his birthday.

"You don't have to answer this if you don't want to, but how's your mom?"

"She's okay."

"She knows what you're going to do?"

"No."

"You mean you haven't told her."

"No."

"Son, I'm no one to talk, but your mom's a good woman. I'm sure she's given you everything she could. Don't you think you owe her the respect of telling her the truth? I'm sorry. I don't mean to preach at you. I have no right to. It's just that I broke your grandmother's heart when I did exactly what you're about to do. And I'd hate to see you do the same thing to your mom."

Pax was silent for several seconds. "Where are you living, Dad?"

"In Arizona. Town of Black Mesa."

"Desert."

"Sort of. I'm right at the base of a mountain range."

"What are you doing there?"

140

"I work with Native American children in a medical center called Banner Desert."

Pax didn't say anything for a long time. "Kids. You're working with kids."

"Well, mostly babies who are really sick."

"I've got one question, Dad, which is really why I called. If you'd never left us, what would you tell me to do today?"

"You mean about signing up?"

"Yeah."

"Nothing."

"That's what I figured you'd say. You never really gave a shit anyway. That's why you left, isn't it? Mom's ready to have a heart attack and she doesn't even know I'm signing up. I got it, Dad, got it. Sorry if I bothered you. Maybe I'll call again in eleven years."

"Son, you didn't understand what I meant."

"Yeah, I did."

# ✦✦ CHAPTER THIRTY ✦✦

Jake opened his pack and pulled out a sleeping bag. He nodded toward Howie. "There's one in your pack."

"Thanks. What time do you think it is?"

"I don't know; I didn't wear a watch. Hang on, I'll check my cell. 3:15 a.m."

"I've been looking at that petroglyph with the spear stuck in the buck. When do you think that was drawn?"

"I looked on the internet a few years ago. Apparently most glyphs found around New York are about a thousand years old."

"What a thing to sit in the same place as that artist who painted this a thousand years ago," said Howie. "The same shadows on the cave walls, the same fire keeping us warm that kept him warm. The artist, whoever he was, was one of my people."

"True," Jake said, gazing at the ochre drawing. He fixed his eyes on Howie's. "We're going back in the morning, but before that happens we need to come up with a plan. There's a lot to clean up."

Howie was silent for a few moments. "I feel bad about Pax. I mean, that he had to be a part of all this. It has to be spinning his head. Maybe it will keep him from signing up," Howie said.

"You think so? I don't," Jake said, sliding into his sleeping bag.

"I don't have a clue, Jake. I really like the kid. It'll destroy me if he goes and gets himself killed."

"No shit. I'm gonna try and speak with him tomorrow. I'm taking the rest of the week off from school. I thought that you and I might keep meeting every day until we come up with some way to work through this. You know what will happen if the Marines find out about this?"

"Yeah, I can kiss my career goodbye."

"In my opinion, your lips should get sore from kissing your Marine career goodbye. Shit, Howie! You almost kissed your own ass goodbye! If you think the Marines are going to change for you. Check into the hospital right now. From my perspective it sure as hell looks like *keeping* your Marine career would be like putting one foot into the same shit you put the other foot in when you *started* your career."

"So I just walk away from it, huh? Thanks a lot. What do I know how to do? I know how to kill and I know how to sign up kids to kill. Do you know of a job in the civilian sector that needs someone like me? If I leave the Corps, man, I'll be flipping burgers at McDonald's in no time."

"I think there's an awareness in the military now about PTSD," said Jake. "If you go to the hospital they can help you, and you can get some compensation."

"The hospital's not the problem, it's the men I'd be stationed with. When they find out you've been to a shrink, that's it. Who wants to be in a foxhole with a whack-job. Seriously. Would you? It would take a year to get evaluated and I'd be living with assholes pointing at their heads when I wasn't looking."

"I was surrounded by whack-jobs when I was in. Never met crazier men in my life than when I was in the Marines," said Jake. "It felt like I was home."

"Right. But none of them ever went to sickbay for what was going on in their heads, did they?"

"No." Jake looked away.

Howie settled into his sleeping bag. The men lay in silence for several minute until Howie spoke. "How do I convince you that I don't want to kill myself?" He asked.

"You can't just give me your word. It's going to take more than that." Jake raised himself on one elbow and looked over at the lumpy outline of Howie in the dark. "For Christ sake, Howie, look at what you're giving up! A lovely wife and two beautiful kids. You were ready to leave them forever. You want me to believe that was a casual decision? I don't believe what you did was a casual decision. So don't tell me everything's fine now."

Howie swallowed, "What do you want from me, Lieutenant?"

Jake drew in a breath, not convinced that Howie would be truly open to the suggestion he was about to make. What alternative did he have? "Put in for a thirty-day leave when we get back, That'll give you some time to sort out what comes next," Jake said pulling at his beard.

"Oh, I get it. You want me to do what you do, is that it? Rely on the wife. Right."

Jake's head snapped toward Howie. "My wife's not a widow," he said.

Howie rolled over in his sleeping bag, turning his back.

Jake settled into his sleeping bag again and the two men lay in silence.

After a few minutes Jake lifted himself up again. Reaching toward the cave opening, he pushed the pine boughs aside. "The rain's stopped," he said quietly.

The morning fog was thick when they slogged out of the cave wearing their packs. The twittering of small birds in the low brush carried the promise of a sunny day. All the way down the mountain to the car both men were quiet.

Howie, in the lead, felt the softness of the moist earth under his boots. He handed branches back to Jake so he wouldn't be slapped. The care that Howie took in doing this, caused tears to run down Jake's cheeks. Something inside him was breaking up, like rivers of ice in spring bouncing off the banks. Big chunks of emotion were sliding through a cold channel, and then fanning out to open water.

At the car Jake popped the trunk and they dropped their packs in. They settled into their seats, Jake on the driver's side.

His keys gripped in his hand, Jake stared straight ahead at the mountain they'd just descended. "Before we go home," he began. "I just want to say – I'm here for you. It might take a long time for things to get back to normal at your house. I'll be around if you need me." He started to put the key into the ignition but stopped and pulled it out.

Turning his head toward the driver's side window, he gazed at the road that lead home. "That's not all I wanted to say," he said. "I meant it when I said I'm here for you. But it's not altruism. This time that I'm spending with you – is helping me too." He turned and faced Howie.

"When I found out you were signing up, Pax, I hated you. I've lost three students in Iraq and one in Afghanistan," he said, his voice starting to crack.

The two men looked at one another in silence for a long moment.

Jake turned away and looked out at the road again. "But who am I to complain about loss of life? I'm the guy who called in coordinates on an orphanage." He paused.

"We'd been pursuing three VC snipers for hours when we came upon a small village. One of my men saw gooks in black pajamas slip into a reed covered hootch. I didn't want to lose any of my men, so I decided to call in a Cobra to do our work for us.

The pilot had given us an earlier sighting of the VC and was still in the vicinity. He was there in five minutes. He fired all nineteen of his Hydra 70 rockets. The place cooked! And when the sound of the explosions died, we heard screams. We stood there watching little kids, on fire, running out of the hootch.  Later I found out it was an orphanage."

Howie glimpsed Jake's wet cheeks.  "I've read a lot about your unit and what they did in Nam," he said quietly.

Jake wiped his eyes with the back of his hand.  "Yeah, well, don't believe everything you read.  Most of that so-called 'history' is bullshit."  He took a deep breath.  "Thanks for listening, man.  I guess I needed to talk about that."

"No problem," Howie replied.

Jake noticed a catch in his Howie's voice.  "You okay?"

"Yeah, I'm fine," said Howie.  "You just reminded me of my old man."

"Yeah?" Jake asked, surprised.  "He tell you what he did in the war?"

"You kidding?" Howie asked.  "No way.  I wish he could've told me – the way you just did.  I think his stories might've been like yours.  That's where the resemblance comes in. History dictating life, that's what it seems like you're doing.  We all watched him suffer and we paid for it.  I didn't want to be like him and I could see I was turning out just like him, that's why I had the rope around my neck.  He was a good Marine, doing what all good Marines do.  Keep your mouth shut about the past. And have another drink!"

# ✧✦ CHAPTER THIRTY-ONE ✧✦

Shiloh sat on an aluminum lawn chair looking out at the ginger colored mountains, wireless phone in his lap. His son had just hung up on him and he was smiling for the fact that he'd made contact after so long. He realized he'd been waiting for years for this call.

He'd yearned for news of his only child. But he'd felt too embarrassed to ever call his ex-wife, Phyllis. He was sure the town of Reeve was still telling the chain-saw story. He'd seen the online version of the story, illustrated by photos of his house cut in half. He'd read the number of views and it was clear that the YouTube had gone viral.

What Pax did not know was Shiloh left him and his mother because it was the best thing he could figure out to do for them at the time. There were enough brain cells left for him to realize his war rage and drinking were so intense that he couldn't control himself. As he was drilling holes in their marriage boat Phyllis was right behind him, plugging them as fast as he made them. Her efforts for some reason made him drill even faster.

Shiloh knew his son grew up better with his mother raising him alone. She was a good woman and loved him. He'd also loved the boy, which is how he rationalized leaving him.

He looked at the mountain and recalling the sound of his son's deep voice was a bittersweet reminder of how long it had taken him to make the other choice of sobriety.

Six years ago Shiloh had gotten sober for the first time since leaving Nam. He was still sober. He'd found meaning again in his life. Somehow taking care of babies suffering from AIDS and fetal-alcohol syndrome at the local medical center changed him. He could feel the difference he made in the babies' lives. They gave him a kind of love he could not block out.

The inspiration for his vocation came in his sixth sweat lodge, which he'd learned to call the inipi. He'd been raising the pipe to the west, the symbolic direction of death – the place of thunder. A tectonic shift occurred, the slightest realignment that he knew allowed the sun into his heart again. He'd been alone in the inipi and stayed longer than usual. When he crawled through the flap into the cool night air he collapsed on the earth. He could feel the stars in the night sky on his skin, and he knew the job offer he been given at the hospital was one that would change him.

His body started shaking and he couldn't stop it. Gurgling sounds came out of him as though layers of self-hatred were melting off and liquefying from the intense hear of the inipi. Drool came running out of his mouth, snot from his nose. He began peeing and couldn't stop. His ability to prevent what was happening in his body was gone. He was free falling, having lost the tenuous grip on the tree limb he'd grabbed years ago after jumping off the cliff called the Vietnam War.

To his amazement he woke up in the medical center. He was told by his friend Wallingford standing at his bed side that he found him in the morning unconscious outside the inipi. During his two day recovery he made his way to the nursery where he watched the AIDS babies. He noticed that some days they were picked up only two or three times by the busy nurses. A week later he started working in the hospital nursery.

Shiloh pressed the received-call button on the phone and up came his son's number: 671-136-1019. He repeated it over and over, filing it in his memory.

He knew there was nothing he could have done to stop Pax from signing up even if he'd stayed married to his mother. Eighteen-year olds believe the slogan: Marines make men.

Shiloh knew the slogan well. Marines destroyed childhoods and shaped new Marines into human killing machines, not men. Marine's and soldiers have one purpose that gets disguised innendless rhetoric, their primary function as a soldier is to kill the enemy. He only recently learned the distinction between a Marine and a man from Standing Deer. Standing Deer's birth name was Gary Whiting and he was the head doctor at the AIDS clinic at the hospital who'd invited him to his first sweat lodge.

The heat in that sweat lodge was worse than any he'd encountered in Nam. Standing Deer had encouraged him to tolerate it and eventually Shiloh realized that the physical pain of the heat was a doorway to healing. He was forced to focus on the pain in his body and no matter how hard he tried his active self -hating mind had no energy to keep generating self-hate. He was literally forced to stop hating himself because it took all his focus and liveliness to stay in the lodge. The relief he felt from lifting this internal pressure astounded him when he left the inipi. At the same time, Standing Deer's tribe honored Shiloh as a warrior in a way that left him feeling appreciated.

These inipi experiences had given his chaotic world an anchor. He became an active member of the Native American community. He found out that it made little difference to the folks in the community if you had Native American heritage or not. There were people from many aspects of life and many nationalities. The unifying energy of the community was authenticity; telling personal truth and being seen for who you are. Using the traditions and wisdom of a nature-based belief system to facilitate and support an authentic way of living.

Shiloh had been in training to become a pipe carrier and would be completing that training within weeks. He then would be allowed to lead ceremonies.

He sat with the phone in his lap, and recalled another lesson he'd learned from Standing Deer: anger always lives near caring. Thinking of this he was glad to have heard the anger in Pax.

# ✧✦ CHAPTER THIRTY-TWO ✧✦

Pax sat in his bedroom squeezing the phone in his hand as hard as he could. He couldn't believe his father wasn't drunk. He couldn't believe his father had no argument with his decision to sign up. He was surprised by how infuriated felt.

It would have been easier if his dad had been drunk. Pax would have hung up and that would've been the end of it. Instead, his father had told him exactly what he'd wanted to hear from his mom.

Looking at the phone in his hand he felt like throwing it through the window. He knew his mom would buy him another one, though so he put it back in the cradle.

Ten minutes later Pax was a mile down the road, pumping the pedals hard, feeling the tension in his chest starting to ease up. He looked at his watch as he zigzagged around the puddles on the side of the road. He'd be at the recruiting office before eleven.

When he reached Abner he turned onto Main Street and headed toward the post office building. He parked and locked his bike on a light pole. Looking around, he stiffened his back and headed for the door with the poster of an eagle attacking a plane. The caption below read, "Wear the FIGHTINGEST wings in the service. Fly with the Marines!"

Pax entered the office; in front of him was a desk with nothing on it. A dress-blue jacket blouse hung on the back of the chair. No one seemed to be there. "Anyone home?" he called loudly.

"Give me a minute," echoed a voice from behind a door with a bathroom sign on it.

Two seconds later a tall man came out. His bubble-shaped head was perfectly bald; his long face ended in a point of a chin.

"Good morning, sir," said Pax.

Good morning, young man. What can I do to help you? I'm Staff Sergeant Epidemius," he said reaching for his dress-blue blouse.

"I came to sign up," said Pax.

"Really?" said the sergeant, looking him over. "How old are you?"

"Eighteen. I'm graduating from high school in two months."

"You don't look familiar. Where are you from?"

"Reeve."

"That's Sergeant Howie Watkins's territory. Have you met with him?"

"I have."

"How come you didn't sign with him?"

"He's away right now and I'm ready to go."

"Sounds great. How many times did you and Sergeant Watkins talk?"

"A lot of times. I had dinner at his house last week."

"Well, before we go any further, tell me your name."

"Pax" he said, taking hold of the powerful hand being offered.

"Pax, I'd like to sign you up, but I'll have to speak to Sergeant Watkins first. It's not right for him to do all the work and then let me get the credit for signing you, if you see what I mean."

"Yes, sir. Like I said, he's not around right now."

"No one told me he was taking leave. Usually he calls me so I can cover his territory."

Pax realized he'd just made a problem for Mr. Watkins. "Sergeant Epidemius, I think I'll wait to see Sergeant Watkins. I didn't realize how recruiting works."

"Why don't you sit down while I give him a call? If I don't get him, I'll call headquarters. They'll know what to do. Maybe I can sign you up and make sure he gets the credit."

"Ahh, I'm not sure I want to do that."

"Really? A minute ago all I needed to do was put the paper in front of you and you'd have signed it, right?"

Pax felt heat coming into his face. He wanted to scream "Leave me alone." Instead he said, "Sir, I really like Sergeant Watkins and I want him to get credit for signing me. I came here because my mom went to work this morning and I had a chance to come over here without her knowing it."

"Does that mean you haven't told your mom you're signing up?"

"Not exactly. She knows I'm exploring the idea."

"Not a good plan. Why don't you go home and tell your mom and dad what you're doing? Then if you still can't find Sergeant Watkins, come back and sign up with me, and I'll make sure he gets credit."

Pax headed for the door, then turned. "Thanks, Sergeant Epidemius." He paused. "Can I ask you what your name means?"

"Sure. War seer."

The sergeant stared right into the boy's eyes. "You, my friend, have the name every warrior wants, Pax, Roman for peace." Sergeant Epidemius saluted as Pax closed the door.

# ✦✦ CHAPTER THIRTY-THREE ✦✦

Two days had passed since Alma stayed the night at Naomi's. The men came home wet but calmer. They'd agreed to meet every day for the rest of the week. Jake had left to have breakfast with Howie at eight, and Naomi was sitting alone in front of a bowl of oatmeal. Outside the window she watched the green leaves of the trees and bushes vibrate in the gentle wind. She breathed in deeply and murmured, "Thank you."

Only two days left till the weekend, she thought. She'd taken sick days and canceled all her private therapy clients for the week. Her evening conversations with Jake had centered on what he and Howie were doing. He'd been asking her opinion on how he could help Howie. Naomi didn't think Jake's man-to-man or Marine-to-Marine talks with Howie would help in any lasting way, but she was afraid to say so. Howie needed understanding and support, and she was glad that Jake could provide it. But she felt the Marines caused the problem; they couldn't be trusted to solve it.

In addition, she was still living under a shadow of self-reproach for not following the social workers' code.

She was watering houseplants when the phone rang.

"Hello? Hi, Alma. No, no particular plans. Sure, I'd be happy to ride to the airport with you. When are you leaving? I'll leave Jake a note. We won't be much more than two hours, will we?"

Alma and Naomi were waiting in the baggage claim area when a tall woman with a long white braid waved to them. Her face was round with a smooth forehead and crow's feet drawing attention to her dark eyes. She walked over to them quickly, wrapped her arms around Alma and rocked her gently. Opening her eyes, she smiled. The two women unfolded. "Mom, I want you to meet my new friend, Naomi. Naomi, this is Elu."

Naomi took hold of the outstretched hand offered her and was pulled forward into open arms. "Naomi, I'm so happy to meet you. Alma has told me about how much you've been helping her. Thank you!" Naomi sank into the softness of Elu's embrace. During the drive home Elu's presence felt to Naomi like a blanket that someone had draped over her cold shoulders on a winter evening.

By the time Alma pulled into Naomi's driveway, Elu had heard the full story of Howie's suicide attempt, as well as a lot of Naomi's experiences with Jake. She didn't ask many questions. Instead she listened, nodded and made cooing sounds like a morning dove.

Naomi climbed out of the back of the car and stood in her driveway. Elu lowered the car window. "Will you come to dinner on Saturday, my dear?"

"I'll need to check with my husband."

Elu nodded. "It will be just us women," Elu cooed.

Smiling, Naomi said, "I'll make it happen."

"Bring your pajamas. You'll stay the night."

"You only have two bedrooms and the kids will be home. How's Howie going to deal with such a crowd?"

Alma grinned. "Elu's here. He will."

# ✦✦ CHAPTER THIRTY-FOUR ✦✦

On the deck of the Gola Restaurant the sound of clattering dishes and silverware mixed with the whoosh of a steady wind coming off the mountain.

"What's going on at your house?" asked Jake.

"What do you mean?"

"Naomi told me she's staying there tonight."

"Oh, yeah. I was supposed to ask you if the kids and I could stay at your house tonight. My mother-in-law wants us out of my place."

"Sure, why not? What's going on at your place?"

"She's going to perform some kind of women's purification ritual. She and Alma have been working in the backyard for the past two days, building a lodge and a fire ring."

"You're kidding me."

"No, this is how Alma was raised. Her folks actually live by the Indian culture. They hold sweat lodges and ceremonies for every change in season. They sweat if the tribe needs to make an important decision. Sweat lodge is called an inipi which is a sacred space."

"So Naomi's going to sit in a sweat lodge, eh?" Jake smiled. "I can't wait to hear her report! What time you want to bring the kids over?"

"Five o'clock too early?"

"No, that'd be fine."

"You have enough room?"

"We'll make it work," Jake replied. "Pizza okay?"

"Sure," Howie nodded. "I can stop at Rodolfo's on the way over."

Jake waved at the waitress and held up his coffee cup for a refill. "You're a Native American," he said, turning back to Howie. "Why don't you do sweat lodges?"

"My dad wouldn't let my mom teach us anything about our native roots. When he was a kid he was taken out of his home and sent to a Christian school. Apparently it was really hard on him. He begged his parents to take him out, but they never did. Once he joined the Marines, they became his tribe – the only one he believed in."

"You ever do a sweat lodge?" Jake asked.

"Yeah, once – before I married Alma. Her dad made a sweat for just me and him."

"What was that like?"

"Hotter than hell. We were in there for at least three hours. He was basically giving me an introductory course. He explained the meaning of the four directions on the compass and prayed to each one. I thought I was going to pass out after the first direction.

"He'd asked a friend of his to stay outside the inipi and tend the fire and bring water. Every half hour the guy would bring in new hot rocks, and my father-in-law would pour water on them. The steam was incredible, man! It felt like my skin was being peeled off. Didn't seem to bother old Shuman a bit, though. He was too busy praying.

"I remember only one of the prayers. It was about welcoming the disturbance of the heat. That cracked me up. I'm sitting there praying to get out while my father-in-law's praying for the heat to get in. I mean, he's praying for the pain! This made no sense to me. I had plenty of disturbances in my life, courtesy of the USMC. I kept thinking, I don't need any more shit, man."

"Is that what Elu's going to put Naomi and Alma through?" Jake asked.

"I don't know. I asked Elu but she said it wasn't any of my business. She said if I wanted to know more about Indian traditions I should ask Shuman."

"I thought that taking you up to that Indian cave was a big deal," said Jake. "I thought that maybe there was some ghost of a warrior there that would offer us a blessing."

"I don't know, Jake," Howie replied. "I don't know what real Native American tradition is. I imagine a lot of people's understanding of it got screwed up by all that New Age crap about free love and going native in the sixties."

"What do you mean?" Jake asked, forking the last of his eggs into his mouth.

"Shuman said that in the sixties hippies did sweat lodges just to see each other naked, not to invite disturbance into their lives. Looking for wisdom in a traditional lodge is not exactly a fun experience. Shuman calls it a cleansing that forces you to look inside yourself. It's not about staring at nude bodies."

"I thought you said you didn't know anything about it."

"I couldn't be married to Alma without knowing something."

Jake thought for a moment. "There was this enlisted kid in my squad," he said.

"Ethete!" Howie said.

"Yeah! How do you know that?"

"I told you I did some research on your unit. He was a tough kid. But he didn't make it."

"No. He used to tell me what life was like in his tribe. He was from Ohio. He said that before he was deployed to Nam, the tribe held a week-long ceremony for him. Every man in the tribe spent time alone with him before he left. He spoke about how the women looked at him with a respect he'd never felt before. He couldn't say exactly what they did in their ceremonies, but he did say that the bond he felt with the other men in his tribe was like the bond we all had in the bush. Their understanding of everyday life included death as well as life."

"He was Shawnee, wasn't he?" Howie asked. "And if I remember right, no one ever found him. He's still listed as missing."

"You remember right," Jake said. "I sent him on a night ops deep in country. We had intel on troop movement and command needed to know what was going on. I told them the full moon made it dangerous to do surveillance. I must've been talking to someone who'd never gotten his boots muddy. He was a captain. Can't remember his name. He said, 'If we don't figure out what's going on out there tonight, I'm sending the entire squad in the morning.'

"Ethete was standing next to me and overheard the whole conversation. He looked at the clouds for a long time and said, 'I'll take it. Give me the heads up when to start.' That was the last time I saw him. We did get one radio transmission from him. He said he'd seen troop movement. He guessed a thousand NVA were moving equipment toward Hue.

"A few days later we had the shit surprised out of us. Apparently Captain Shit-for-Brains had never reported the intel. When I confronted him, he said he'd overridden Ethete's report with another report of no activity in the area.

"Later I found out that the recon squad that reported the bogus intel had been burned by this captain two other times. So they only went out into the bush a couple hundred yards, set up camp and reported as if they were at location."

"I didn't know that," Howie said quietly.

"Now you do, professor."

# ✥✦ CHAPTER THIRTY-FIVE ✥✦

Epidemius's salute was the first acknowledgement he had ever received for why he thought his parents had named him Pax. The road was dry on his way back. His legs seemed to operate independently of his mind; it felt like they'd decided, on their own, to pump the pedals harder and harder. His only thought was that he must have made a mess for Sergeant Watkins. The long hill before him had become a challenge. Near the top, his legs cramped as he made one last surge.

Coasting downhill with his head bent over the handlebars, trees flashed by. He felt like someone had hooked him up to a remote. He flew through an intersection with his eyes straight ahead, without checking for oncoming traffic. He raced down the street headed to Alma and Howie's house not really sure why.

Wheeling into the driveway, he saw Alma coming around the side of the house. "Pax, what's going on? Nice to see you."

"Good to see you, Mrs. Watkins. I was riding by and thought I'd stop and say hello."

Alma squinted and shaded her eyes with her hand to take a better look at him. "Everything okay? You seem out of breath."

"Is Sergeant Watkins around?"

"Not right now. He's with Mr. Finn. Can I help you?"

"Nah, I think I'd better tell him myself."

Alma's eyes narrowed, and she took a gulp of air. "You know how hard a time he's having. Maybe you ought to tell me and let me pass it on. What do you think?"

Pax looked away and bit his lower lip. "Okay."

"Mind waiting here for a minute? I'll be right back. Then we can go in the house to talk."

Alma found Elu in the backyard. "Ma, I have to speak with a young man who stopped by looking for Howie. Can you make sure no one interrupts us?"

Elu looked hard at her daughter and nodded. Alma was touched.

She returned to Pax. "Come on inside," she said.

The two walked into the living room and sat down. Alma couldn't believe that in a month this boy in front of her might be in boot camp, being prepared for the battlefield.

"I'm surprised to see you," Alma said. "Don't you have school today?"

"I took a sick day."

"You don't look sick."

"I'm not. I rode my bike over to the recruiter in Abner."

"Sergeant Epidemius."

"Yeah."

"Howie and I know him and his wife. Why'd you go over there?"

"To sign up," he said, looking down.

"Did you?"

"No. I found out that if I did, Sergeant Watkins would lose me from his quota. But Sergeant Epidemius got curious about why I was there. He told me he was going to call Sergeant Watkins to find out what was going on. I told him he wasn't home or at work. So he said he was going to call headquarters."

Alma flinched.

"I told him I didn't understand how the quota thing worked," Pax continued. "And that I'd wait until Sergeant Watkins came home and then sign up with him. I think he was okay with that. I'm really sorry, Mrs. Watkins. I didn't mean to make trouble," Pax said, lacing his fingers together and squeezing them until they turned white.

"It's not your fault," Alma reassured him. "You're doing what you need to. *I'm* the one who's sorry. It wasn't right of us to let you become involved in all this. It has to be really hard to watch the adults in your life falling apart in front of you. Sergeant Watkins will take responsibility for his life. It's not your job," she said.

"But he's having a hard time. I can see it," Pax said.

"Yes, he is. But he's an adult. And a Marine. If he wants to, he can do almost anything." She paused and added, "If he wants to." She focused on Pax again. "Sergeant Watkins should be home on Sunday. Would you like to come back and speak with him then?"

"Okay. Any particular time?"

"About noon would be good."

"Okay." He wiped his eyes with the back of his hand.

Reaching over, she touched his arm. "Come on out to the backyard. I want to show you something."

"All right." He stood up and followed her to the back door.

"Whoa! What's that?" Pax asked, catching sight of the small dome, constructed of branches and twigs, in the middle of the lawn.

"An inipi."

"A what?"

"Inipi. A Native American sweat lodge," Alma replied.

"What's it for?"

"Ceremonies – sacred Native American ceremonies. People sit inside and pray. It's called a sweat lodge because you bring red-hot rocks inside while you pray. The heat makes you uncomfortable and being uncomfortable helps you think about your life in ways that you normally don't. So the sweat lodge really gives you a way of getting to know yourself better."

"Are you going to use it?"

"Oh yeah. We're having a women's ceremony tonight. My mother's inside there right now, getting it ready." Alma raised her voice. "Ma, could you come out? I'd like you to meet Pax."

"Be right out, sweetheart. I'm almost done."

Elu backed out of the inipi and stood up, brushing off her hands on her sweatshirt. Then she looked at Pax and smiled. "Alma, you didn't tell me he was so handsome!" She strode across the lawn toward the visitor. "My name is Elu," she said, offering her hand.

"I'm Pax. Nice to meet you."

"And you. Alma tells me you're joining the Marines."

"I am."

"You'll make a good warrior. I can feel it in your hand: strong and gentle."

Pax raised his eyebrows and smiled.

Elu turned to face the inipi. "We're going to start a fire in a few minutes. We put rocks among the branches and let them heat in the wood coals. Then we move them into the inipi."

"Mrs. Watkins was telling me how you go inside and pray together. Do you do this regularly or just on special occasions, like holidays?" Pax asked.

"It's not like going to church on Sundays, if that's what you mean," Elu replied. "I guess you could say that we use the inipi for special occasions, but that doesn't necessarily mean holidays like Christmas. A special occasion might be a time when we have to make an important decision. Or interrupt our everyday lives to step back and get some perspective." A playful smile appeared on Elu's face. "This weekend we're taking time out to get some perspective on our husbands!"

Pax, shrugged his shoulders. These women want to get to know their husbands better, so they're going to sit in a homemade dome filled with hot rocks. Didn't make much sense to him.

"I have to get going," he said aloud. "Have a good – have a good time!"

# ✧✦ CHAPTER THIRTY-SIX ✧✦

Two eagle feathers dangled from Standing Deer's red stone pipe. Shiloh watched them tremble in the dark shadows of the inipi. He could feel himself resisting the heat. The more he pushed against it the more painful it became.

Standing Deer spoke. "It was the first people who harvested our great wisdom. They knew the earth lived so they could live. The music that flowed in their blood was no different than the music of the flowing streams and oceans of the planet. Elk feed on the mountain grasses and buffalo graze on the plains, but mountains and plains were all part of one."

Standing Deer raised his pipe to the East, inhaled and passed it to the woman sitting next to him. He then reached for an ear of corn. Holding it in both hands, he said, "This gift is from all of mankind. Man has built his body with the flesh of this plant. Corn is a mother, making her the same as earth."

"The first people knew their father had two faces. One face was the sun, a solar god of the cosmos who first became visible in the red light of Talawva. In his face they saw their creator, Taiowa.

"The second face of the father was the sun's night face: the moon. There, out of shadows, spirits incubate beauty.

"The corn mother and the sun father are the real parents of every human. When a human mother bears a child, we place, beside the child, a perfect ear of corn – one with a tip that ends in four kernels. There it rests for twenty days, a sign that the child is being protected by his or her universal parents."

Again the pipe was packed, lit and passed. When it came to Shiloh, he began coughing. His face contorted as he tried to stop, but he couldn't. The women next to him patted his back as though he were a child with food caught in his throat. A thin wail rose out of his frame. He shook for a long time. No one in the dark inipi could see him. He got to his knees to leave.

"Please stay," said Chief Standing Deer. "Thank you for this gift from your soul for the new child among us now."

Shiloh sat down again. His crying deepened as he began to see all the AIDS babies he had cradled in his arms as his benefactors, helping his soul on its journey home.

Shiloh was a good twenty miles into the fifty-mile bike ride home. He began to understand what had come to him in the sweat. The birth ceremony for the new child coming brought him back to Pax's birth. Pulling his bike to the side of the road, he lowered the kickstand. He drank from his water bottle and sat down in the shadow of a large saguaro cactus. Running his hand through his thinning gray hair, he still felt his wails echoing in his chest.

When his son came into the world, for a moment, life was beautiful. He and Phyllis brought Pax home from the hospital and settled him in the room Shiloh had painted. Phyllis had been happy during her pregnancy. The child was healthy, Shiloh's job was good and he had not yet started drinking hard. He was still able to keep the war more or less at bay. In conversation, the new parents' dreams poured out of them freely. Both of them fed and changed their baby. Both enjoyed rocking Pax to sleep in the bentwood rocker.

Pax was two weeks old when the phone rang late one night. Phyllis heard Shiloh answer it.

"Hello?"

"Captain DuBois?" asked the caller. Shiloh recognized the voice of his radio operator.

"Caddock!" said Shiloh. "It's me."

"I'm in some deep shit."

Caddock gave Shiloh a telephone number but no details about his situation. The next day was a Saturday. Shiloh left around noon and didn't come home until ten on Sunday morning.

He told Phyllis he'd gone down to the VFW and had a few drinks with Caddock. The incident was so typical that Phyllis was not alarmed. Her only complaint was that they'd missed their "date" to take the baby out.

"Sorry," he'd said.

A week later he didn't come home for three days. When he did, his clothes were soiled and his face, scratched. His eyes were filled with jungle.

He joined the VFW and six months later was elected commander of the post. His drinking became a nightly event.

The shadow cast by the saguaro had disappeared. He slowly returned to the present and thought, with gratitude, about how different his life had become. He was sitting in a sweat-lodge circle where an ear of corn laid next to him. Resting his head on his bent knees, he felt the heat of the day leaving as the sun sank below the bluffs.

Pax was starting down the same path that Shiloh had once walked. Iraq and Afghanistan were consuming young men and women daily. The reasons for fighting these two wars had long ago faded for Shiloh. The patriotism stirred by 9/11 seemed to be drowned out by iPods, reality TV and shopping. Terror was real: 919,967 Afghanistan and Iraqi people had been killed. He wondered if that number was high enough to compensate for the 2,819 Americans lost on September 11th.

Once again he told himself that even if he hadn't left his family, there would be nothing he could do to stop Pax from joining the Marines. He was learning from the tribe that in the darkness of night we see the brightest lights, and it was clear that Pax was headed into the blackness of war. He could only hope his son would see the light he'd been unable to see.

It had taken forty years for Shiloh to turn his war in Vietnam into something other than a dragon eating his insides. He hadn't believed, until now, that anything good could possibly come from Nam. But the heat in the inipi was schooling him that pain can be a powerful teacher, not just a disabler. He'd seen beauty in the night sky, beauty in old folks' wrinkles, and beauty in a young man's tears. He could feel beauty nearby.

## ✧✦ CHAPTER THIRTY-SEVEN ✧✦

Jake had been so occupied with Howie that he hadn't checked his email in days. He glanced at the clock on the kitchen wall. Howie and the kids would be arriving in a half hour. More than enough time to catch up.

Turning on the computer, he watched the blank screen come to life. In the bottom left-hand corner, gmail alerts flashed the names of senders. He tried not to look at these, knowing that if he saw certain names he'd be hooked into reading messages he shouldn't. But he looked, anyway. There it was: another email from Tom. As though tuned to a frequency that controlled an internal mechanism, he clicked on the Juba follow-up email.

The hair on his neck rose as he moved the cursor to start the YouTube video. The film began with Juba returning for a new sniping mission. Jake watched him add a new mark to the three hundred marks already etched on a wall: the number of Americans killed.

This segment was followed by clips of U.S. soldiers being sniped, while Naheed music played in the background.

Finally, an insurgent commander spoke about training his men with a textbook called *The Ultimate Sniper* by U.S. sniper and retired Army Major John Plaster.

Jake heard tapping on the window. His head snapped up and he found himself face-to-face with Howie, who was right outside the window, car keys in hand. "Can I come in?" he asked. He motioned toward the driveway. "I've got the kids in the car."

Jake swallowed hard and tried to answer but couldn't. He nodded. Getting up he went to unlock the back door.

"Hey, you okay? I knocked several times on the back and front doors." Howie handed Jake two pizza boxes.

"Sorry! I got myself hooked on one of those YouTube pieces about Juba."

"I know about that cat. Mind if I take the kids into the living room and turn on the TV?"

"Not at all. Go ahead and get them settled," said Jake. "You need anything?"

"You have any paper plates for the pizza?"

"Top cabinet. On the right."

Once the TV was on, Jake poured soda for the kids and Howie served the pizza. In the kitchen, the two of them sat down at the table with their own paper plates of pizza.

"So you were watching Juba, huh?" said Howie. "That's some heavy shit, man," said Howie. "I saw one of those videos when I was in Iraq. The only thing that made me feel better afterward was to clean my M-4." He took a breath and turned away.

"It really stirs up my shit," said Jake. "I was on both sides of the sniper game. Sometimes I told our snipers when and who to kill, and sometimes we were the targets for Charlie's snipers. I can't get into it right now with the kids here."

Howie noticed the stress line on Jake's forehead and the distance in his eyes. "I think you've got something, partner. Let's take a breather and eat pizza. But sometime I'd like to come back to this conversation. I have my own bag of shit I'd like to dump on the table. You cool with that?"

Jake nodded. The two men ate in silence for several minutes.

Jake felt strange with kids in the house. He loved children, but he wasn't accustomed to having them around. He and Naomi were disappointed that circumstances had stopped them from having any. He remembered telling her, "Kids are like ducklings after birth. They're imprinted onto you. If you're at least nice in the beginning they'll love you."

"You're right," Naomi had said. "Some of the kids I work with in the hospital protect their parents from some unbelievable things they've done. If we had a kid – " She'd stopped.

He'd never been able to finish her sentences, so he didn't know what she had in mind. As usual, he didn't ask.

He never said it out loud but he thought it was fortunate that they didn't have kids. He wasn't at all sure that he could keep Vietnam in the bag and no child wanted to see what was in that bag. He would have either scared the hell out of them or protected them so much that they'd never have been able to grow up.

After turning off the TV, Jake got Howie and the kids settled in the guest bedroom. He blew up the inflatable mattress for the girls and put clean linens on the bed for Howie. Closing the door, he said, "I'm going to put a night light in the bathroom so no one falls down the stairs."

"Go ahead – if you think I need it," said Howie, teasingly. "These two are gone. They won't budge until the sun comes in the windows."

Jake smiled. "Lucky little girls," he said, gently envious of the children's ability to sleep so soundly and easily. "Good night, Howie." Jake softly pulled the door closed.

"Good night, Lieutenant."

Jake was unsure of how many hours had passed when he descended the stairs on his toes. With his hand on the door knob, he opened the door slowly, holding his foot against the bottom to keep it from springing.

A three-quarter moon with dim umbra hung in the sky. In the south the starlight was crisp. Slowly he walked along the hedge until reaching the corner, where he stepped on the lawn.

He was ten feet from the side of the house, staring into the shadows made by the eves of the house. The property line, which went back two hundred feet, was marked by a fence he'd built of five-quarter pressure-treated lumber. No one could punch through it. He'd built it two feet above the building inspector's height requirement, making it really hard to climb. Leaning against the fence, he surveyed the house. A soft light glowed in the upstairs bathroom window. Otherwise it stood in darkness.

He would have a hard time explaining to anyone why this place was where he felt safe. He often came out here at night. Naomi knew he was doing it but, after many arguments, she'd stopped asking him why.

Jake felt comfort in knowing that no one would expect a homeowner to be standing at the back fence at 3:00 in the morning. Therefore he held the element of surprise if he had to move toward an aggressor.

He'd learned to let himself become the fence. Allowing his vision to soften into a blur he followed the lines of the house. Lifting his head he stared at the moon's penumbra.

Counting to four seconds he breathed in through his nose, with the tip of his tongue resting lightly on the protruding bone at the roof of his mouth, holding his breath to the count of four he exhaled through his mouth, making a slight vibration in his throat to the count of eight. Naomi had taught him this sequence of breathing to center him. He'd been practicing it for years. It worked well whenever he was teetering on the boundary between himself and the world around him.

He could feel the tight protective emotional binding in which he'd wrapped himself beginning to loosen. He let himself imagine a penumbra, like the moon's, around his body.

Faces began to appear in his mind's eye: first, those of Howie's two kids, Andee and Bella, and then Pax's, with his unshaven stubble. Then the ghosts came. The first appeared without features, a small figure floating like billowing smoke. Faceless Vietnamese orphans whirled into the sky, shrouded in silent screams. Children, it was always children that came to him. He knew he was a teacher because it put him with children. They did not know hatred fully yet. They lived with love still not completely hidden. When he was with children, he knew the Vietnamese ghost orphans would smile.

A light rain was falling when Jake opened the back door with the morning paper under his arm. He found Howie sitting at the kitchen table with a coffee cup in his hand. A quick glance at the wall clock told him it was 6:00 a.m.

"Anything get through the wire?" Howie whispered.

Jake stared at him. "How long have you been up?"

"I got up ten minutes after you went out the back door."

# ✧✦ CHAPTER THIRTY-EIGHT ✧✦

Pax came flying up his driveway, pulling up the handlebars at the bump in the asphalt. The bike went airborne. He'd been doing that jump since he learned to ride. He put his bike in the garage and opened the kitchen door. "Hey, Ma."

"Hey, Pax."

"How come you're home?" he asked.

"They found someone who wanted overtime more than I did, and let me go home. What was that smell in the garage? Did you start the lawnmower?"

He turned to go into the living room. "Yeah." But before he got to the couch, he came back into the kitchen and stood near her chair.

"No," he said. "It wasn't the lawnmower." Trying to keep his eyes on hers, he went on, "I didn't start the lawnmower. I started the chainsaw that was under the bench."

"The chainsaw? I didn't even know we still had it."

"I don't know why, but I started it."

Phyllis stared at him. "You need to shave."

Pax ignored her comment. "I didn't mean to bring up all that stuff about Dad again. I just wanted to feel what it was like to have it in my hands."

"Yeah? What did it feel like?"

He shrugged, "Like a chainsaw."

"There's a call from the school principal on the machine. Wondering why you weren't at school today."

"I skipped. I've only got three days left. It's called senior skip. Everyone in my class is doing it."

"Is that right? Why did they call me then?"

"I don't know. Probably it's the law or something."

"Mmm. I'm sure. Where did you go?"

Pax headed to the living room without answering.

"Is that it, Pax? You're just going to walk away from me? What's going on with you? You look like you haven't slept in days. You walk around scowling and every time I ask you a serious question you've got some wise-ass remark. Come back in here and talk to me. Now!"

Before she could lower the hand she'd been running through her hair, he was standing right in front of her, his jaw clenched and a piercing light in his blue eyes. She saw words gathering in his pulsing jaw muscles. He looked like Shiloh. She felt the fine hairs along her backbone rise.

Holding her eyes on his, she yelled, "You're turning out like your father. I saw it when you were a kid. You followed him around like a puppy. You'd cry for hours when he didn't come home." Reaching out, she put her hand on his chest and pushed him back so she could get up from the chair.

"You think I don't know what you've been doing the last few weeks? Remember, I grew up in this town. I know a lot of people. I went to school with Peggy Evans!" naming the school secretary. She had stopped, noticing his nostrils flaring.

"So you know!" he shouted, taking a step back from her.

"Did you ever think to tell me? Or were you going to just disappear – like your father?"

"What do you mean 'like my father'? He left us because you told him to!" Pax yelled.

"Is that what you think?" Phyllis asked.

"That's what everyone in this town thinks! So why shouldn't I?"

"You might start by asking me for the facts."

"Come on, Ma. I'm tired of you making shit up to protect me. I'm going in the Marines in a few days and it's time you told me the truth." He saw her face flush and tears pool in her eyes. She reached for him but he pulled away.

"Stop it, Ma! Tell me what happened, goddamn it!"

Phyllis broke her gaze, walked back to her chair and sat down. "Sit down," she said. "I'll tell you."

"No, I won't sit down. You can tell me while I'm standing," he said wiping his eyes with the back of his hand. "I want to be ready to walk out if you make up some new story. And by the way, just so you know, I called him."

"Who?"

"Dad. I called him. I asked him what he'd do if he was still with us and I told him I was signing up with the Marines."

Phyllis gasped and raised a hand to her heart.

"He told me he would have done nothing," Pax spat. "*Nothing*! Just like he did nothing my whole life!"

She heard a small sound and looked at him.

"He asked me if I'd told you. He said he'd hurt his mother by doing the same thing."

Putting her head in her hands she shook. Reaching for the dishtowel on the fridge handle she buried her face in it. The silence in the kitchen lengthened. The second hand on the old electric clock framed each beat. Pax didn't know what to say. He swallowed.

"I knew someday it would come to this," she said in a loud whisper. "Get this into your head, young man. I *never* asked your father to leave. You have no idea what kind of man he is. What he saw and did in that fucking war destroyed him. He carries a huge amount of guilt. And he believes that if he stops feeling guilty, he'll be seen as a killer.

"Another thing you don't know is that I'm still getting calls from men in his squad from Nam. They love him. He risked his life every day for them. He crawled a mile and a half, alone, on the jungle floor, through snakes and spiders, to bring back the *body* of one of his men. The *body*, Pax!

"Your father gave his beautiful soul to his men and to his country. I've never met another man with his courage. Even when he was drunk he held on to enough discipline to keep from hitting me. Oh, in case you want the real truth, I *wanted* him to hit me. I'd throw the most hurtful words I knew at him, trying to provoke him. I thought that hitting me might help him get rid of his pain. Was that crazy or what? I was just turning into another *source* of pain for him.

"So he left me. When he cut the house in half he made it easier for me. He wanted everyone to see that he was crazy. He wanted everyone to think I *had* to leave him to protect you. Well, he did a good job. They all swallowed the whole thing. And so did you."

Pax was sitting very still, his eyes on the table. "Go on," he said quietly.

"Well, the truth is, he left because of you. He knew the pain that he carried would eventually come out directly on you. Either that or his drinking would destroy all of us. I begged him to stay. I told him I'd go to meetings with him. I told him I'd wait for him while he went to rehab. The last thing he said to me was, 'I love you in my bones, but no human being deserves to see what I have inside me.'"

She looked up to see her son sitting with his eyes closed. "Pax, I've been protecting you from a man who loved you so much that he left you. He knew you'd hate him, but he also knew that losing him would be better than what would have happened if he'd stayed. He made me promise not to tell you any of this until you grew up.

"The last time he called you, eleven years ago, he was actually sober. But he pretended he was drunk just to make sure you wouldn't reach out to him. I was listening on the extension."

## ✧✦ CHAPTER THIRTY-NINE ✧✦

Pax's last class of the day was a senior study hall. Half the seats were empty. He looked out the tall windows he'd stared through for the last four years, examining the floor's black asphalt tiles with faint white specks that many times served his imagination for neighborhoods in outer space. He recalled how many times he found it easy to escape – and travel a make believe galactic world. USS Boredom he named the starship he rode to the farthest reaches of the cosmos beneath his feet. With relief he remembered in two more days he'd no longer need to escape. He'd be free of this room, free of school – and free of home.

Pax unlocked his bike from the rack and rolled it onto the sidewalk, coasting with his left foot on the pedal, while tilting the bike to the right. Reaching the street, he lifted his right leg over the seat and started pedaling toward Sergeant Watkins's house.

He was nervous; he didn't want to upset Sergeant Watkins. He realized he was giving himself the same argument every time he found himself in a difficult situation: "If I'm not afraid to join the Marines, why should I be afraid to talk to Watkins?" He pulled into the Watkinses' driveway, parked his bike, and as he walked to the door he wondered whether the sweat dome was still standing in the backyard.

Walking to the front door he noticed that the hedge, once perfectly clipped, was now looking a little ragged. On the front steps, he saw what looked like a fat green cigar. He heard kids' voices coming from the backyard as he knocked. Sergeant Watkins opened the door in a T-shirt and shorts.

"Hello, Pax. Come on in."

"Hello, Sir. Sorry I didn't show up yesterday."

"Let's sit in the living room. Alma's out back with the kids."

Sergeant Watkins settled into an armchair and gestured for Pax to take the chair beside him. "Let's get to it," Sergeant Watkins said, scratching his head. "I have to start by thanking you for saving my life."

"Come on, Sergeant Watkins. Mr. Finn did that."

"Yes, but if you hadn't noticed and had the guts to speak up, everything would have turned out differently. I feel obligated to say a few things to you. Will you let me do that?"

"Sure."

"It's unfair to you to have been caught in the middle of this. You're an innocent young man who came to me to sign up with the Marines. I have to get something off my chest. The truth is, Pax, ever since I came off the battlefield, every time I sign up a new recruit I feel like I've cut off one of my own fingers."

Pax's eyebrows scrunched up.

"This is my shit, not yours, so just hear me out. I'm not telling you what to do. I've signed up over seventy-five kids in the past year. Six of them are already dead. Two are amputees and four are in the hospital with TBI – Tramatic Brain Injury. The kind of injury that happens when you're near an explosion and your brain gets rattled around in your skull. Did I tell you any of this while I was giving you an overview of the Marines?"

"No."

"That's right. Why do you think I didn't?"

Pax lifted his shoulders and dropped them. "I don't know."

"Because you might not have signed up. And then I might not have met my quota. They have monthly quotas for each recruiter. If you fail to meet them, they ship you overseas again," said Sergeant Watkins, slumping in his chair.

"Can I say something?" asked Pax.

"Yeah, sure. There's more I want to say, but it can wait. Go ahead."

"I told the recruiter in Abner that you were not around and that's why I came to him to sign up," Pax explained.

"Did you sign with him?"

"No. He said he didn't want to steal one of your recruits. He was going to call to see if you wanted him to sign me. If he couldn't find you he was going to call headquarters."

"Oh, I get it. You're worried the Marines are going to find out what I did?"

Pax nodded.

"That could happen. But I'm not worried about that now." He looked at the picture on the mantel of himself in dress-blues. "Alma and I have made a decision. I'm getting out."

Pax folded his arms across his chest and looked at the floor. "You're getting out?"

"That's right. I always thought I was cut out for it. My dad, like yours, was a Marine. I worked hard to follow him. But somewhere out there in the woods something happened, and I'm not willing to go on. I have to quit."

"What happened?" Pax asked.

Sergeant Watkins hesitated. "I put a rope around my neck, and –" he said, and then stopped, his voice starting to crack. He took a breath and continued. "And then I started hearing the voices of my girls. That's what it took for me, to hear them calling me. I mean, I could literally hear them saying, 'Daddy! Daddy!' I realized that if I killed myself I would've left – " He choked on the names of his daughters and took a moment to collect himself. "You can hear them playing in the backyard right now, can't you?"

"Yeah, I can," said Pax.

"This is a lot to unload on you. But since you've been in the middle of it, I owe you a truthful explanation."

Pax stood up and looked out the window. "I still want to join."

"Good. You want me to bring you the papers?"

"No. If it's okay with you I'd like to have Sergeant Epidemius do it. I don't know him, and it'll be easier."

"I understand. I'm fine with that. I want you to know that what I'm doing has nothing to do with you. I didn't try and take my life because of you. I loved the Corps, but it doesn't work for me anymore. I figured that out myself the hard way. You have your own life to figure out."

"Thank you, Sergeant Watkins," Pax said, offering his hand.

Sergeant Watkins shook Pax's hand. "Go well, my friend."

# ✧✦ CHAPTER FORTY ✧✦

Elu's coiled white braid looked like a hat of white fur. Her dark eyes held Naomi's. Both women were on their knees, facing one another, in front of the inipi. Elu put her hands on Naomi's shoulders and bowed her head in the inipi opening.

"You're entering a sacred place," Elu said. "Allow the heat to embrace you. Listen to the prayers of the four directions with your heart. Let go what you know in your mind and listen to your body. Feel the soil beneath you; draw her energy in. We shall pray for beauty. We shall pray for disturbance. We shall pray for our ancestors to visit with their wisdom. Go in, my dear. I'll be right behind you."

Alma was still outside the inipi, pulling rocks out of the fire. There was a tap on the tarp. Elu opened the flap and Alma handed her a short-handled shovel with a glowing stone.

Elu slid the shovel along the ground toward the wakicagapi, the shallow pit in the center of the inipi. Elu said, "This is where beloved relatives visit when they return to the earth after death." At the edge of the pit she tipped her shovel, allowing the rock to tumble into the pit dug in the ground. It took twenty minutes to fill the pit with hissing, shimmering stones. Naomi felt sweat running down her neck and between her breasts.

When Alma entered the inipi, she and Elu began a soft chant. Elu lit the pipe and raised it starting with the south. She had explained that they would be honoring all Four Directions as well as father sky, mother earth and the ancestors. At each honoring Elu would open the inipi flap to let cool air in.

After honoring the south Elu explained that the inipi was the inner world or the womb of Grandmother Earth, and the opening in the lodge was the entry to both the underworld and the upper world.

Alma's hand touched Naomi's knee. "We are about to close the door and honor the east."

Elu intoned, "Anything said in this lodge is sacred. Anger, love, confusion, pain – it's all sacred. If feelings come, you are encouraged to express them. If nothing comes, you are encouraged to accept this. We are all here to open the doorway within ourselves to the power of all animals and ancestors who have come before us."

Naomi's skin burned. Her face and eyes hurt. There was a pain in her back from sitting crouched over. Each breath seared her lungs and she was about to ask to leave when she heard a growl. Naomi recognized the sound; she'd heard it, once, from an anguished client. She couldn't tell where it had come from. From Alma? From Elu?

She heard the growl once more. This time she knew it had come from inside herself. The growl continued, growing louder. It slowly built into harmonics that she felt in her stomach. It rose and softened, touching places inside that she'd long ago forgotten. No words.

Finally when it stopped. Her back pain was gone. She felt as though she were standing on a cliff, a vast expanse open before her.

Cool air entered the inipi, and she realized Alma was leaving to get more rocks.

"Are you all right, dear?" she heard Elu ask.

"I wanted to leave, and then I forgot I wanted to leave," Naomi replied.

"Yes."

With new heat building up on her back, she let herself imagine the earth finger gathering and taking years of back tension.

She'd lost track of how much time had passed, when she was shocked back to reality by screeching in the darkness: "I'll break his fucking neck! Selfish bastard!" Then an earsplitting wail: "I hate him!" This phrase was repeated over and over until it became a whisper, "He hates me, I wasn't worth living for. Oh God, Oh Great Father show me a path."

Naomi heard a rustle and imagined that Elu had reached out a comforting hand to her daughter.

"Tell us what you feel Alma," came Elu's soft voice.

"I gave everything I had to Howie. What I wouldn't give to Daddy I gave to him. And he trashed it the same way Daddy did. Can't loving someone be more important than what the war steels from them?"

"Oh if it were only that simple, my love. I can only tell you that feeling like no one could possibly love you after what you did in war is part of what has happened to our men. For now lets let the silences hold us."

After stillness entered the inipi the great pain seemed to dissolve into the darkness.

After their time in the inipi, each woman sat alone outside leaning their back against the inipi canvas. Sipping bottles of water letting the air dry their skin. Then Elu stood and they gathered their things and headed for Alma's kitchen where a candle that set on the table was lit. Its soft glow lit up their faces. Elu was sitting between Alma and Naomi, holding hands with each of them. One at a time they'd showered, and the floral smells of shampoo and soap sweetened the air around them.

Naomi was not used to allowing explosive feelings to be expressed. She was a social worker and dealt with feelings at work every day – but not like this. The purpose of the inipi ritual seemed to be encouraging you to be with your feelings, not to fix them. To reach beyond your surroundings into other worlds you almost never allow yourself to touch.

"Thank you – both of you," said Naomi.

"Ho Mitakuye oysin," said Elu.

"Ho Mitakuye oysin," Naomi whispered back, bowing her head and squeezing her companions' hands. "Elu, I will take this lodge with me."

Naomi had not once thought of Jake that night. She was not worried about whether he'd be triggered by email or one of the kids at school. She was sleeping in the house of someone she'd met only two weeks before and, in this moment, she felt closer to Alma and Elu than to any of her friends.

## ✦✦ CHAPTER FORTY-ONE ✦✦

Shiloh lowered his coffee cup to the wooden arm of the lawn chair and raised his eyes to the sky above the umber hills. A golden eagle tipped its wings, and corkscrewed down into the winds rising off the bluff. Thousands of feet directly above it a white line of vapor steadily grew. A needle of light glinted off what he guessed was an AV-8B Harrier out of Yuma. In one glance, Shiloh saw his two worlds.

He heard a ring. Cupping his hand behind his ear, he confirmed the sound of the phone. Other than calls related to work, he got almost none. He sauntered into the house, guessing the hospital was calling to ask him to come in because someone didn't show.

"Hello?"

"Shi."

Shiloh was speechless for a moment. "Phyllis, is that you?"

"It's me."

"Something the matter?"

"Plenty. Our son is joining the Marines."

"I know. He called me a few days ago. I was so glad to hear his voice.

And so surprised to hear how deep it is now, how grown up he sounds. He got off the phone really pissed at me."

"What did he tell you?"

"That he was joining the Marines and he wanted to know how *I* felt about it. I told him it was his life and he was a man. Somehow that really upset him. Maybe he wanted me to tell him not to go."

"He wants you, to tell him not to go and, at the same time, he wants me, to tell him its okay."

Shiloh was silent for a moment. "Phyllis, I don't know where to begin; it's been so many years since we've spoken. Are you okay? I mean aside from Pax and this Marine business? I know how you must feel about this. Don't blame yourself. I was the idiot who ruined a beautiful family. I'm so sorry this is all getting stirred up again."

"So am I. But it was going to happen, wasn't it? Because he's so much *like* you, Shi. In big ways and small. It's eerie to me because he can look just like you at times, or move in some way that looks like he's imitating you. And I know he hasn't seen you in years. The other day when we were arguing about his going in, he planted his feet and put his hands on his hips, and in that moment I thought he *was* you."

"Do you think there's something I can do? Is that why you called?"

"No. I called because no one knows better than you that he may not come home. There are two wars going on and he wants to be a– what do you call it? A Marine on the ground."

"A grunt."

"Right. He wants to be a grunt like his dad."

Shiloh's quiet was longer this time. "It's different now. The "frontline" is everywhere, what with IEDs and suicide bombers."

"Do you want to see him before he goes?" Phyllis asked.

"He hates me."

"I talked with him about you."

Shiloh considered this, and then asked, "You hate me, too?"

A long stillness followed. Shiloh could hear cars passing Phyllis's house. Phyllis heard sparrows tweeting in Shiloh's yard.

"I never hated *you*," she finally said. I hated alcohol, I hated war. Sure, I was pissed off at the time. But even then I didn't really *hate* you. I felt sorry for you."

"I've been sober for over eleven years, Phyllis."

"I know. I used to pray that you'd find a way to get your life back. And now it sounds like maybe you have." She paused. "Shiloh, I need to change the subject now, okay?"

"Go ahead. If you don't, I'm going to cry."

Phyllis closed her eyes. "I made Pax speak to Jake Finn. Do you remember him?"

"Jake Finn? Sure! He was a marine lieutenant in the Recon and a teacher at the high school. He came to the post a few times. He still in Reeve?"

"Yeah, he's still here. Still teaching. He's been telling Pax about the Marines."

"That's only going to make him want to join more."

"Why do you say that?"

"Young men seek danger, and the more you tell them about how dangerous a situation is the more they want to head right into it. Parents have failed to understand this since the beginning of time."

"I hope you're wrong."

"So do I. Maybe you could have Jake give me a call. I doubt that I'll be able to say anything to him that could help, but I'd be glad to give it a try."

"Okay, I'll ask him." Phyllis paused. "I have to go, now," she said.

"So good to hear your voice, Phyllis," Shiloh said quietly. "Call me if there's anything I can do to help. It's got to be your worst nightmare coming true. I guess it's payback for what I did. I'm sorry you're the one who's still paying."

"I got to go," she said again.

Before Phyllis's phone hit the receiver, Shiloh could hear sobbing.

# ✦✦ CHAPTER FORTY-TWO ✦✦

The morning sun turned the fine hairs on the backs of Jake's hands golden. He sat at the kitchen table looking at the age spots on his skin. It felt good to have Howie and the kids out of the house. He'd been worried that something bad would happen. Now the weight was off his shoulders.

He was thinking of taking a nap when the back door opened.

"Hey, baby," Jake said.

Naomi smiled, bent and kissed him on the cheek. "How was last night?"

"Great kids. Once they were in bed they didn't make a peep."

"How did Howie do?"

"He's coming around. The kids love him. For them, staying here was an adventure with their dad."

"Sounds great. But you look tired."

"I didn't get much sleep. How did the sweat lodge go?"

Naomi smiled and nodded. "Really well."

"Would you mind if I lay down for a few minutes?" asked Jake. "I don't mean to run away as soon as you come home, but I'm beat."

"Go ahead, that's fine!" Naomi replied. "Actually, I might take a nap myself."

Naomi took her vitamins, put the empty pizza boxes in the trash and made her way upstairs. She was surprised to see the bed made. She put a pillow under her knees and began a breathing exercise to relax. The feelings she'd experienced at Alma's house returned and she allowed them to wash over her.

A dream came like a breeze out of a dense forest, carrying smells of living things. From a thick pattern of green, gray and brown, a pair of tiny yellow eyes anchored her gaze. She made out the outline of a hawk. Traveling the light waves between their eyes was a sensation she felt in her solar plexus. A faint sound, like a distant school bell, carried her toward wakefulness. The phone was ringing. Her right hand was resting on her chest and she imagined the softly beating wings of a red-tailed hawk before she picked up the phone.

"Hello?"

"Hello, Mrs. Finn. This is Phyllis, Pax's mother."

"Is he okay?"

"He's fine. Is this a bad time?"

"No, I was just napping."

"I'll call back later."

"No, it's okay, really. It's all right. What can I do for you?"

"Are you sure, Mrs. Finn?"

"Phyllis, I'm very sure. And please call me Naomi."

"Okay, Naomi. You must know that I asked your husband to speak with Pax."

"Yes."

"I needed someone besides the recruiter to tell him about what the Marines are really like. You know about Pax's dad, Shiloh?"

"I know he was a Marine Recon, just like Jake."

"Right. I'm calling to ask your husband if he'd be willing to speak with Shiloh. I just got off the phone with him, and he asked me to ask Jake to call him. What do you think? Would that be all right?"

"I'm glad you checked with me," Naomi said, suddenly alert. "Jake gets worked up when he's reminded of the past."

"Oh, do I know about that!" said Phyllis.

"I'm sure you do. I'll ask him, though. I'd really like to help Pax. He's a great kid."

"Thank you, Naomi."

"I'll give you a call in the morning. Or maybe we could meet for a cup of coffee. Would you have time?"

"Sure," Phyllis said. "I'd like that. Should we meet at Tilly's?"

"I don't know. That place has too much testosterone for my taste," Naomi replied. "How about Clumet's, instead?"

"Great. I like that place," said Phyllis. "Ten o'clock okay?"

"Sure. See you then. Goodbye."

Naomi hung up the phone and lay back on the bed.

# ✧✦ CHAPTER FORTY-THREE ✧✦

The front door of Clumet's was hand-carved wood with the bottoms of wine bottles embedded in the wood. At night the lights from inside lit the glass. The morning sun sparkled on the green, blue, and clear wine bottle punts when Naomi opened the door. She liked the ample space between the tables and the well-cushioned chairs. A hand waved from a sunken area in the back, and she made her way toward Phyllis.

"Good morning."

"Hi. Good to see you, Naomi."

"Good to see you, too. It's been a while since we last ran into each other in the hospital."

"I've been working a lot of weekends and nights," Phyllis said, unfolding her napkin.

"Isn't this music nice?" asked Naomi.

Phyllis raised her head. "It's George Winston, isn't it?"

"His 'Spring album,' I think."

Phyllis nodded, and then sat up in her seat. "If you don't mind," she said, "I'd like to say what's on my mind. Then maybe I can enjoy this place and you."

"Go ahead," replied Naomi. "Makes sense to me."

"Did you talk with Jake?" Phyllis asked.

"I did. He's willing to speak to Shiloh," Naomi said. "He told me that Shiloh's some kind of hero to many Marines. Do you know anything about that?"

"He never really talked about what he did in the war. But I figured as much because I keep getting calls from men he served with in Vietnam. What I do know is that war changed him. After he came back he couldn't live with himself – or with us."

"Sorry, I didn't mean to open that door," Naomi said as she sipped the coffee the waitress had just delivered.

"Shiloh told me he's been sober eleven years."

"You believe him?"

"I do," Phyllis said, lifting a wisp of gray hair from her forehead.

Naomi saw the hurt. She laid her hand on top of Phyllis's. "Sorry," she whispered.

Phyllis nodded. "I just can't stand the idea that another man I love is going into that soul-eating Marine machine."

Naomi felt the bite in her words. "Do you know Alma Watkins?" she asked?

"The recruiter's wife?"

"Yes."

"I don't know her and I don't want to," Phyllis said, removing her hand from under Naomi's.

"Oh." Naomi then realized Phyllis didn't know anything about what her son had been through. Pax had kept his word. "I've just gotten to know both of them and they're not anything like who I thought they'd be."

"They may be nice people but Watkins wants my son as one of his quota," Phyllis said.

"Do you have Shiloh's phone number?"

Phyllis reached for a yellow Post-It note in her handbag and handed it to Naomi.

"Jake said he'd call today. Would you like me or him to get back to you?"

"Would you mind?"

"Not at all. I'll give you a call after Jake talks to Shiloh."

Phyllis nodded. "Sorry I barked about the Watkinses."

✦✦ CHAPTER FORTY-FOUR ✦✦

Shiloh's kitchen table had two ears of corn on a white plate, a few jalapeño peppers in a small stainless steel bowl, a bag of corn meal from the health food store, salt and a cast-iron skillet. Shiloh was bending to look in a low cabinet for a large bowl when the phone rang. Instinctively he turned off the oven before answering it.

"Hello?"

"Captain Shiloh DuBois?"

Surprised, Shiloh took a moment to respond. "Yes. Who's this?"

"Jake Finn."

"Oh, man, thanks for calling. Phyllis must have spoken to you."

"She and my wife, Naomi, talked."

"What a lovely name. Jake, I really don't want to pull you any further into this than Phyllis already has."

"Captain DuBois, I don't mind. To be up front with you, I really don't want to see your son go into the Corps. I don't want to see any kid go to either one of these wars."

"I hear you. I feel the same way. But I don't think I have any say in the matter. I remember what was going on when I was Pax's age. I don't know about you, but I wasn't paying any attention to politics when I went in."

"No, I was the same way. Politics had nothing to do with it. Anyway, to cut to the chase, what would you like me to say to your son?" Jake asked.

"I don't know. I was trying to help Phyllis feel some hope that he might not go. The kid hates me, and I've never blamed him for that. I'm sure you tried to scare him with stories about the reality of war."

"I did, but I don't think it helped. In fact, it may have pushed him closer to joining."

"Boys have a spring-loaded lever that flips at the age of eighteen. Whatever loving care their parents have given them gets pushed into history at that point."

"Never heard it expressed like that, but that sounds right to me," said Jake. "What would you like me to do, Captain DuBois?"

"Nothing. Just tell Phyllis we spoke. And if you think of something, try it!"

"I've tried everything I know, including confronting his recruiter."

"Really? I appreciate that. I've been in recovery long enough to know that there's nothing you can say or do to make someone sober. I'm afraid the same idea applies here." He paused. "Come to think of it, there *is* something you could say to Pax from me."

"What's that?"

Shiloh hesitated. "Never mind. Thanks, Jake."

"You're welcome."

"Listen, Jake, as long as I've got you on the phone, I want to tell you something you might like to know about. Nothing to do with Pax."

"I'm involved with a Native American tribe out here. I've been learning their ceremonies and their ways of dealing with life. It's been a very healing experience for me, Jake. Really feeds my soul."

"And you think I might find it useful, too?" Jake asked.

"As a warrior, yes. They have an attitude to warriors that I haven't run across anywhere else. For example, before every ceremony they honor all the warriors in the group."

"You're kidding me. *Every* ceremony? Not just war-related events? Shit, it took thirty-five years for me to even tell anyone that I'd been to war."

"You and me and all the other so called 'baby killers' have been in hiding. It's time we come out before we die," said Shiloh. "I've been working with a man named Standing Deer, a chief. He recently asked if I'd be willing to work with vets, using the knowledge of indigenous peoples. Up until now I've been a student, but he thinks I'm ready to start applying this knowledge. This wisdom, really. Anyway, I want to reach out to other warriors, so I've agreed to present a workshop. Would you have any interest?"

"No, not really. Not now, anyway – I've got a lot going on. I'm a schoolteacher and my job keeps me busy. There are some other things happening, too, that I can't talk about. Maybe if you do it again, I'd consider it. Let me know how it works out."

"Gotcha. Listen, I got to run. I need to leave for work in a few minutes."

"Okay. If anything comes up when I talk to Pax, I'll give you a call."

# ✧✦ CHAPTER FORTY-FIVE ✧✦

Pax opened his sock drawer, pulled up the liner paper the socks sat on and took out a business card. Holding it under the desk lamp, he ran his thumb over the embossed globe and anchor. He lifted the phone and dialed.

"United States Marine Recruiter Sergeant Epidemius speaking."

"Hello, sir."

"Who's speaking?"

"Sorry, sir. It's Pax DuBois."

"Hello, Pax. Did you get things ironed out with Sergeant Watkins?"

"Yes, sir. I did. I'd like to come over to your office and sign up. Sergeant said he's taking a leave and would be happy to have you sign me up. He said you could call him at home if you need to."

"Great, I'll do that. When would you like to come in?"

"I'm ready now."

"How about I come pick you up? Then I can speak with your parents for a few minutes before you sign, okay?"

"Sir, I'm eighteen years old," Pax said. "And even if you came over here you couldn't see my parents. They're not around. I haven't seen my dad in years. But he was in the Marines himself; I don't think he'd have a problem with my signing up. My mom's working, and I don't want to bother her."

"Can I call you back, Pax?"

"Yeah, but I'd like to get this done now."

"No problem. I just need to do a few things before I can come pick you up."

"I can ride my bike to your office. I'd rather do that."

"All right, but wait until I get back to you."

Pax tossed the phone on the bed and flopped down hard on his back. "Shit, shit, shit," he hissed. "What the fuck's the matter with me?" He'd figured out that Epidemius was calling Sergeant Watkins.

He reached for his iPod headphones and began slipping them over his ears when he realized that if he were listening to music, he wouldn't be able to hear the phone. He lay on the bed, tapping the phone on the side of his bent knee. When it rang he dropped it as if it had come alive.

"Hello?"

"Hello, Pax. It's Sergeant Epidemius. We're clear."

"Clear? What do you mean?"

"I have a contract on my desk waiting for your signature."

"I'll be right over."

"How about I meet you somewhere and drive you back to the office? I want to be able to spend some time telling you what to expect. Sergeant Watkins was very impressed with you and he asked if I'd spend some extra time with you. I told him I would."

"I really don't want anything special. Can't I just sign and go home?"

"I'd like to buy you lunch at Tilly's. Then I can bring you to the office. Speaking Marine to almost Marine, trust me: it'll be better this way."

"Okay, sir. What time?"

"How long will it take you to walk to Tilly's?"

"Fifteen minutes."

"Okay. Then see you there in a half hour."

"Yes, sir."

Pax pushed the heavy oak door open. Squinting, he scanned the booths and tables. No sign of any Marines in dress blues. He sat at the same table where he and Mr. Finn had sat when they'd first talked. Running his hand over graffiti carved into the wooden table, he looked at his Swiss Army watch. He wasn't sure how he felt about Epidemius giving him some kind of private lessons on signing up. He sat with his eyes on the door and hands on the table.

He felt a touch on his shoulder and turned. "Hey, Nabi."

"Hi, Pax. Do you want anything? Or are you waiting for someone?"

"Oh, I'm waiting."

"I thought you might be – the way you were staring at the door. Want me to get you a Coke or something?"

"I'm good. How you doing? I haven't seen you around in school."

"I graduated in January and started community college."

"Hey, that's great. You like it?"

She tilted her head. "I don't know. I kind of wanted a break. What about you? You going to college?"

"No, I'm joining the Marines. As a matter of fact, I'm waiting, right now, for the Marine recruiter."

"Wooh." Her eyes widened and she smiled. "I'll be right back."

Pax watched her walk toward the swinging kitchen door. Her long brown hair, reaching midway down her back, was full of ruby highlights. He took in her tight blue jeans.

"What are you looking at, Marine?"

Quickly standing up and extending his hand, Pax said, "Nothing, sir."

"Right! How about some lunch?"

"Fine with me."

"I bet it is." Epidemius lifted his eyes to the kitchen door and watched Nabi coming toward them, a large Coke in her hand. She set it down in front of Pax. "Ned told us that any customer who's active military gets a free Heavy Weapon Burger – if they want." You want one?"

Epidemius smiled and nodded at Pax. "I like the sound of that. How about you, Pax?"

"Yeah, that would be good," he said. He looked up at Nabi quickly. "Thanks for the Coke."

Nabi looked at Pax, her cheeks flushed and eyes bright. "It will be a few minutes," she said, and walked back to the kitchen.

"Is that your girlfriend?" asked Epidemius.

"I wish. I mean, no, sir."

# ✧✦ CHAPTER FORTY-SIX ✧✦

Jake listened carefully to the church bell, counting the hours with each soft note. The bell stopped at the count of seven. Jake opened his eyes. Reaching over to Naomi's side of the bed, he noticed the sheets were still warm.

He lay thinking about the day ahead. It was Sunday, his last free day before returning to work. He wouldn't be able to take any more time off from school. His plan was to speak with Howie today to assess whether he could be on his own. At the end of the week, Howie had told him that he and Alma had made a new game plan. Howie would leave the Marines.

Jake knew, all too well, how strong the desire for a return to normal life could be. In his experience it seemed that as soon as a sense of normalcy was established, some crisis snatched it away before it could really take root. And a crisis could arise without even any particular event. All it took was a memory, some old guilt that came wheeling out of a closet in which he'd tried to lock it. At times, it was shame that shattered his short-lived tranquility.

Maybe Pax would be different. But, as Shiloh had said, there was very little anyone could do to get a grown man to change his mind. It would be up to Pax and that was that.

Jake had tried to use what the Marines had taught him by becoming

Howie's drill instructor. When Howie tried to commit suicide in front of him, he'd grabbed him and pulled him off the battlefield. What happened after that was not supposed to worry him, but it did. It was painful to hear Howie tell him that his Marine drill instructor behavior was just a game Howie played with Jake.

He made his way to the bathroom thinking about his conversation with Shiloh. The latter's voice had been steady and calm; no echoes of his Marine past were audible. Most ex-Marines kept the Corps lingo alive. It never took long to hear the leatherneck edge.

Jake had never gone to any of the workshops that Naomi had recommended to him; workshops run by therapists who hadn't a clue about the issues faced by soldiers returning from war. "What the hell do those people know about the insides of a soldier?" he'd asked Naomi the last time he turned down her suggestion.

"Why don't you go and give them that point of view?" she'd replied.

Downstairs Jake found Naomi sitting at the dining room table, a cup of tea steaming in her hands, a book lying on the coffee table.

"Hey, sweetheart," Jake said, leaning over to kiss her on the forehead. "Have you eaten?"

"Yes. There's oatmeal on the stove, if you want some."

"Yeah, I guess so."

Naomi got up and went to the cabinet for a bowl. "Get yourself a spoon."

"Got it. What are you reading?"

"A book called *Star Heart*. Alma's mom, Elu, recommended it. It's by this Native American psychotherapist, Will Taegel. He believes we should blend ancient native learning and present day psychology to fight global warming and pollution."

"You like it?"

"Yeah, I do."

"Listen," Jake said, changing the subject. "Would you mind if I asked you a few questions about Howie?"

"No, of course not. What's up?"

"I can't follow him anymore," said Jake. "I have to go back to work. I'm going to tell him that today."

"Of course. You have your own responsibilities. Howie's a lucky man to have had your support all week. And Alma says he's doing well. Not just well; he acts like a different man. She's grateful to you, Jake."

"I don't think she knows the whole story," he said.

"What do you mean?"

Jake looked out the window for a moment and then turned back to Naomi. "He didn't say this to me," Jake explained, "but I get the strong impression that he feels completely lost about what to do when he gets out. On top of that he's worried that his old man's going to disown him. That scares me."

Naomi sighed. "Sounds like you're pretty worried about him."

"I am."

"I'm worried about *you*," Naomi said. "You've been doing great with him. You and Pax saved Howie's life. Of course I'm happy about that. Howie was lucky you were there for him. But now I'm waiting to see what happens to *you* when the adrenaline wears off. And I think that's about to happen. Am I wrong?"

Jake's lips tightened into a thin line, and he didn't answer.

"How did the call with Shiloh go?" Naomi asked.

"It was strange. I thought he was going to ask me to say something in particular to his son. But he never did. Instead we talked about how impossible it was to change the mind of an eighteen-year-old. He was concerned about Pax, but he didn't think there was much he could do since he'd only talked to him once in eleven years. He said the reason he spoke with me was to make Phyllis feel better."

"Do you really think you can't change the mind of an eighteen-year old?"

"Yeah. I do," said Jake.

"Was Shiloh sober?"

"Sounded like it to me. He told me he's been sober for years and Phyllis says she believes him. In fact, he's now trying to help *other* vets sober up."

"Yeah? What's he doing?" asked Naomi.

"He's planning a workshop for vets. Sounds like he's been attending a lot of Native American ceremonies. He thinks they've helped him a lot in terms of healing from his war experiences, so now he wants to introduce other vets to them. Anyway, he invited me, but I told him I'm too busy — between school and other things."

"When's the workshop?"

"I don't know. I didn't ask."

"Then how did you know you couldn't go because of school?"

Jake shrugged. "I don't believe in that kind of New Age shit."

"You're telling me Shiloh's gone New Age?"

"Hard to believe, isn't it? Last time I saw the guy he was about as New Age as I am."

Naomi was silent for a moment. "Well, in any event, I don't think there's anything you can do for Pax. I think you just have to let him be."

# ✦✦ CHAPTER FORTY-SEVEN ✦✦

Shadows thrown by the June sun skittered in patterns on the living-room rug. The room was free of toys; the children were playing contentedly in their rooms.

Alma was lying on the couch, wearing her iPod ear-buds. Howie had a book on his lap but was staring at the wall. Pulling out the ear-buds, Alma asked, "You okay, hon?"

"I'm good. Not interested in this book, though."

"What is it?" Alma asked.

"*The Accidental Leader: What to Do When You're Suddenly in Charge*, by Harvey Robbins and Michael Finley."

"Sounds heavy."

"It's not bad. I just can't focus on it right now." He paused. "I wasn't planning on being out of a job this year. Much less out of the Corps."

"Howie," He looked at her. "I love you, sweetheart," she said.

He smiled. "Am I a crazy guy, or what? Why do I want to spend all my time worrying about what's coming when I could be appreciating what's right in front of me?"

Alma smiled back. "You want to appreciate? Come on over here," she said, sliding to the inside of the couch and patting the cushion beside her. "I'll help you practice."

That evening at dinner Howie told Alma about a conversation with Jake. "I thanked him for helping me and it was now time for me to take charge of my own life. He knows about our plans. We shook hands and that was it."

"How many more days do you have before your leave is up?"

"Three more weeks before I have to report to headquarters."

"Okay, then that's how much time we have to figure out what we're going to do," Alma said, putting broccoli on Bella's and Andee's plates.

"Maybe I can finish reading that book by then," Howie muttered.

"I want to go out for lunch with Naomi tomorrow. Can you stay with the kids? There's no school because of a teachers' conference."

"Sure."

"How would you girls like to spend the afternoon with your dad tomorrow?"

Their mouths full, both children nodded. Howie smiled.

Howie woke feeling rested. He and Alma ate breakfast slowly while the kids slept. Getting up from the table, he said, "I have a few things to put in order at my desk. Can you keep the kids out of my hair until you leave for lunch?"

Alma nodded. "I'll feed them breakfast and get them dressed."

"Thanks, sweetheart."

Before he knew it, it was noon and Alma was knocking on the

bedroom door. "I'm leaving in a minute." Howie followed her to the front door. The kids were busy with a game in the living room. "I'll see you guys after lunch," she called to them. "Don't go into the backyard unless you tell Daddy," she warned, closing the door.

"We'll be fine." Howie's reply bounced off the closing door.

He sat down, picked up his book and watched the kids go into Andee's room. He felt able to focus on the book and read quietly for a while. Taking a break, he got up and looked in on the kids. They were watching a DVD. Howie returned to the living room and picked up the book again, eager to continue reading. He was beginning to realize that all the discipline he'd learned in the Marines would be valuable in the business world.

Looking up from the page, he saw Bella near the end of the couch. She'd picked something up and was heading back to her bedroom.

A half hour passed before Howie got up again to check on the kids. Andee was still watching the DVD in her room. The door to Bella's room was closed. Tapping lightly on the door, Howie said, "Bella, open the door." No answer. He tapped harder and raised his voice. "Open the door, Bella!" Still no answer. He grabbed the doorknob, it was locked, and he shook it hard.

Returning to Andee's bedroom, he asked "What's your sister doing in there?" Andee looked up, her eyes widening in response to the tone in his voice.

Before she could reply, he was back at Bella's door, pounding hard enough to dent it. In one second a frenzied fear tore loose in his chest. Narrowing his eyes, he leaned back from the door. Andee was standing in the hallway staring at him.

Howie lunged, shoulder first, into the door, breaking it free. He fell forward and the door landed on the floor with the squeal of splintering wood. He'd fallen with the door and looked up to see Bella was huddled in the corner, her little knees pulled up to protect her chest. Alma's iPod was in her hand and the ear-bud wires dangled from her ears.

# ✦✦ CHAPTER FORTY-EIGHT ✦✦

Alma was the first to arrive at Clumet's, and she found a table. She admired the flower-patterned placemats, and the ivory walls, topped with a wallpaper strip of serpentine green vines. Beautiful harp music completed the atmosphere. She rubbed her fingertips against her temples.

Naomi came through the door. Her hair was held back by a silver barrette in the shape of a turtle, embedded with red, amber and green stones. The two women exchanged smiles.

"How was the first day of post-Marine life?" Naomi asked.

"I'm afraid to tell you how good it was. It was like having my whole family together again for the first time in years!"

"I'm so happy to hear that, Alma! For all of you!" Naomi beamed at her friend. "On a more selfish note, I've been wondering if you plan to leave Reeve after Howie gets out?"

"We're not sure yet. We're still talking about what he might do."

"I feel like I've just made a good friend and I would hate to lose her."

"I know what you mean. But after what just happened I have no choice but to keep an open mind," Alma said.

"I didn't mean to make you feel guilty," Naomi said quickly. "I just wanted you to know how happy I am that we've become friends."

"Thanks," said Alma. "The waitress is right there. Do you know what you want?"

Naomi nodded. "Are you in a hurry?"

Alma waved to the waitress. "I left Howie with the kids and a DVD that lasts about an hour and a half. Howie hasn't had much practice being alone with the kids."

"Got it. Let's order then."

They both ordered the vegetable soup. Alma had a mesclun salad with fresh figs, goat cheese and lemon dressing. Naomi followed her soup with a stir-fry of tofu, snow peas, bell peppers and fresh ginger on soba noodles.

Naomi lifted her fork toward Alma. "This isn't Tilly's, is it?" she smiled.

Alma laughed and picked up her china teacup. "I love these. There must be fifty different kinds of yard-sale china here." She drained the cup, looked at her wristwatch, "I have to leave in a few minutes."

"I want to ask you something before you go," Naomi said.

"Sure."

"Jake mentioned that Pax's dad, Shiloh, has been working with a Native American man named Standing Deer. I was wondering if you might have heard of him. I remember what you told me about your dad."

"The name's not familiar. Would you like me to call my folks and see if they know him?"

"No, no. It's not that important."

"What did Jake tell you about him?"

"He said this man has been encouraging Shiloh to hold a workshop for vets out in Arizona."

"What did Jake say? Is he going?"

"No, he said he was too busy."

"I'll call my folks and get back to you." She paused. "Do you think we could meet here again?"

"I'd love to make it a regular date if you would."

"I'd love that, too. Would Saturday mornings work for you?"

"I'll speak to Jake, and I'll make it happen," said Naomi.

Alma leaned over and kissed her friend on the cheek.

As Alma made her way up the front walk to the house, the sound of sobs quickened her steps. Opening the front door she saw Howie sitting on the couch with Bella in his arms, her head shaking in the crook of his neck. Andee was tucked under his arm, crying softly. Howie was saying, "Its okay, it's okay."

"What happened?" Alma asked, craning to see Bella's face. "What's the matter, sweetheart?" Her words were soft and strained.

Howie answered, "I scared them. I knocked down the bedroom door when Bella locked herself inside and didn't answer. I thought something was wrong."

Alma turned and walked down the hallway. "My god, Howie!"

"I'll take care of it in a few minutes."

"All right," Alma said, sitting down next to him. "Let me have her."

## ✧✦ CHAPTER FORTY-NINE ✧✦

"I knocked the door down because she didn't answer. She had your iPod ear buds on. She must have had the volume turned up so loud she couldn't hear me. I don't know why she locked the door. Maybe she didn't want me to know she was using the iPod. She knows she's not supposed to."

"I understand you had your reasons," Alma said. "But they were scared out of their minds. They were still shaking when I put them to bed. They didn't want me to leave their rooms."

When Alma told her mother, Elu immediately asked, "He's not drinking, is he?"

"No," Alma said. "He really thought something was wrong and panicked."

"Have you told Naomi?"

"Not yet. I don't know what to do. She and her husband have already done so much to help."

"Well, I don't think she'd mind talking to you. Why don't you call her and make it clear that you don't need her and her husband to come over, that you'd just like to talk with her?"

"Yeah, I guess it couldn't hurt to ask. I'll give her a call," Alma said. "Oh, by the way, she asked if I knew of a tribal teacher named Standing Deer. I said I'd ask you."

"Yes, I know him," Elu said warmly. "He's a good man. Your Uncle Pete spent some time with his group, learning tribal ceremonies. Standing Deer gave him the name Hawk Wings after his initiation, in honor of his service in Korea. It made a huge difference for Pete. He's not the same guy. He's still not exactly a party animal, but he seems a lot more sociable now, and a lot more relaxed. He still participates in tribal ceremonies, too. He's a pipe carrier now. He and your dad have grown close. So what did you hear about Standing Deer?"

"Remember Pax? The kid who wants to join the Marines after high school? Well his father, Shiloh, lives in Arizona now. Jake, Naomi's husband knew him from VFW here years ago, before he moved away. Apparently Shiloh has been learning about tribal customs from Standing Deer. And now Standing Deer is encouraging him to lead some kind of veterans' workshop, based on sacred ceremonies."

"Really?" said Elu. "Pu Ha. Have you told Howie about this?"

"No."

"Don't. I have an idea."

"What's that, Ma?"

"Let me think a minute," Elu said. "Tell you what. Let me speak with dad and I'll call you right back. Okay?"

"Okay. I'll be here."

Elu called back in fifteen minutes and told Alma that she and Alma's dad were going to come out to Reeve for a visit – soon. They would stay in a nearby hotel; there was no need for Alma to entertain them. "Dad wants to spend a little time with Howie," Elu explained. "Don't worry."

Alma asked, "What's he going to say to him?"

"Men's talk. Don't tell him we're coming."

216

## ✧✦ CHAPTER FIFTY ✧✦

The streetlights in front of Pax's house made his white sneakers glow as he ran across the front lawn. Pax wore his favorite T-shirt. The shirt was black. The front featured a toothy white skull, pierced by two KA-BAR knives. The letters "USMC" were stamped across the top. At the bottom, a slogan was draped over the KA-BAR blades: "We fight what you fear." A set of dog tags dangled between the blades of the knifes. He'd ordered the T-shirt months ago and had kept it hidden in the bottom of the toy box in his room. This was the first time he'd worn it.

He was heading to the elementary school to meet Nabi on the playground behind it. His mom had left for her night shift an hour earlier. She wouldn't be back until late morning.

June gardens scented the night air as Pax made his way from street to street. The slapping of his sneakers on the asphalt created a rhythm and a song popped into his head. He began softly singing:

*Well, we're droppin' our bombs*
*In the southern hemisphere,*
*And people are starving*
*That live right here.*
*And they're tearing down walls*

217

*In the name of peace,*
*And they're killing each other*
*In the Middle East.*
*But love and happiness*
*Have forgotten our names,*
*And there's no value left*
*In love and happiness.*
*They raise the price of oil*
*and they censor our mouths . . .*

Pax danced down Millrock Road to the playground. His black shirt and pants made his body blend into the darkness. From a distance the only visible movement was a pair of fast-moving sneakers skimming the sidewalk.

He stopped before he hit the grass of the playground. Waiting for his eyes to adjust better to the dark, he looked around. No Nabi.

He walked over to the swings and took hold of a pair of chains. A familiar voice spoke from behind him. "Mellencaamp, right? 'Love and Happiness'?"

"Holy shit! Where'd you come from?"

"Sorry," Nabi giggled. "I was right behind you almost all the way here. When I saw you start dancing and singing, I just wanted to watch."

"You sneak!" Pax complained, but looking pleased. "How did you know it was 'Love and Happiness'?"

"I was copying your moves and the words just came out of the rhythms. That song has the best rhythms."

"It does. I used to dance to it a lot when I was a kid. My mom still plays the CD."

The night sky spiraled in their eyes as they unfurled in their swing seats, the twisted chains unraveling and gravity pulling their heads back on their necks. Above them Orion, Ursa Minor and Cassiopeia tangled into trailing lights. The only music was their soft laughter.

The wet grass soaked through the back of Pax's T-shirt, Nabi's breasts pressing on the skull on the front of his shirt. He held her for a long time, not moving, letting her warmth sink into him. He felt her muscles relax. She lowered her head on his shoulder. "I'm scared, Pax," she whispered into his ear. "I'm not sure we should be doing this."

"Don't be scared," he murmured back. "Everything'll be fine. Besides, what if we weren't doing this? A week from now I'll be gone. I don't want to look back and know we didn't get together when we had the chance. That's what *I'm* scared of. I don't want you to be the girl I lost, the girl I walked away from."

Running his fingers through her thick hair he lifted her face and kissed her – softly and slowly. He could feel her surrender. A few minutes later there was no place their bodies were not connected.

# ✦✦ CHAPTER FIFTY-ONE ✦✦

Alma was eating breakfast, waiting for the kids to get up, when she saw an orange truck pull into the driveway. A young man with a nametag on his shirt came to the front door. "Hello," he said as Alma opened the door.

"Joseph," Alma said, reading his nametag. "You must be bringing the new door from Home Depot."

"Yes, ma'am."

"Would you put it in the garage?" Alma asked.

"Sure. Could you open it up, please?"

"Yes. It's paid for, isn't it?"

"It is, ma'am."

Alma had called Naomi the day Howie broke down the door. As Elu had suggested, she hadn't asked for help other than an opportunity to talk. Naomi listened on the phone as Alma described what had happened at her house while the two friends had been having lunch.

Naomi must have told Jake, because he'd shown up on the Watkins' doorstep an hour earlier and taken Howie away in his car. Alma knew, then, that she'd been mistaken to think they'd reached the end of their problems.

Later that afternoon Howie came home in a better mood than she'd expected. She was even more surprised when she told him the new door was sitting in the garage, and he immediately said, "I'll put it in tomorrow."

The next day was Saturday. Alma decided to take the kids to the playground. Before they left, Howie brought his toolbox in from the garage and started prying off the remaining pieces of the door fame. The sharp squeal of the nails being pulled out made the kids shudder. "Howie, can't you wait until we leave?" Naomi asked.

"Sorry."

After they left, Howie opened the bedroom window. Sweat was already running down the sides of his face. Once all the broken lumber was out of the house and piled up at the curb, he headed into the garage to get the new door.

He was carrying the door out of the garage when he saw a taxi pull up to the curb. A man's hand reached from the back seat to pay the driver. The passenger looked familiar.

The cab door opened and Howie saw his father-in-law, Shuman. Shuman quickly glanced at the pile of wood before looking at Howie. He walked up the driveway smiling. Howie stuck out his hand. Shuman pushed it aside and took the younger man into a bear hug. "Good to see you, son," he said, ignoring Howie's tool belt in his eagerness.

"What are you doing here?" asked Howie. "Where's Elu?"

"At the hotel."

"The hotel?" Howie asked, bewildered.

"Yeah, we wanted to visit for a few days, but we don't want to intrude. So we got a room at the Holiday Inn. Where are Alma and the kids?"

"Down at the playground.," said Howie. "Alma got them out of here so I could have some time to install the new door."

"Good, good," said Shuman, nodding.

Howie looked at his father-in-law. "Did Alma know you guys were coming?"

"Elu told her we were thinking about a visit, but I don't think she gave her a date. Listen, Howie. I'd really like to have a few minutes alone with you. Could we take a short walk? I tell you what. If you spend a few minutes walking with me, I'll give you a hand with that door. It'll go much faster with two of us."

"I think I'd better get the door in before Alma gets back with the girls. It's just easier when they're not around."

"Yeah, I understand. So listen. How about I give you a hand right now, and *then* you take a few minutes to walk down to the river with me. What do you say?"

Howie felt trapped. "All right."

The door was a pre-hung and went in quickly. Shuman was skilled; he had the trim attached before Howie finished picking up the tools and cardboard.

Howie was trying to find out why his in-laws had shown up. When Shuman said, "Sometimes a bird from the west carries love." Howie had never mastered the code of such Native American metaphors, but he knew two important beliefs about the West: it's the direction from which disturbance often comes and the direction in which death resides. And on the other hand he didn't know if this statement came from Shuman's imagination and had nothing to do with Native American lingo.

Howie said, "Let's drive to the river."

Shuman replied, "What's the matter you can't walk and talk?"

Shuman's large frame bent forward, gray hair covering his ears. His dark eyes were barely visible in squinting folds. He placed his hand on Howie's shoulder and guided him down the driveway. They walked in silence for twenty minutes. Finally, Shuman spoke.

"Lot's going on."

"Yeah," Howie, looked away.

"I didn't come here to lecture."

"Good," Howie said.

"I came to tell you some things about myself."

"I hurt my daughter when she was a child. I buried my killing in drink."

"Your killing?" Howie cringed and raised his shoulders.

"Yeah. I've got Korean blood all over me. I didn't know how to get it off when I got home. So I smeared it on my wife and kids. They didn't realize what was going on until it got physical — until they saw their own blood when I started hitting them."

"Shuman, you don't have to tell me this."

"I know. You don't have to listen, either."

Howie stopped and turned to his father-in-law. "In that case, Shuman, leave me – "

Shuman interrupted. "When a man kills, Howie, he must dig two graves: one in the earth, for the dead, and one in his heart, for his own spirit. If he doesn't, he will not return. That's all I came here to say. If you think that's a lecture, fine; you can throw it out. Now let's go back. My legs hurt."

# ✦✦ CHAPTER FIFTY-TWO ✦✦

"Where we going?" Howie asked, as Jake drove away from the Watkins' house.

"No idea! I came over to tell you I'm as confused as you. At first I thought I could help you. But I'm realizing I need as much help as you do." Howie shifted in his seat so he could see his Jake's face.

Tears were on his cheeks, he continued. "Man, I'm sorry. I feel like I haven't been honest with you. You didn't even know who I was until you showed up in school, and then you went and read all that bullshit Marine history. I know what it says about me. And it's all crap; it's not true. I should've told you that right in the beginning. I'm no hero. And I didn't come back in any better shape than you did. I've got my demons, my nightmares. I'm scared more than most."

"I pretended only one of us needed help. I made you the patient, the wounded Marine on the battlefield who I could drag off. I told you to quit the Marines, to take off your uniform, while I kept mine on. The real truth is, the goddamn uniform isn't *ever* coming off either one of us. The frigging thing's super-glued on. And another thing." Jake paused. "What you tried to do on the mountain – I've been thinking about for years. I just never had the courage."

Howie stared at Jake. "You talking about suicide?"

Jake nodded.

"Does Naomi know?"

"She knows I made an attempt once, years ago. But she doesn't know what's been going on lately. And I don't want to tell her, either. Because then she might actually make it worse." He was quiet for a moment. "That's not really fair. It's because of her that I'm still alive. But when she gets scared, she tries to control every single move I make. And there's only so much of that I can stand, said Jake whipping the back of his wrist across his eyes."

"Want me to drive?" Howie asked.

"Yeah," Jake said, pulling up to a curb and opening his door.

They switched seats and got back on the road. "What I want you to know," Howie said, "is that you helped me. You knew how to tune in to the only frequency I could pay any attention to. If someone had offered me some kind of therapy shit it would have been a waste of time."

"Turn right, here," Jake said.

"Looks like an old apple orchard."

"I used to come up here as a kid. I'd get into these horrendous fights with my old man and then have to get out of the house. I'd come up to these orchards and look out at the mountains until I didn't want to kill him anymore."

The two men sat in the car, gazing out at the mountains in the distance.

"Do you think two sick Marines can help each other?" Howie asked.

"No!" Jake said. "But I do have an idea."

"What?"

"I found out that Pax's father, Shiloh, is working with a Native American shaman in Arizona. Your in-laws know the shaman and vouch for him. Apparently Shiloh has become a powerful man in the Native American community."

"Wait a minute. How do you know all this? Have Naomi and Alma been talking about it?" Howie asked.

"Maybe. *I* told Naomi about a conversation I had with Shiloh a few days ago. He told me he was planning a workshop using Native American ceremonies to help heal veterans. I told Naomi that he'd invited me."

Howie ran his hand through his hair and said, "Let's open the windows. It must be ninety in here."

Jake agreed, "See the heat shimmering between here and the mountains?"

"Our women are becoming good friends," Howie continued.

"Yeah," said Jake.

"You know they're still talking about Shiloh in the Marines today? There are a couple old-timers keeping his Nam stories alive. I've even heard that at one point he was being considered for the Medal of Honor."

"I didn't know that," Jake said. "Anyway, Naomi told me that the Native American man who's training Shiloh as a shaman is named Standing Deer, and your in-laws respect him."

"I don't know much about Shiloh," he continued. "Actually all I know is that he became a drunk and cut his house in half with a chain saw. He seems like the last person on earth to be helping veterans. But if he's really changed, and if I were to look honestly at you and me, I'd have to say it makes perfect sense," Jake said, rolling up his shirtsleeves.

"Only thing is," he added, "I don't know anything about Native American rituals. You're closer to that than I am; what do you think? You think these 'ceremonies' can make any difference?"

"Like I said," Howie replied, "My father thought it was a bunch of crap. On the other hand, my mother used to tell us bed-time stories about the power of the four directions."

"What about Alma's family?" asked Jake.

"They're deeply committed to their traditions. They don't make any important decisions without going to the sweat lodge and then sitting in council."

"Hmm," said Jake. "Have you heard anything about how they treat warriors? Shiloh said that before every ceremony the tribe honors their warriors. Have you heard anything like that?"

"Yeah, it's true," Howie replied. "Warriors have the most important role in the tribe. They risk their lives to protect the women and children and the elderly. Without the warriors there would be no tribe."

Jake sat for a moment, absorbing Howie's responses. Then he looked at his friend. "Let's go."

Howie started the engine, pushed the buttons to raise the windows and turned on the air conditioner.

"Nothing like that happened to me when I got home from Nam," Jake said. "The first thing I did was grow a beard so nobody would know I'd been in the military. What happened to you when you came home?"

"Yellow ribbons and all that shit. It lasted about two weeks. It feels to me like patriotism hit a high point right after 9/11, and it's been draining away every since. So when I first got back, I was welcomed as a patriot. But now the American public sees its soldiers as mercenaries."

"Thank God for air conditioners," said Jake, holding his hand in front of the vent. "That baby's kicking out now. Howie, what would you think of going to Shiloh's workshop? It's clear that neither one of us has been able to change much. Our wives understand some things we don't. The workshop happens next week. I would have to take a few sick days off. I'm willing to make that happen, though I am sure they will be pissed because I just took a week off."

"The truth is, Jake, I'm feeling pretty good. But if my going with you would help you, I'd consider it."

"Pardon the expression, but you're full of shit! Two weeks ago you're ready to check out. A couple of days ago you almost crushed your daughter under a door. Yeah, you're doing great. Right.

"Wake up man! You're in the same place I am! And today that might be a fine place to be! But what about tomorrow, Howie? Will we be in a good place tomorrow? I haven't a fucking clue!"

Howie's face was red, and he swallowed repeatedly. "Fuck you, man! Fuck you! Who the fuck are you to be telling me what to do?"

"I'm not telling you what to do, Sergeant!" said Jake. "I'm just letting you know that you have zero credibility with me when you tell me that you're just fine now. Do what you want! I don't care! But don't expect me to believe your bullshit story. I'm not buying it!"

Howie pulled the car off the road, into a small parking lot adjacent to a hiking trail. He turned off the engine and sat with his head in his hands.

Jake got out of the car and walked up the first few hundred feet of the trail.

By the time Jake returned to the car, Howie's eyes were red. Jake sat in the passenger's seat and put on his seatbelt. The two men sat in silence for another five minutes.

Finally, Howie spoke. "Do you have Shiloh's number?" he asked.

"Yeah."

"I'll give him a call and find out more about his workshop. I'm not making any promises. But I'll call."

"Okay," said Jake. "Let's go home. Sorry I yanked your chain so hard. The truth is I need help as much as you do. It's just easier seeing your troubles than my own."

## ✧✦ CHAPTER FIFTY-THREE ✧✦

Cumulus clouds were building, their dark floors teasing the dry prairies. Shiloh was reminded of the cumulous nimbus clouds piling the sky's in Nam before the monsoons. He'd tell his men, "This is the safest time to be in the jungle. Not even the North Vietnamese like to get wet."

Getting up from his lawn chair, he walked into the kitchen and filled the teapot. He knew these kinds of memories would never leave. But they no longer tormenting him like they once had.

It took many sweat lodges before he could reach the core of his war pain. He'd eventually confessed, in detail, his actions during the war. The healing was that the tribe witnessed these confessions and continued their acceptances of him. He was now an honored warrior in the tribe. And, most importantly, he could finally accept himself in this role. Even so, the upcoming workshop was something he'd never imagined doing.

During his last vision quest he'd stayed out for five nights. A black widow spider, a coral snake and a nest of yellow jackets had all entered his vision-quest circle. When he returned home, he told the elders about these participants and was given the nature-name "Piercing Medicine."

He took his nature-name seriously, especially in his work with AIDS babies. He'd let his work grow into a sacred practice. He found the only way to form bonds with these infants who knew no words was through touch and sound. Nurses from other hospitals came to witness him interacting with the AIDS babies. They said his eyes spilled love. He seemed to know something about these children that no one else did.

He was profoundly glad to become a common man again and saw this as a deep blessing. Fear had been the prescription he'd forced himself to take everyday for most of his life, and he was such a good soldier he had taken every dose available. Things had changed; he'd called his ex-wife and was not afraid. For years she had refused to accept his phone calls, knowing the war was still raging inside him. But today she answered the phone and they spoke for two hours. She accepted his apologies.

Shiloh told Phyllis about his workshop. He explained that he was advertising his event as a "workshop" because he was afraid that no one would come if it were called a "ceremony." Phyllis told him she'd consider bringing Pax.

They spoke about Jake and the recruiter. She told him that Pax had divulged to her the recruiters suicide attempt.

Shiloh turned off the burner under and poured hot water over chamomile flowers he'd picked behind his house. Raising the teacup to his lips, he heard the pelting of large raindrops on the deck outside the kitchen. Shiloh doubted that Pax would attend. He understood the reasons why his son was unlikely to come, and he felt deeply saddened.

## ✧✦ CHAPTER FIFTY-FOUR ✧✦

Four days had passed since Alma's parents returned home. Alma had spoken to Elu that morning and found out that Shuman had contacted Standing Deer. Elu made it clear that neither she nor Shuman would attend the workshop. Alma was relieved because she knew Howie wouldn't show up if he knew his in-laws were participating. Shuman must have realized this, too.

Elu had asked whether Howie was going, but Alma still didn't know. Howie said he was going to call Shiloh to find out more about the workshop. Alma didn't know whether he had. Elu said she was willing to pay for plane tickets, but they'd have to buy them in the next two days and Alma was still figuring out who could take care of the kids for an entire week if she and Howie went to Arizona.

Alma paced back and forth across the kitchen. The kids were napping, but would get up in a few minutes. She was surprised by Howie's interest in Shiloh's workshop. When it came to his Native American heritage, he responded like his father more than his mom.

Alma had loved his mother, a kind woman who tolerated her husband's enormous ego. She'd been dead now for almost ten years. Howie's dad had waited for only nine months before finding himself a new woman.

Alma considered calling Naomi to see whether Jake was planning to attend. But a voice inside her said, "Leave it alone." It was her habit to ignore such voices, but this time she knew the voice was right. Sitting alone in the kitchen, she said to herself, "Let *them* figure it out."

Folding her hands in front of her, she closed her eyes and said, "Thank you. Thank you God, thank you Great Mystery, and thank you to all living beings." She'd heard her father say this after he'd gotten sober.

Shuman had worked hard apologizing to her for his drunken behavior. She saw how much he wanted a relationship with her. He taught her native prayers and songs, and for years they prayed together.

Shuman's prayers were simple to remember and had made her feel good. Alma wished now that she'd allowed him to come closer when she was younger. She began to recite "As I Walk with Beauty," a traditional Navaho prayer she'd learned from her dad and still loved:

*As I walk, as I walk,*

*The universe is walking with me.*

*In beauty it walks before me.*

*In beauty it walks behind me.*

*In beauty it walks below me.*

*In beauty it walks above me.*

*Beauty is on every side.*

*As I walk, I walk with Beauty.*

Absorbed in her prayer, she let the phone ring three times before answering.

"Hello?"

"Hi, Mrs. Watkins. This is Pax. How are you?"

"I'm fine, Pax. What's up?"

"Could I speak to Mr. Watkins?"

"He's not here right now. Can I help you with something?"

"I think you've heard about the workshop that my father, Shiloh, is giving next week, right? He and my mother want me to go. But I'm not going. Could you tell Mr. Watkins for me?"

"You know he's going to ask me why."

"I'm sorry, Mrs. Watkins, but that's not anybody's business but mine."

"I understand," said Alma. "I'll give him the message."

"My mother said you and Mr. Watkins might go. Is that true?"

"It looks like we *are* going."

"Oh," said Pax, surprised. "Well, have a good trip."

"Thank you, Pax. Please stop by sometime. Howie would really like to see you."

"I will if I can. Goodbye, Mrs. Watkins."

# ✧✦ CHAPTER FIFTY-FIVE ✧✦

Wisps of clouds wreathed the moon. A steady, dry wind carried a bouquet of scents: whitethorn acacia, saguaro, desert hackberry, fernbush and desert willow. As Shiloh approached the encampment, the smell of wood smoke cancelled the other fragrances. A few hours remained before people were due to arrive.

The encampment was a one-mile walk into the desert from the parking lot. The moon would be bright; flashlights shouldn't be necessary for people walking in. Birds were settling for the night. The red flash of a Vermilion flycatcher caught his eye, and then the chuck of a burrowing owl slid among the lengthened shadows.

The cloud cover was thickening in the west. Shiloh imagined that by the time the ceremony started, the clouds might dim the light so much that it would be difficult for people to recognize each other. This would help keep the focus on the ceremony.

He'd stationed his good friend, Wallingford, at the trailhead to greet arriving participants and give them towels, water jugs and instructions to keep conversations quiet as they entered sacred space. Wallingford would encourage them to feel the desert air and be aware of the sounds of all living beings. Shiloh imagined Wallingford's quiet voice: "Allow the noise of the airport, the noise of the city to fall away from you as you walk toward the Great Mystery."

Shiloh had asked another friend, Harrington, to play his native flute to guide people to the inipi. Of the thirty-five people he expected, half were combat veterans; the others, friends and family.

On the workshop website Shiloh had provided a description of the inipi: a dome-shaped structure made of bent saplings, covered by multiple layers of tarps. The door of the inipi faced the west, the direction from which the light of new growth and wisdom comes. The website also defined the word "inipi" itself: a sacred space of spirits, sometimes known as a sweat lodge or sweat house.

Shiloh's friend, Brown Dove, had recently written him an explanation of how the ancients used the inipi for cleansing the body, mind and spirit. In ancient times women did not participate in sweat lodges because it was assumed that they were cleansed naturally during the "moon time" of their menstrual cycle.

Men, however, were not so lucky. Those given responsibility for protecting their people had to fight and sometimes kill. They needed a way to cleanse, so they could approach their Creator with 'clean hands.'

Another woman from the tribe had taught Shiloh to use the dirt removed from the inipi pit to form a little ridge, a path for the spirits, leading about ten steps out of the inipi. A small mound was formed from the dirt from the center pit for the stones. It was called *"unci"* in honor of grandmother earth. The center pit also represents *wakicagapi*, the beloved dead relative who have returned to the earth. You have to remember him when you put rocks into that hole. This pit is a circle within the circle; it stands for life, for that which has no end. Plants, animals and men are born and die, but the Indian people will live.

Shiloh hoped that participants would use the website to learn about the ceremony in which they'd take part, before they arrived, so that he would have less to explain once they were all together inside the inipi.

He let everyone know that staying in the lodge was voluntary; no one would need to stay in the lodge if they did not want to. He also wanted to convey some idea of what the ceremony had meant to him and the tribe. So he invited tribe members to write short essays about their inipi experiences, and he posted them online.

Shiloh would provide a simple meal after the ceremony. Several tribe members agreed to help build the "peta" (the fire used for heating the stones), place tarps over the inipis, and provide leadership and guidance for those who'd never experienced such a ceremony. Three volunteers were designated "doorkeepers," responsible for delivering rocks to the pits in the three inipi's. The doorkeeper assigned to the inipi that Shiloh would oversee was Jasper. Shiloh sat on a large stone surveying the encampment. He said aloud "I'm ready."

Shiloh looked toward the fire where Philco had just tossed a stick and saw the first shadowy outline of a person coming up the path. Philco was standing at the end of the path welcoming folks as they arrived. He would guide each person to a seat in the circle around the fire. Shiloh left the rock and sat by the closest of the three inipi. Closing his eyes and taking in the night sounds, he waited. Harrington's flute music floated on the air, circling, dipping and connecting all the force fields.

The first person made his way to Shiloh's side. He felt a hand on his shoulder and opened his eyes to find Digby, his radio operator in Nam. "Lieutenant!" Digby barked.

"Shhh! Great to see you, Dig," Shiloh whispered. "Keep your voice down. Lots to talk about when this is over, man. I'm so glad you came."

The two men did a thumb-to-thumb handshake.

Slowly, others arrived. Shiloh looked at the sky, noticing his prediction coming true. The clouds from the west shadowed the encampment so that the only light illuminating faces was the faint glow of the fire. Shiloh counted thirty shadows. He stood and walked around the inside of the circle.

"Welcome, my friends," he said. "I'm delighted you're here. I'll start by asking all of you to stand and face the west. Would you folks from the Plains Tribe please help me with the prayers?" Within a few minutes they honored all four directions – north, south, east and west, as well as the sky, the earth and the ancestors.

"We have three inipis. I will lead the sweat in this one. Sinclair, here, will lead in the second one, and my brother Wilson will cover the third. No one is required to enter the inipi. You'll benefit from this experience even if you don't enter."

Shiloh walked the inner circle for twenty minutes, explaining the meaning of the four directions and the procedure for welcoming a disturbance. Again he repeated that there was no requirement to enter an inipi. When he'd finished speaking, he lit the pipe and passed it around the group while Wilson made sure it stayed lit. He'd recognized only a few people when the moonlight had broken through the clouds. Neither his ex-wife nor his son was among them.

"Before we enter the inipi I want to acknowledge the veterans who are here. If you're a veteran, would you please step forward and make a circle around the fire?"

As the silhouettes moved, Shiloh continued speaking. "Warriors are the reason we can have this ceremony this evening. Their protection of us is a sacred act. As they move to this inner circle, pray for them, as well as for the warriors who are on battlefields today."

About fifteen men surrounded the fire. Shiloh stepped into their circle. The man beside him put his arm over his shoulder and the others followed suit. In a moment the entire group was linked.

"Ho! Brothers!" called Shiloh.

"Ho!" the group replied in unison.

"We are about to enter a timeless world," Shiloh began. "Warriors who have given life, taken life and bled for this land, it is with honor that I welcome you. Whatever you may find in the darkness of the inipi is all right for you to touch. The faces that may come before you are there to help, no matter how much pain they bring with them. You are not at war with the heat in the inipi. We have learned that the heat's disturbance brings change. If you become frightened, try and welcome what the fear brings you. The healing is in surrender. Questions?"

"Lieutenant?"

"Is that Ives?"

"Yes, it's me. What are we supposed to be getting out of this?"

"Same thing I told you in the jungle. You'll get dirty and exhausted. You'll appreciate the fact that you got another day to live, and you'll realize it's time to figure out what you're going to do with it. What you find in the inipi is that the leeches, snakes and North Vietnamese are all inside you. Your job might be to let them out. Most of us including myself have lived in cages inside ourselves and the strange thing is that many of us hold the doors shut, afraid to release what wants to come out."

"Can't see you, Lieutenant, but I know it's you from that answer."

"Let me give you the last heads up before I speak with the civilians standing around us. The womenfolk will go into the inipi first. If you came with your family, have them with you in the inipi. And I'm going to say this one more time: NO ONE *HAS* TO DO THIS, this includes you guys!"

The vets grunted as if to say they'd do the sweat or die.

Shiloh divided the veterans equally in front of the three inipis. He then gathered the civilians in their own circle and instructed them.

"What's important for you to know is that without you here there would be no reason for this ceremony. You have been the ones holding the harmony, peace, safety and love. Those values were compromised, ruptured and sacrificed when your loved ones returned from war, bringing your life into the same disharmony as theirs. It's because of your courage in coming here that these soldiers can find meaning in what they were asked to do. Everyone is equal in this ceremony. No veteran's story or civilian's story is greater or lesser then anyone else's. No story is greater or lesser than someone's silence."

Shiloh yelled, "Ho!" When there was no reply, he asked, "Are you with me? Ho!"

"Ho!" the group shouted back, the sound of their voices filling the encampment.

Shiloh pointed out that the inipi doors face west. He called to Philco, "Will you bring any latecomers to my inipi?"

"Will do, Piercing Medicine."

Shiloh stood before his small group. To his right were two forked sticks, supporting his sacred pipe. Spent sweat rocks were lined up, north to south. The lodge was covered with more than a dozen tarps.

He crawled into the inipi, closed the flap and inspected the walls and ceiling to make sure no light was getting in. After spreading sage on the floor he crawled out and found the doorkeeper. "After I'm inside, please have the women enter first, and then the men."

He turned and faced the waiting group, who stood with towels over their shoulders. "The inipi is ready," he said. I'll go in first. Once we're all inside, the doorkeeper will bring in the stones, hand us water and close the flap. Remember, if any of you don't want to come in, this is a good time to stand aside."

Shiloh lowered his head to the ground in the doorway of the inipi and said, "Ho Mitakuye Oyas." Then he crawled into the inipi. The participants followed. He counted six people. Then the ancestor rocks were eased in with a pitchfork, while sage and cedar were sprinkled on them. The pipe was handed in. Shiloh lit it and held it up to the four directions. He then passed it, clockwise, around the lodge.

Shiloh waved the smoke of sweet grass around the lodge with a hawk wing as people settled in.

"Welcome. This is a good way to pray," started Shiloh.

There was a light tapping on the flap, followed by a soft voice: "Five more folks just got here. They said their plane was late."

"Take five minutes to orient them to what we're doing and then let them in."

"We have; they're ready."

The flap opened and the faint movement of bodies was heard.

"Welcome, friends. I'm so glad you came. We're saying prayers to the four directions. Any questions?"

A newcomer spoke up: "How hot is it going to get?"

"Very," Shiloh said. "Keep in mind that you can leave at any time. Just ask to have the flap opened."

"Okay," came a frightened voice.

"We are not in this sweat lodge for ourselves," Shiloh said. "We are here for the healing of our people. Only if you are here for them, will change come to you." Lowering his voice, he began reciting:

> *From the west, look there!*
> *Your grandfathers are looking there! Pray! Pray!*
> *Looking around, sitting there, he says that!*

It was clear to all that Shiloh was to recite prayers to the South, North and East, to the sky and to the earth calling for the flap to be opened at the end of each prayer. "Open the flap," Shiloh called and the cool night air rushed in, drawing murmurs of appreciation from the group.

The flap was shut again and Shiloh started another prayer. In this one, addressed to the South, he requested help for victims of drugs, alcohol and domestic violence. "I am unworthy to ask for this," he said, "but I beg you, Great Spirit of the South, to forgive me for what I have done to those I love. Bring strength and beauty to them. Feed their open hearts."

A whimper was heard, with halting breath. Shiloh began whispering a prayer in support. When he let his voice stop, the silence of the dark felt more like a cosmic expanse than a claustrophobic cave. One of the rocks cracked, sending up sparks. Shiloh saw Phyllis's face.

After the flap had closed for the third time, words started popping up, in short phrases:

"I'm so, so sorry."

"I've lied to you and myself."

"I feel that I'm still a killer."

"If you really knew me, you'd leave."

"I still love you. I just hate myself!"

By the time they reached the North, longer sentences started emerging.

"Great Spirit of the West, help me," said a man. "Please help me to let go. I can't change anything or help anyone when I hold on." The words gave way to deep sobbing.

"Daddy, I'm so sorry I didn't let you in. I've needed you desperately. I need you right now!"

"How many kids have died because I lied to them?"

"Ho, Grandfather. I left my son because I had to protect him from myself. I know now that I hurt him more deeply than if I had stayed there, drunk."

"Help me, Great Spirit, to find the courage to open the cage of hatred that I've grown to love."

Shiloh held his face in his hands and wept loudly. A choir of whimpering, choking, sniffling and soft wailing began to produce harmonies. Then a voice started singing.

*I am sending a voice to my Grandfather.*
*I am sending a voice to my Grandfather.*

*Hear me!*
*Together with all things of the universe,*
*I am sending a voice to Wakan Tanka.*

Black Elk's song had found it's way to them out of the darkness. For a long time they all sang, the melody rising and sinking with emotion.

When the inipi flap opened for the last time, a billow of intense heat rose into the night sky, carrying with it prayers, pains and losses. Shiloh was the last to crawl out of the inipi. Looking up, he saw pain-ghosts forming a cloud that blanketed the moon.

He walked a good distance from the lodge and sank to the cool sand, knowing that Pax had not come. No matter how hard he worked at accepting his son's choice, he felt overwhelming pain and knew he was facing yet another lesson. This knowledge collapsed on him. On his knees he pushed his face into the sand so no one could hear his grief. His whole body shook between sobs.

Cool water was being dribbled on the back of his neck and he stiffened. "It's okay. Let it come. It's okay, Shi," Phyllis said, pouring more water onto his steaming back.

Alma sat on the ground, her back against the inipi, toweling her face dry. Howie stood over her and she reached for his hand. He pulled her up and then collapsed in her arms. They said nothing to each other. Alma could feel, in her body, that her husband was present in a way she remembered from long ago. "You're home, Howie," she murmured. "You're home."

Naomi sat alone on a flat rock, holding her head in her hands. She'd seen Jake's white shorts when he crawled out of the inipi and was surprised that he hadn't looked for her. She walked toward the parking lot – as best she could figure out where it was.

Toweling herself off as she walked, she moved in and out of the trance of the sweat. It had been about twenty minutes since she'd seen Jake. He was not at the fire pit. She heard Shiloh's voice calling the group together.

She debated whether to go back or find Jake.

Her mind found its familiar patter. "You'd better go find him," said the voice in her head. "He could have been triggered. The only reason he came here was because you wanted him to, and now he's out there having flashbacks."

Suddenly a new voice, a voice she'd first heard in the sweat, joined the conversation. "There's nothing you can do to help him," she said. "He's a grown man. You can't control what he does to himself." Naomi turned and made her way back toward Shiloh's deep voice.

# ✧✦ CHAPTER FIFTY-SIX ✧✦

An orange glow highlighted the mountains. Bird song was carried on a light wind. Jake picked up the faint smell of wood smoke before he opened the door to the van and got into the driver's seat. Naomi sat next to him. Alma and Howie climbed into the seats furthest in the back.

"Did Phyllis say she's not going to the hotel with us?" Jake asked.

"That's right," Naomi said. "She's still talking to Shiloh and he said he'd get her a ride."

"I don't think he's even got a car," Howie said.

"She's a grownup," Naomi replied. "Let's just leave it alone and get going."

"You got it," said Howie.

The flight back to New York took three and a half hours. Jake and Naomi were sitting several rows ahead of Alma and Howie.

"Look at those two," Howie said to Alma as he squeezed her hand.

"Looks like something intense is going on."

"A few weeks ago Jake told me he'd been in the same shape I was. He said he's kept a lot of it hidden from Naomi because she could be so controlling, which made it worse."

"What do you think's going to happen?" Alma asked.

"Jake told me, on the way to the van, that something happened to him in the sweat. When I asked him about it, he would only say, 'It's good. That's all I'm telling you.' But from the look on Naomi's face right now, I don't think so."

A flight attendant parked a cart in the aisle beside Howie. "Something to drink?" he asked. Howie and Alma took cups of coffee.

"I was wondering how you'd feel about taking a trip out to see my mom and dad after you leave the Marines?" Alma asked.

"Sure. I think I'm ready for that. Your dad was on my mind in the sweat. I'd like to see him."

"He was on my mind, too. You heard what I said in there, didn't you?"

"Every word."

Shiloh was leaning against a rock. Phyllis sat so close to him that their knees touched. Philco was policing the area and making sure the fire was out. As he walked by on his last round, he asked, "You need anything, Shiloh, before I go home?"

"I was wondering if you might give us a ride."

"Love to."

"How do you think it went?"

"The vets in Wilson's lodge said this was the first time since they got home that they could speak safely in front of civilians."

"Great! Really good. Listen, I'd like to introduce you to Phyllis. We've known each other a long time. Phyllis, this is my dear friend, Philco. We know each other from the hospital where I work. Philco's a doctor

245

there."

Phyllis stuck out her hand. "Pleasure to meet you, Philco."

"Pleasure's mine, ma'am." Philco began making his way to the parking lot but stopped and called back to Shiloh and Phyllis. "I've got some things to pack up," he said. "Take your time. I'll meet you at my truck."

"Thanks. We'll be just a few minutes," Shiloh said, standing and offering his hand to Phyllis to help her up.

The smell of exhaust burned their nostrils as the long-term parking bus pulled away from the terminal at Newark Airport. Jake got to the car first and opened the door for Naomi. She put her hand on his arm when she got in, but he didn't cover her hand with his own, as he usually did.

They were on the Sawmill Parkway when she said, "Please tell me what's happening."

"I'm not sure I can. All I know is that what's been happening between us for years is no longer working for me. I find myself getting angry without a good reason. Whatever I brought home from the war has been between us forever. Even if you say it's okay, I know it's not. I'm tired of pretending. When Shiloh said that many of us were holding the war in a cage inside, he was talking to me."

"Wait a minute, Jake. Are you saying our marriage is over?"

"No, I'm not saying that. But I *am* saying that I need to open the cage in me; there's not enough room for both of us in it. Listen, there's stuff going on inside me that you have no idea about. Not because you're not a good therapist, but because I've never told you. Until I sort that out life is going to continue the way it's been."

"Do I get to vote on this?"

"Of course, you do. It's just that you get to vote *only* for you. You don't get to vote for me, too."

"What are you planning to do?"

"I got an email from a high school friend who's living in Cape Hatteras. I thought I'd spend a little time down there near the ocean and sort things out. I've only got one day of school left when I get back."

"What's her name?"

"Alvin."

"Alvin? How come I've never heard of him?"

"There are a lot of things you haven't heard of." He entered the exit lane to leave the Parkway. "This will be a test for both of us."

"Your right, there are a lot of things I haven't heard," Naomi said, looking out the passenger's window.

The shadows on the floor near the east window were short when Shiloh woke. He looked through the bedroom door and saw Phyllis's arm dangling over the arm of the couch. He got up, put on his jeans and strapped tee shirt and sat down in the rocking chair across from the couch. And waited.

"Hey, you," he said, when he saw Phyllis's eyes open.

"Whoa! I had some wild dreams," she said.

"That can happen after a sweat."

"What time is it?"

"I don't know. From the shadows I'd guess it's almost noon."

"Shit. Is it too late for me to get to the airport?" Phyllis asked.

Shiloh's smile widened.

"What are *you* smiling about?" Phyllis asked.

"Well, I won't lie to you. You won't get any sympathy from me if you miss your plane." Shiloh's smile got even wider. "I've never stopped loving you, Phyll."

Phyllis sat up, suddenly awake. "Stop it, Shiloh. It's too late for that."

Shiloh nodded but kept smiling. "I just had to say that. I'm in no hurry."

"Hurry for what?"

"For you to come back. But I plan on trying everything I know to make it happen."

"That's enough. You're being ridiculous."

"Maybe," Shiloh admitted. "But maybe being ridiculous is the best way to be right now. Don't you think?"

"What are you talking about?" Phyllis said. She avoided looking at him.

"How would you feel if I were to come back to New York with you, so I could have a talk with Pax?"

"I don't know," Phyllis said thoughtfully.

"Don't get nervous. I wouldn't ask you to put me up. I could crash with Digby, the guy I was speaking to after the sweat. He lives in Kingston. I could take the bus."

"Are you serious? I think that would be great."

Shiloh got up from the chair and sat beside Phyllis on the couch. He covered her hand with his own. "Thanks."

Together, Phyllis and Shiloh walked up the path to the front door. Shiloh couldn't help acknowledging the elephant in the room. "New siding," he said.

Phyllis smirked at him and put her key in the lock. Shiloh touched her arm. "You think he's home?"

"I don't know. I called the house several times, but there was no answer. He's been getting more and more remote lately. My guess is that he's got a girlfriend and he's with her."

"Sounds good to me," Shiloh said.

The house was familiar to him. Not many changes, he thought. Phyllis walked back to the kitchen and saw a note on the table. She picked it up and read:

Mom,

I feel bad doing this but I think it will make it easier on both of us. I left this morning for NYC for my Marine physical. I should be in Parris Island by tomorrow evening. I love you. I know how hard it is for you to watch me do the same thing Dad did, but I'm not him!

Speaking of Dad, the envelope on the table contains his diary. Mr. Finn stuck it in our mailbox before he left for Arizona. I just read it and for the first time in my life I feel like I know who my father is. Read it, Ma!

I hope you had a good trip. Sorry I wouldn't go with you.

I'll call you the first time they let me.

Love,
Pax

# ✦✦ CHAPTER FIFTY-SEVEN ✦✦

Phyllis reached for a tissue and passed the note to Shiloh. Then, taking the envelope, she headed into the living room. Shiloh read the note in silence, carefully folded it and put it in his breast pocket. Phyllis sat down in her favorite arm chair, turned on a lamp and began to read.

## *Notes from Nam*

*A tin cup sat on one of the flat stones surrounding a hand-dug well. Perspiration accumulated on my finger as I drew it across my forehead. Careful to keep the drops from dripping, holding my finger above my mouth I let the salty sweat drip onto my parched tongue. It tasted of mildew and jungle decay. From the protection of the tree line I'd been fixating on the tin cup for over two hours. I must have been hallucinating because when I closed my eyes, the cup was the size of a swimming pool with silvery light shimmering up from its blue bottom. Thirst was becoming an overwhelming power, pushing aside all the danger my mind knew was present.*

*I must have gone blank because I suddenly found myself at the edge of the well without any memory of how I got there. My brain must have stopped screaming: "You're dead, man! You are fucking dead!" I scanned the tree line for shooters, I flattened my back against the stones of the well. A wind gust picked up fine grains of sand that stuck to my damp skin. A short clump of elephant grass that was growing around the well brushed my trousers, making a ticking sound – the sound of a clock, counting the last seconds of my life. I could feel the protective shadows of the jungle pulling me back. Crouching below the rim of the stone, I realized this was the first time in three days I'd been in sunlight.*

*It would have been safer to wait until after dark to drink. The green bananas I'd eaten hours before had left a coating like dry cement in my mouth.*

*Beside the well I found a hemp rope. One end was tied to an iron peg; the other, to a hollow bamboo tube. Keeping my head down, I lowered the tube into the well. I heard it splash. Flicking my wrist, I made a loop that traveled the length of the rope and tilted the bamboo tube so it would fill. I had seen this done in a village by an elderly Vietnamese man. I pulled the rope and felt the heft; it worked! The bamboo clanked against the stone walls of the well, reminding me of the elephant bones I'd knocked together a few days before while picking them for edible meat. A line of holes pierced the animal's hide, evidence of a chopper's door gunner practicing on something that couldn't shoot back.*

*The rope wet my hands making me pull faster. Lifting the bamboo tube over the well rim, I tucked myself down into a small angle of shadow. Pressing my back against the cool stones, I hurriedly lifted the tube to my mouth, stopping when I saw the rotting rim of the tube. I imagined Vietnamese women with decaying black teeth drinking from it. I lowered the tube between my thighs and reached over my shoulder for the cup resting on the stone rim. With shaking hands, I filled the cup and was bringing it to my mouth, after the first drip of water on my white-coated tongue I stopped. A small green head had risen above the surface of the water. I dropped the cup. The water spilled and I watched a tiny bamboo viper wiggling inside the cup. Marines know this snake as "the two-step snake."*

*After peering into the tube to make sure it was empty, I drank, sloshing water on the front of my shirt. After I had my fill, I carefully picked up the cup and held it at arm's length. Turning it over I expected the snake to drop out. Instead, a circular cut green leaf floated out of the cup landing on the wet spot. The snake stayed inside, even after I shook the cup hard. Then I noticed two holes in the bottom of the cup, with a fine "thread" running between them. The snake's tail had been tied into the bottom of the cup with just enough room for its head to reach the drinkers face.*

*I tossed the cup to the side muttering, "Fucking gooks." The cup landed on its side. I watched the snake attempt to dart to freedom with only a few inches of its head protruding. It wiggled relentlessly, trying to escape. With each wiggle, though, it succeeded only in embedding the rim of the cup more deeply in the sand.*

*The voice in my head was screaming again: "Get your ass back in the jungle!" I low-crawled to the protection of the tree line, taking the bamboo tube of water with me. Parting the thick elephant-eared leaves, I entered the safety of not being seen.*

*When my breathing returned to normal I surveyed the clearing. I was in "Oklahoma Territory," the Vietnamese equivalent of the US Calvary term for Indian* country. I heard, a week ago, some guy at a recon briefing say: "There are so many gooks in Oklahoma Territory that you can walk on their backs – all the way to Hill 55 never touching the ground." That's the hill I had to get to if I wanted to make it out of this fucking mess alive.

Everyone said shit about "Oklahoma Territory" just to keep up the fear level. The more afraid we were, the more vigilant we were. When I was telling Digby about this he didn't know what "vigilant" meant, so I explained it to him. When he put it in his own words it made a lot of sense.

"You mean," he said, "being so afraid of dying, you'll do anything to stay alive."

"That's it, Dig. Vigilant means you go home from Nam with your ass on an airplane seat, not in a body bag."

My mind drifted back to the Recon camp at Hill 55. I was proud to be a sniper. No one could question my contribution to the war; they were on my rifle stock. The men on the squad respected me. Just before I left, a bunch of them watched me kill a VC sniper at over twenty-five hundred yards. One of them said I'd taken the place of Sergeant Hathcock, the famous sniper, when he left for the States.

Hathcock invented the idea of attaching an 8-powered scope to a 50-Cal rifle. The rounds from that two-and-a-half inch, 700-grain, 50-Cal gave double the reach of a .30-06. In three months Hathcock killed more VC than an entire platoon.

It was hard trying to get comfortable in the hide I'd made. The damp rotting leaves stuck to me, along with the crawling insects. The only way I found to stay still was to let my mind drift back over my past life. I learned to do this while keeping my eyes open and continuously scanning the scenery around me – all 360 degrees of it.

A picture of my mother's face came to mind. She was crying. I remembered saying goodbye to her before I left for Nam. We were standing in the bus terminal. She faced me, her back to my stepfather. Tears ran down her cheeks. I watched my stepfather grab his crotch. Hefting his balls, he looked over mom's shoulder at me and said, "You'd better come back with a set of these, boy."

"You'd better hope I don't come back, asshole!" I said under my breath.

I hated leaving my mother with him, but there was nothing else I could do. The man dominated both of us. Leaving was an option she seemed not to want to take. I was hoping the Marines would teach me to stop being afraid of the bastard.

*I was half Indian and kept my hair cropped close. That way nobody seemed to be able to pin my race. Some people thought I looked gook. Once when I was dressed in Vietnamese clothes, an old man from the ville came up to me and asked, in Vietnamese, where I was from. I replied in Vietnamese, "Sir, I'm from New York." He just nodded.*

*After my first tour I was given two bronze stars and a silver star, and they made me a sniper trainer.*

*I am writing this in the VFW not sure that Phyllis and I are going to make it. Maybe our son Pax will read this someday.*

*The Marines loved that I could put bullet holes where they wanted them. At sniper school someone started a rumor that I'd killed more Viet Cong than I'd trained snipers. It was crap.*

*At the time, I thought I was a good Marine who did my job very well. I'd tell my class, "If you beat a man for doing wrong, he's more likely to do wrong again – but this time out of spite, instead of by mistake. What we're doing with these high-powered rifles is taking human life. You have the most deadly Job –MOS-0317 in the Marines. And you're the one they want to kill the most."*

*At sniper school I'd been given a new nickname: "Eyes." My instructor, Sergeant Hathcock, said, "You've got the long reach. You play it right, ain't no one ever gonna get close enough to take you out. You'll never get blood on those hands." How wrong he was.*

*"Say a prayer for that long rifle, boy," Hathcock said. I wondered what he meant. My friend, Digby, was in training with me. He started to use Hathcock's mantra each time he pulled the trigger. "Say a prayer!" he'd say. He told me he was just giving Mr. Charlie one last piece of advice before he gave up his life for Dig's.*

*A few days ago I was sitting in a tree watching a VC patrol below me, praying they wouldn't gun me down like a treed coon. I killed six of them and they had no idea where the shots were coming from. After the rest of them left, I searched the bodies for food, but all I found was a small bag of rice and a little salt.*

*The stench of rotting vegetation rolled in like waves over the jungle floor. I debated whether to spend the night in the hide I'd just made or to carve out a good spot in the undergrowth. I remembered Hathcock saying, "Never hunt the same ground twice. And always change your patterns. Never be predictable. Habit will get you killed in this business." I decided to leave and was pushing myself up just as the sharp crack of a rifle buckled my knees.*

*Pointing the muzzle of my rifle into the clearing, I tried to discern where the shot had come from. Then a jungle hat whirled, like a Frisbee, into the clearing. Two seconds later a man dressed in camouflage, holding his rifle over his head, stepped into the clearing saying, "Cho hoy."*

*I lowered my rifle as Digby walked toward me.*

*"What the hell you doing here?" I asked.*

*"You've been out over a week. We thought you were dead or that some VC might be driving stakes into you, getting you ready for one of them sniper barbeques. I thought I'd come out and look."*

*"Thanks. Now tell me the real reason."*

*"CIA thinks you know too much. They're afraid you'll get caught and telegraph it to Uncle Ho. It's hard to know what a man might say when someone's threatening to chop off his fingers."*

*"You put that fucking snake in that cup over there, Dig?"*

*Digby smiled.*

*"No," he said, looking over his shoulder at the well and handing me a plastic bag of dehydrated food. "Better get some of this in you. We've got ten miles to hike tonight."*

*I poured water from Dig's canteen into the plastic bag. Digby watched me wolf down the powdered food while he worked his KA-BAR knife into the end of a stick. With one quick stroke he made a sharp point. Reaching into his shirt pocket, he removed a thin black ribbon that was about a foot long. Carefully, he drove the stick point through the snake in two places. After lighting a small can of Sterno, he grilled the snake over the clear blue flame.*

*"Aren't you taking this living-off-the-land shit a little far?" I asked. "Found your little fire where you rousted that rotten elephant meat. Should've hidden it better."*

*I watched Digby's white teeth close on the charred snake. Then, his meal finished, he leaned against a tree and wiped sweat from his forehead with the back of his wrist. I could barely make out his face in the faint moonlight that was now sifting through the canopy.*

*When it was time to move, the half moon looked like it was playing in the treetops. Dig insisted we walk separately, so we agreed on two rendezvous points and headed off in different directions. I watched Dig move out, stepping quietly in his Vietnamese-style rubber thongs, body flowing around trees and vines.*

*I was late to the first rendezvous point. Digby stepped out of the landscape, walking toward me. He asked if I'd seen anything. I told him I'd been delayed by a small stream that was deeper than it looked.*

*At the second rendezvous, too, I was last to arrive. Dig was in a tree over my head. When he came down I noticed he was limping. He made his way to a banana tree and sat down under it. I didn't ask him what had happened. I just peered into the darkness of the jungle. We sat together as the din of night sounds throbbed on our skin like an infection waiting to break out.*

*"Let's talk about our next meeting place," I said.*

*"I'm feeling beat. Why don't we wait here till dawn?"*

*"Sure. Makes sense. There's a VC patrol near here that should be making its way back to their ville before sunup. Not a bad idea to sit tight." I paused. "You know that means we won't move again till tomorrow night, right?"*

*Dig didn't answer. He rubbed his eyes with his forefinger and thumb. I wanted to ask if the leg was bothering him, but didn't.*

*"Why don't you go get some sleep?" I suggested. "I'll sit the first watch."*

*"Thanks, I'll take you up on that. Here's what you need to know. The ville's off to the north and there's a footpath a couple hundred yards to our east. I'll sleep for an hour."*

*I cut sight lines through the undergrowth with my knife, checked the safety on my weapon and cleared a place to sit. Dig slid his back down a few inches against the banana tree.*

*I was trying to sort out the calls and yells in the night. A high-pitched squeal was either a night bird's claws sinking into the flesh of a rodent, or some VC signal call. The distant roar might be a tiger. It felt like the jungle was breathing.*

*I kept thinking that if I were there much longer I'd be slowly digested by the jungle itself. The skin between my toes was rotting. My calves were covered with scars and bleeding from leech bites. My armpits were red with rash. But my eyes and ears were fixed on the jungle, while I tried to control my mind by mentally checking my body, one part at a time, trying to calm the itching and the fear.*

*Dig broke the silence. "My mother was a full-blooded Sioux. She wore her hair in one long braid down the center of her back."*

*In the years I'd known Dig he'd never told me anything about his life outside the Corps. We'd sat next to each other on the flight over to Nam and all I'd found out was that he'd been married once and had a son he never saw.*

*We were silent awhile. For some reason he went on, "My father was black. I saw him grab hold of mom's braid and swing her off her feet and up against a wall. He'd been drinking. I got hold of his leg and sunk my teeth in. He kicked me off like I was a small dog. When she didn't get up, he left. I ran next door to get the old lady who lived there. She came over and waited, with me, for Mom to wake up. When Mom opened her eyes, they were crossed. She whispered, "Hold my hand. Please boy, hold my hand."*

*I grunted.*

*"I never saw my old man again. Mom's eyes got better and she started working two jobs. She'd leave my little brother, Roger, and me home alone every night while she went to work. She was a nurse's aide at Mercy Hospital. Mostly she emptied bedpans. She'd bring home food that patients left on their trays.*

*"When Roger and I were alone, we'd play cowboys and Indians. We'd argue who was going to be the Indian. My dad hated Indians. There was this closet in the house that was always locked. Mom told us never to open it. Of course, then we had to get in there. Roger managed to get it open with a knife.*

*"My father's two shotguns were inside. We each took one and started running around the house. We wound up at opposite ends of the hallway at the same time. Roger aimed at me and pulled the trigger. The gun clicked. I aimed at him and pulled the trigger. The blast blew me against the wall."*

*After a long time Dig said, "You remind me of Roger sometimes. You trust that someone's always covering you."*

*"Hey, man. Something just slid over my boot," I said in a loud whisper. "I think it was some kind of snake."*

*Dig leaned toward me, looking intently at the ground near my feet. "There he goes, back into the bush. We don't have to worry about him," he said.*

*The sun was lighting the crowns of the trees. Neither of us had spoken in an hour. Dig had fallen asleep again and I decided not to wake him. Daylight was eating away the shadows when I noticed a large spot of dried blood on the bottom of Dig's left leg. I never really understood Dig's explanation for wearing Ho Chi Minh sandals instead of his jungle boots. He told me the sandals prevented jungle rot and enabled him to walk silently. He seemed unworried about the possible drawbacks of exposing his feet and ankles to punji stakes and snakebites.*

*I looked at my watch — not yet 1100. I felt sweat rolling under my clothes. The picture left in my mind from Dig's story quivered among thousands of shadows trembling on the jungle floor. When a fleck of black passed my sight line, I tightened my grip on my rifle. I inched my foot toward Dig and tapped his boot lightly with mine. He didn't wake. Then another movement — a dark shape against a lighter background — and I made out a man in black silk, slinking through the brush, low to the ground.*

*A small group of VC was moving toward the ville. I reached for Dig's shoulder. When my fingers brushed his shirt, his eyes flashed and his arm shot reflexively to my throat. He didn't stop until he realized it was me and my windpipe was being crushed. His face was inches from mine. I tried to speak but could only raise my eyebrows. Then I realized Dig was still not sure it was me. I let go of my rifle, drove both my arms up between Dig's and broke the hold.*

*Sucking in hard to regain breath, I tried to speak but my voice box felt crushed. I motioned with my head toward the path and held up four fingers. Dig's eyes cleared.*

*Rubbing my throat, I watched Dig stand slowly. He started his ritual of checking his rifle, feeling for his knife and looking down at his forty-five pistol strapped to his outer thigh. To my surprise Dig moved with the grace of a performing Tai Chi master. Raising his hand, he gestured for me to cover him. Then he dropped down into a low crouch and slipped around the tree on his belly, like the snake we'd seen in the night.*

*Looking up, I searched the trees for hanging vines I could climb. When I stood up, the bones of my knees popped. I pressed into the tree and froze, hoping no one heard. Several minutes passed before I got to the vine tree and climbed, my rifle slung diagonally across my back. I grasped the vines and pulled myself upward. I was resting ten feet above the ground when I spotted an overhead branch that was large enough to stand on. From my perch on that tree limb I surveyed the thick jungle.*

*Easing my head around the side of the tree for a better look, I saw Dig. The four VC in black pajamas were strung out in a line about ten yards apart. They were moving cautiously, rifles at the ready.*

*A soft popping noise, like tapping on an empty cardboard box, was audible. I saw the VC at the end of the column raise his hand to the back of his head as if to push an insect away. Then he folded onto himself, his knees buckling and his face hitting the ground.*

*I jerked my rifle to my shoulder, sighting on the closest VC, who was leaning against an acacia tree. I expected him to run, but it appeared that he hadn't heard the muted shot. I drew in my breath and let it out through tense lips. Slowly, my index finger caressed the trigger. The scope was so powerful I could see a pimple on the right cheek of the VC. I looked at the man's eyes darting around the undergrowth. On my second breath the VC slipped further around the tree, obscuring my shot. Pressing my cheek against the rifle stock until my cheekbone connected, I waited, taking long deliberate breaths. The man's face came back into view.*

*A quick flash of color and movement drew my eyes toward Dig. He was making a stealthy leap over dew-soaked leaves onto the back of a VC. He hooked the man's neck from behind with his right arm, caught his left forearm and, with one quick jerk, snapped his neck.*

*The head of the VC visible in my scope jerked toward the sound of Digby's attack. Biting my lip, I watched him stretch his neck around the side of the tree. His ear came into view. I eased off a round. The VC instantly collapsed.*

*The last VC was now crouched behind a large elephant-leaf plant. My shot made him jump from the trail into a thick tangle. By the time I got my sights on his position there was nothing but bobbing leaves.*

*A voice drifted up from the impenetrable vegetation: "Say a prayer."*

*The events of the last half hour had been like scenes in a movie. I felt like a cameraman shooting film. I was climbing down the vine-covered tree to go on a break. While behind me, back on the set, I could hear the filming of the next scene — the one in which the fourth VC is being killed.*

*I sat against the tree and let my chin drop onto my chest. God knows how many men I'd killed as a sniper, but I'd never been close enough to see them clearly. The VC's pimpled face was spinning around in my mind. Hathcock had once told me, "Never look at the eyes if you want to kill." I'd looked. I'd shot the man's face instead of his chest.*

*My thoughts were interrupted when Dig parted the leaves with the barrel of his rifle. Looking into my face, he sat down. I saw nothing there that I hadn't seen before. I wondered if he felt regret. Didn't seem to. Dig's face was blank.*

*"Why didn't you let them pass?" I blurted in a raspy voice.*

*Dig took off his tattered camouflage jungle hat and ran his fingers through his short-cropped hair. He said nothing.*

*My eyes wouldn't leave him alone until he said, "Drop it."*

*"Want me to take a look at the leg?" I asked.*

*"No! It'll be fine. Just part of the game," Dig replied.*

*"So is first aid," I said. "You get something out of killing people?" I asked.*

*Dig's forehead wrinkled. "I said drop it."*

*Then he started talking. "Shi. It's never easy killing, but it's what we're here to do. It's what we're paid to do. Someone's got to justify the numbers they're putting on the news every night."*

*I said, "Who really gives a shit about the numbers? We didn't have to kill them. They were just going home to their village."*

*"Sure, we could have let them walk. Just like the guy you let walk at Cu Chi. Let' em go home to get fed and get laid by their mama sans. Then they'll be bright and chipper tomorrow, so they can blow the head off some unsuspecting Marine."*

*"Fuck you, Dig. The only reason I didn't get that guy up in Cu Chi was because*

*my scope got knocked and I didn't have time to sight him in the rifle."*

*"It's just that we're either going to kill first or be killed," Dig said, reaching for the rifle sling and lifting it off his shoulder.*

*"Let me get this right. You're saying everything boils down to the same solution? Kill them before they kill us? Come on, man. There aren't enough bullets in the world to do that." Jake paused and looked at Dig with new curiosity. "Tell me, why'd you come out here anyway? I know it wasn't to save my ass. Weren't there enough gooks to kill back at base camp? Did you need a death fix? You know what I think? I think killing's gone to your brain."*

*I spit on the ground. "You kill like it's a sport. I don't buy that shit about doing your job. It my job, too, and I hate it. In fact, I'm quitting this fucking job. I'm going the fuck home the minute I step out of this fucking infested jungle."*

*Dig pushed his finger into my chest, trying to quiet me. His gesture had the opposite effect. "I'm sick of putting holes in people!" I yelled.*

*"Sit back down," Dig barked.*

*I remember lowering my head into my hands. "I want out! I mean it, man! I count my kills, instead of sheep, when I go to sleep." Words streamed out of me while Dig sat like stone, facing away from me.*

*With my teeth locked shut a raw whisper was leaking out of my injured throat. "I've been here two months and twenty four people are dead because of me. I should be in college screwing coeds. Instead I'm in this fucking hell hole blowing the faces off people."*

*Dig's hand gripped my forearm. "Shut up!"*

*We sat in a shroud of sounds. I slowly released the clip from my rifle, removed a round from my bandolier and replaced it. I noticed Dig's leg was looking bad. When his adrenaline dissipated after the ambush, his limp had become more pronounced.*

*Dig stared down the sightlines, his eyes bugging. Wet blotches grew below his armpits. Fever beads had formed on his upper lip, and his mouth hung open. I knew the wound was infected. He'd pulled a punji stake out of his lower calf muscle. I was sure it had been smeared with human shit.*

*We had hours ahead of us before sundown, when it would be safe to start heading*

260

*back to camp. But I couldn't sit still. I could feel something crawling inside my body. I wiggled my ass on the damp ground, but the intruder didn't stop moving. I could still feel it moving around inside.*

*A grunting sound came from something rutting in the underbrush.*

*"It's a wild pig," Dig said, pointing. "See the snout?" We both knew it wouldn't be long before the animal found the dead VC.*

*"Your turn to get some sleep," he told me.*

*"That leg's not looking any better. Why don't you let me look at it?"*

*"You still don't get it, do you?"*

*"Get what?" I asked.*

*"I'm not leaving this jungle."*

*"What the fuck you talking about?"*

*"I'm not leaving."*

*"Well, I'm sure as hell leaving."*

*"I ain't stopping you," Dig whispered hoarsely.*

*"What the fuck do you mean when you say you ain't leaving? Stay out here and you're dead."*

*"No shit!"*

*Wiping my forehead with the sleeve of my shirt, I said, "You're talking shit."*

*"I ain't talking shit," Dig said, fingering the forty-five on his knee.*

*The bark crackled when Dig moved his back against the tree. Shifting my butt, I felt the muscles of my anus tighten as if protecting me from a jungle slug trying to crawl inside me.*

*A loud snort arrowed through the underbrush. "They found one," Dig said.*

*As the grunting sounds increased, Dig sat like a yogi I'd once seen on TV. The yogi had sat in the snow for twenty-four hours wearing nothing but a loose robe. He was demonstrating a technique for speeding up his metabolism to avoid freezing. Right now Dig's eyes looked like the yogi's: connected to something beyond the earth.*

*Dig reached inside his utility shirt and handed me a small piece of paper. "This is the way out of here."*

*Unfolding the paper, I saw a mass of pen scratches and tried to orient myself. "Where the hell are we?"*

*"In the valley just below Hill 55. That long line is the river," Dig said, pointing. "It's the fastest way out. But the hill's safer."*

*"So you're really not coming with me?" I asked. "Dig, what am I supposed to tell 'em when I get back?"*

*"Nothing! You never saw me. You didn't even know I came looking for you." Dig's voice fell away.*

*"You're fucking crazy."*

*A light breeze bent the leaves above us, and a shaft of sunlight flashed across Dig's face. "When a man blows the heart out of his brother with a shotgun, I'd say it has something to do with being crazy."*

*"That's what I'm saying, man," I said, startled. "I thought you were voting with the guy who told us, 'All your bullet's doing is bringing that necessity to hand,'" I said, quoting a line we'd both heard — seemingly in a previous lifetime. "You telling me you disagree?"*

*Dig smirked. "You remember all that boot camp shit? All that crap they tell young boys to get them to do the impossible."*

*"What's so impossible?"*

*"You think it's natural to kill your own kind? Gooks are no different from you or me. Put their pants on one leg at a time. You surprised to hear that shit out of me?" Dig asked.*

*"So why are you telling me you're going to stay out here and die? That you're gonna take as many VC down with you as you can? That's thinking with half your ass,*

*man." I stuck the piece of paper inside my breast pocket.*

*"When I first came out here, I used to think this was a picnic, a vacation from the house I grew up in," Dig said. "Then I ran into you and you taught me all I have to do is stand a thousand yards away and pull a trigger to kill any fucker I've got in my sights. When you stare at me for killing those VC, Shi, it don't change a fucking thing. Dead is dead. You've just never been close enough to see a face, right? This is the first time, isn't it?" Dig stopped talking, closed his eyes and let out a low moan.*

*"You got a fever!" Shiloh said. "You ain't gonna kill any VC. Let me take a look at that leg."*

*"Don't you understand, man? I have to spell it out for you? I've been in this jungle more than I've been out. The leg's my handicap. Yes, siree. My handicap — my jungle golf score. Your ticket out is over that hill. But that's not me; I got to go down fighting. My ticket out is this leg."*

*"Let me take a look at it. I might be able to ease up some of the pain. Be a shame for the VC to stumble on you while you're unconscious with fever and take you prisoner. They know who you are."*

*My words must have registered. Dig wrinkled his forehead and, using both hands, lifted his leg closer to me.*

*I took my buck knife out of its scabbard and slit his pants leg up to the knee. His calf muscle was bulging like that of a track star after a race. Faint red lines radiated upward. In the center of the wound was an angry red hole oozing with blood and puss. "Infection. I could lance it."*

*"Do it then!"*

*"Hand me a can of Sterno out of your pack." I lit the can and drew the blade of the knife across the flame several times. A few seconds later, without wiping off the carbon, I sat down between Dig's spread legs, my back to his face. Wedging his left knee under my left armpit, I steadied his calf and lowered the blade. A rush of puss and blood spurted from the wound. Kneading the swollen skin, I flushed the wound with fresh blood.*

*Dig let his head roll back. With my back blocking his view, I bent over the wound and sucked the infection into my mouth. Dig opened his eyes and frowned at me.*

*"What the hell you doing?" he asked. "That punji stake had human shit smeared all over it." I spat and repeated the maneuver several times.*

*I took off my wet camouflage shirt and T-shirt and tore them into strips. Handing the rags to Dig, I said, "Spit on them. You've seen dogs licking their wounds; it's the same thing."*

*A stench of rotted entrails had rolled in, "Someone's gonna come out looking for those VC. We need to be out of here soon. I'm not sure we should wait the two hours to sunset."*

*Dig pulled the ripped pants leg down. "I'm not going! You'd better make your move soon. I think you should take the hill."*

*I nodded and began surveying my immediate area. I took out the canteen that I'd filled at the well and placed it beside Dig.*

*"You'll need that," Dig said.*

*"Get some rest," I replied. I waited for Dig's eyes to close and then slipped my remaining C-rats under the rags torn from my T-shirt.*

*"Leg feels a little better. Thanks," Dig slurred.*

*I fingered my bandolier, feeling the tips of each round until I found the one with the cross-filed on the tip. Working the round out I lay it next to Dig. He'd know it was a magic bullet, one that would blow up your gun, as well as your head. We didn't need to be putting our guns in gook hands.*

*The shadows lengthened. I tried to weigh my fatigue against the profound need to move. My body was throbbing with exhaustion. I hadn't slept more than one hour in the last forty-eight. Over the last several hours of quiet I could feel my adrenaline level dropping. I decided that fifteen minutes of sleep would serve me better than moving out immediately. I nudged Dig. "I'm gonna close my eyes for a few minutes. Can you take the watch?"*

*Dig shifted his position, flicked the safety off his rifle and rested it on his knees.*

*I woke to voices. Vietnamese voices. When I opened my eyes it was absolutely dark. I heard faint snoring to my right. Brief flashes of light flicked on the undersides of leaves. The VC were using flashlights to find their dead, but only for a few seconds at a time.*

*"Time to fucking pray, Mr. Digby," I said under my breath.*

*Squealing broke out. The VC must have disturbed the nest of boars that were sleeping near their abandoned feast. Finally awake, Dig put his hand on my arm.*

*"They're really pissed," I whispered.*

*"We killed their leader," he whispered back. "Some cat named Su Chet. Name mean anything to you?" He put his lips closer to my ear. "Su Chet means death," he went on. "It was the guy's nickname. I read it in an intelligence report. He was a VC sniper, killed over twenty Marines on Hill 55, just south of Elephant Valley."*

*"Shut up, man," I said. We waited until the voices faded.*

*"Shit!" I said. "We should have picked up his rifle!"*

*"Don't worry about it. I cracked the scope's lens," said Dig.*

*"How's the leg?" asked Shiloh.*

*"It's stiffening up, but the swelling's down."*

*"If we don't move out of here soon, they're gonna stumble on us."*

*"I told you I'm staying, man. Can't make it far on this leg anyway. I'll cover you while you crawl out of the hide. Don't get caught up in that Marine-never-leaves-another-Marine-behind shit. I've got a job to do and I'm gonna do it."*

*I slid up the sleeve of my shirt and looked at the luminescent dial of my watch. Four a.m. Daylight would start at five. "Okay, I'm out of here!"*

*I reached my arms out and pulled myself out of our sniper's hide. I crept away from the voices. The earth was soft under my feet and I moved silently.*

*After an hour of painfully slow walking I smelled rot. The Army must have recently sprayed Agent Orange defoliant along the riverbank to expose the VC's hidden boats. Fish were floating on the surface, and leaves dropping from the trees. On my way in I'd looked through my scope and spotted a few Vietnamese farmers gathering the dead fish in baskets.*

*It was past 5:00 a.m. when I reached the river. Just as I stepped into the mud of the riverbank, I heard a shot at some distance behind me. Then more shots. A firefight had broken out. Crouching down in a clump of reeds, I imagined Dig with his wounded leg taking on VC.*

*A sudden movement at the riverbank drew my attention back from the gunfire. I lifted my rifle and skimmed the cross hairs along the tree-lined bank. My scope came to rest on a woman squatting near a large stone. She was rinsing clothes that she took from a basket beside her. Just behind her was a small child, maybe three years old, sitting on a pile of leaves. I watched the woman freeze; she'd heard the shooting. Her raven black hair was tied in a braid that swung from one shoulder to the other as she stood up, tossed the wet clothes in her basket and lifted the child to her hip. She darted toward the jungle path behind her. I followed her, through the scope. As I watched, she cradled the toddler's head close to her breast.*

*I lowered my rifle and stepped deeper into the protectiveness of green cover. I hadn't followed Dig's advice about going over the mountain. I thought the faster way would be better.*

*The rising sun was glinting off the chocolate-colored river. Clusters of decaying fish, belly up, were trapped by bamboo trees that had fallen into the river. The fish reminded me that the purpose of every waking and sleeping hour was to stay alive.*

*I wished I were a child again. I wanted so badly for someone to pick me up, tuck my head into her breast and carry me out of this fucking jungle to safety. I recalled Dig saying, "You'd better be operating on all cylinders at all times. One little mistake, like lighting a cigarette, could cost you your life." That's just how my spotter, David Johnson, bought it.*

*We'd finished a week of reconnaissance in the bush and had returned to base camp, thinking we were out of harm's way. We'd been warned to keep low because of reports of a VC sniper prowling the perimeter of the camp. We'd been functioning at such a high level of fear out in the bush for the last week, surrounded by VC day and night, that base camp seemed like a vacation destination. At base camp men guarded the perimeter at night. We had radio contact to call in air strikes, if needed. We could sleep. It seemed to me more like camping out in someone's backyard – stateside.*

*The night we returned to camp David stepped out of the tent around 9:30 for a cigarette. He could have lit up inside, but he knew I detested smoking and would make fun of him.* He wanted to spare himself that. I heard the click of his Zippo lighter, then the crisp crack of an AK-47 rifle. I crawled out of the tent door to find the top of David's skull gone, smoke still circling up from the cigarette between his lips.

I stared at the river trying to sort out the flood of feelings and pictures that threatened to overwhelm me. I'd never even cried for David when he was killed; there had been no time. The following morning all twelve snipers fanned out into the surrounding area. We stayed out until Sergeant Major sent up a smoke flare to signal that David's sniper had been killed – three days later. I remembered my relief when I saw Sergeant Major holding the sniper's rifle over his head.

By the time I realized it was foolish to leave Dig, only an hour of darkness remained. Only an hour's worth of time in which it was safe to move. But I couldn't bear the tension of sitting still a minute longer. I figured that by now Dig had been killed or had passed out from fever.

I'd waited too long. Looking at the brightness caught by the bamboo, I knew I'd have to stay hidden until dark. It was too dangerous to move. I crawled to a slight rise behind my position and made a sniper's hide. I started waiting.

Time inched by. Blotches of sweat widened from the armpits of my camo shirt. My belly was knotted with hunger and I wondered about the food I'd left for Dig. Should I have taken it because I was the only one who was trying to get back to base camp? Dig was surely dead by now. I felt a deep ache inside. I wanted to vomit, but my mouth felt like it had been filled with cotton and there was nothing in my stomach to come up.

Thirst and hunger were demanding too much of my conscious thought. This distraction was unsafe; all my senses needed to be available for a more fundamental need.

I took off my boots and rolled up my pants to get air to the infected leech bites on my calves. My boots needed airing, too. I took out the insoles and laid them in a spot of sunlight that came through the leaves of the hide.

A sour odor arose from my feet when I spread my toes. A white mold was growing between them. While scanning the riverbank with the high-powered scope I picked at the rotting skin between my toes. Tearing off patches of skin I mindlessly rolled them between forefinger and thumb and flicked them away like spitballs pitched in high school. My mind was somewhere else.

It was back with Digby. As the minutes passed, I became increasingly horrified to recall how easily I'd accepted his refusal to come with me. Marines don't leave fellow Marines behind. This was the one Marine lesson that made sense to me. How did I ever think I'd be able to live with myself in the future if I left Dig alone in the jungle to die? Living with that kind of guilt would be worse than living with the guilt I felt for all the VC I'd killed. I couldn't leave Nam knowing I hadn't done all I could to save my Marine brother.

The sun was beginning its descent over Hill 55 when I decided to put my boots on and go back for Dig, dead or alive.

Darkness fell like black silk over the shoulders of the hill. As shadows rushed toward me I stretched. I went over a plan in my head that I'd broken down into three parts. First, I'd make my way back to the place where I'd left Dig. I'd scout out the area to see if he was alive and try to alert him to my presence. I could be killed by Dig as easily as by the VC.

The second phase was to get to the spot on the river where I'd seen a piece of timber lodged against the shore. It looked like it might have come from a bridge that had been blown up. If Dig and I could make it to the timber, maybe we could float downstream until we reached Min Wa, at an oxbow in the river. From there it was only a few miles through thick jungle to the Recon camp.

In the third phase I would leave Dig in a hide and go for help. If he was dead, I'd make a new plan.

My legs shook with the first steps. The moon peeked out from behind a bank of large cumulus clouds stacked high in the sky. I wondered if I could get back to Dig before the storm. A few steps from the hide I crossed an open area that looked like a bomb crater. Quickly stepping past this opening I made my way to the cover of the tree line.

It felt good to be moving my shoulders. They'd relaxed from being up around my ears. I could taste the sweet night air. I smelled wood smoke with a hint of fish cooking and began salivating.

I'd smeared mud on my face and felt like somehow I belonged to the night. In this war the Americans owned the days; the Viet Cong, the nights. VC attacks always came in the cover of darkness. I let myself think that no self-respecting VC could imagine a white man creeping around in an unknown jungle at night. The extra layer of dark cover provided by the foliage felt like a bulletproof blanket draped over my shoulders.

*I stuck my arm through the rifle sling and swung it over my head and shoulder so it hung diagonally across my back, giving me the use of both arms. I held my arms out in front of me and navigated by touch as much as by looking for landmarks in the mountains and trees. As I got closer it was hard to keep hoping that Dig had survived. He'd seemed almost delirious when I'd left him twelve hours ago. I knew that if he'd been attacked, he wouldn't have been able to do more than empty his clip of ammo. But I pushed on, also knowing that if anyone could have stayed alive, it was Dig.*

*After two hours of inching my way forward, a break in the clouds silhouetted the skyline. I recognized the crowns of two familiar trees against the luminescent night sky. I listened to the echo of a distant boom and wondered if it was artillery or the thunder of the approaching storm. The night sounds of the jungle, the distant barking of a dog and the peeping of small night creatures made nightmare music. My arms out in front, I struck a low limb and pushed it aside.*

*I heard a faint sound, familiar but out of place. I cupped both hands behind my ears and waited for the sound to come again. It was human. Someone was whimpering.*

*Making my way toward the moaning, I stopped between each step and tried to make a picture in my mind's eye. When the whimpering stopped, I stopped. I peered into the dark to see where it was coming from. Moonlight stole through the canopy and glinted off the smooth surface of low-lying leaves. I saw nothing. Crouching, I started a slow crawl, shifting my shoulders back and trying to ease the pressure of the rifle strap, which was cutting into my neck muscles.*

*Now I recognized the sound: it was a woman weeping. Her voice swelled and heaved with emotion. Squatting in the dark I imagined her maybe ten yards away. I caught some Vietnamese words between her sobs. It sounded as if she was singing a lullaby I'd heard once, being sung by a mother to her child in the ville near the Recon camp.*

*The moon came out from behind the clouds and I saw the woman in monochromatic light. She sat behind a man, her arms wrapped around him. The man's head hung down and moved freely, back and forth. A lump came up into my throat. I listened to the woman's sorrowful words. Her voice climbed the scales of the tune, only to fall off into halting, guttural sobs.*

*Little by little I worked the rifle strap over my head and put the rifle to my shoulder. I remembered the woman I'd been watching through my scope at the river.*

*Was this the same woman? Had she come out into the jungle to look for a husband who'd not returned? The picture of her carrying the small child who clung to her breast came to me.*

*Waiting for another break in the clouds, I thought about shooting her. I didn't want to, but there seemed to be nothing else I could do. I had to keep looking for Dig and she was sitting right where I needed to pass. I could see no other choice. If she heard or saw me she'd certainly cry for help. The Viet Cong would cover the place in minutes. The moon broke and I sighted the rifle only to lower it back to my lap – I changed my mind. Even with the sound suppressor, a shot would draw VC from all over the jungle. I'd have to kill her with my hands.*

*I wiped the sweat dripping from my forehead on the sleeve of my forearm. Mouth dry and arms tight with tension, I transferred my weight in order to continue my crawl toward her. I placed my KA-BAR knife in my mouth and had just parted a clump of heavy leaves when a deep roar came from nearby, freezing me. The hair on my neck bristled. Bushes and branches were breaking just beyond where the woman and man had been rocking. Her crying stopped completely. Another cavernous roar and I imagined a tiger. I sat back on my butt, bringing the rifle to my shoulder. Then came the thrashing of bushes, a high squeal and the sound of someone running away.*

*I waited, my rifle at the ready, thinking it was likely the tiger had been stalking the crying woman. I decided to stand and cautiously moved into the small clearing. I squatted beside the dark silhouette in the center. The dead man was hard to see in the moonlight, but I could make out a large splotch on his abdomen. I touched his throat and fingered the epaulets on his collar. He was wearing a uniform; must have been an officer. And an NVA regular. I reached inside the dead man's shirt, checking for documents, and found nothing but a hairless chest.*

*A familiar voice slipped out of the dense layers of night, so casual it sounded like someone picking up the other side of a conversation. "Thought I told you to get the hell out of here."*

*I recognized the voice but my instincts slammed my rifle to my shoulder and pointed it toward the voice. "Dig!"*

*"Yeah, it's me. Not dead, after all."*

*"Shit, man, there's a tiger somewhere around here." As if on cue, a hair-raising roar came from the jungle.*

*Dig was dragging his leg. "I already checked him. He had a map and a few papers that looked important. I only had a match and couldn't read them well," Dig mumbled between forced breaths.*

*"Think that was his wife?" I asked.*

*"Yeah, she was singing him a lullaby to send him off to Buddha land. Didn't want him drifting around as a ghost, never finding any peace. You can be sure she'll be back." Dig looked in the direction of the roar. "Well, maybe not."*

*"There's got to be a lot of those VC souls floating around. What's with the leg?"*

*"You'd have been back home if you hadn't come to find me!"*

*"Yeah, that's right. And if a frog had a body temperature of 360, ate clay and had a square asshole, he'd shit bricks."*

*I heard a soft chuckle. "They teach you that in sniper school?"*

*"No! They taught me that Marines don't leave Marines behind."*

*"This Marine's going to get you killed if you don't get out of here. I can't make the hill. You gotta understand that, man. I can't make it, period. Makes no sense to bring you down with me."*

*"Drop the hero shit. I've got a way out. We don't have to go over Hill 55. I spotted a timber floating in the river. We can use it to float down to Min Wa. Then it's just a few miles to Recon camp. I can put you in a hide and go for help. Maybe we can get a chopper to medevac you."*

*"I told you there were only two ways out, the river or the hill. The odds of making it down to Min Wa are about the same as the odds of Lieutenant Charlie here sitting up and shaking my hand."*

*"Got any water left?" I asked.*

*"Left it behind. Didn't think I'd live long enough to use it."*

*"Stupid, fucking stupid. Listen, man. I'm going to get your ass out of this jungle whether you like it or not. In two minutes we're going to head out. Give me your pack and rifle, so you're free to walk."*

*"Left the pack behind. I buried it."*

*"Give me the goddamn rifle."*

*"There ain't no man gonna take my rifle."*

*"Get your ass up; we're leaving. I'm going to walk point. You stay right behind me."*

*"Aye aye, sir!" Dig softly barked.*

*It took us over three hours to reach the riverbank. Dig's groans let me know how much pain the man was in. I scanned the river, looking for the timber. Faint fires flickered behind the trees, showing me where the village was. I scoured the bank until I spotted the timber in shadows from the moon.*

*I told Dig to sit and rest while I dislodged the tree. It was still several yards to the river and I told Dig I'd be back for him in a few minutes. Dig was silent; he hadn't spoken for a while. I took hold of his arm and felt his strength ebbing.*

*"I'll cover you," he whispered, surprising me. "A whistle means someone's coming."*

*Sliding down the slick, muddy bank, I waded into the warm water. Instantly I thought of a movie I'd seen on TV as a kid. The hero of the story, an explorer, dipped a dead sheep into a piranha-infested river. Two minutes later he brought up the remains: a string of bones. I had no idea if piranha were native to Vietnam. I forced my mind to remember the litany of information I'd heard in jungle training lectures.*

*I started sorting through the seemingly endless stream of words about night navigation, calling in artillery and disarming booby traps. Where were the lessons about the rivers of Vietnam? Nothing came to mind. I decided to take the next step.*

*I reached for the nearest branch. Its wet bark, combined with the subtle undulation of the river, made it feel alive. Yanking it with both hands, I moved the tree limb that had been blocking the timber partially out of the way. Then I let go of the timber and went back to get Dig.*

*I felt the gentle current of the river against my legs and knew we'd be able to travel much faster by floating in the river than by trying to crawl over Hill 55 in the dark. As I climbed the riverbank, my boots made a squishing sound; water squirting out of the vent holes. I found Dig asleep. He look like he wouldn't make it much longer without medical attention. In the dim light I watched as his face twitched. I cleared my throat several times before Dig woke. "Ready? We got to get you down to the bank. The water's warm. It'll feel good on your leg."*

*Dig slid on his butt down the riverbank, his rifle in one hand. Chest deep in the water, he took hold of my free arm and I gently pulled him to the timber. "Wrap your arm around it," I told him.*

*Waist deep in the river, I pulled my belt free of my pants. Looping it under Dig's belt and back around the timber, I secured him to the tree. Then, standing between the tree and the bank with both feet firmly planted in the mud, I shoved the timber toward the center of the river. Reaching up, I took hold of my rifle and sloshed toward Dig, whose left arm floated lifeless at his side while his right hand gripped his rifle tightly.*

*"You okay?" I whispered.*

*"Nice boat. This belt's cutting me in half, but it's a smooth ride," Dig said.*

*I reached over and loosened the belt a little. Then I surveyed the area. The moonlight drew silver streaks on the black water. Trees towered over the river, running long fingers of dark gloom out toward the center. Watching the silhouettes of the trees, I noticed the sky was free of clouds. A soft breeze signaled that a front was moving in. I thought I saw a flicker of firelight between trees on the left bank and guessed it was the place where I'd watched the woman washing her clothes. The silence on the river was absolute. Only occasional distant booms of weaponry broke the stillness.*

# ✦✦ CHAPTER FIFTY-EIGHT ✦✦

"You've been a long time reading. Would you like me to put up some tea?" Shiloh said, getting up from the chair opposite Phyllis.

Phyllis laid the manuscript on the coffee table and stared at him.

"What's the matter?" he asked, sitting down next to her.

"I had no idea of where you truly were back then."

He took her hand in his. "I know. How could you? I never wanted to take you there – even in conversation." The two looked at each other in silence for a moment.

"And you know what?" he continued. "It wouldn't have made any difference if you *had* known. I needed to go back there myself, in order to truly leave that place behind. And I *have*, Phyllis. I *have* left it behind, once and for all." Shiloh smiled. "I tried coming home once before, but I wasn't ready; I hadn't left the war. This time I'm really home."

##  EPILOGUE

The air coming in the open window carried the caw of the split-tailed grackles sitting in the palm tree, and the scent of bougainvillea blooming on the garden fence in Jake's backyard. He sat in front of his laptop, which lay open on the kitchen table. Both hands around a mug of coffee, he read the sentences on the screen aloud.

Naomi, my sweet heart,

I cannot wait for you to arrive. I've been marking off the days on the calendar like I did when I was waiting to leave Nam. I know we have a lot to work out, but during the last nine months I've found important answers to what's been wrong. So I have reason to be full of hope.

Like I told you in other emails, I've been attending an event called the Veteran Civilian Dialogues, or VCD. It's not therapy or self-help. It's just a get-together of folks who are open to talking about the human consequences of war. Our kind of people, huh? God only knows, you and I have been holding meetings like this since forever.

I'm starting to understand that I've been suffering from a

"moral dislocation." It's a term that grew out of one that Jonathan Shay the famous VA psychiatrist came up with "moral injury", in his book *"Odysseus in Vietnam"* I changed it to dislocation, I just didn't want to feel injured. You know how I hate jargon, but this particular term really seems true and necessary to me. Can you think of any other word or phrase that conveys this meaning so precisely?

Talking at the VCD has made it more obvious to me that it's not so much the trauma of war as the *moral pain of killing* that's been tearing me up inside. As a Marine, I've always accepted that I had no choice but to do my job. If I hadn't, I would've been killed. Or one of my men would've been killed. I know the reality was that I had no choice, but still, something inside me could never accept this. I've been finding out that even though my mind – and my body, for that matter – was willing to agree to kill, my soul wouldn't accept the killing I'd done.

I started to really understand this in one of the VCD groups with a World War II vet named Herb. You should have seen the ears on this cat. Huge! And man, could he use them. We were in a discussion group of about six people. I spoke in the group for almost forty-five minutes. Half the time I was weeping into my hands. Herb didn't say a thing, just kept his hand on my shoulder.

When I looked up toward the end he said, "Son, it's an honor to sit with you. A man who has put his life on the line for me as many times as you have gets my deepest respect. God bless you! Now I want you to hear what I have to say. It took me sixty years to recognize all the guilt and shame I'd lashed to my back. I realized that I knew it was wrong to kill."

"Son, I think that's where you are right now. I know you may not believe this, but if you didn't feel the way you do now, we'd know that you'd lost your soul. I thought I'd lost mine. But I found out I hadn't. And listening to you right now has helped me to bring it even closer. Man, I can't tell you how much I've missed it! It feels so good to have it back."

Herb put his hand on the back of my neck and said, "Keep your ears and eyes open. I think the soul who has loved you since birth is waiting just outside your door. He's been walking all the way from the battlefields of Vietnam, and he's about to knock. Open it if you can."

Then he stood up, pulled me to my feet and embraced me in a big bear hug, potbelly and all. He said, "You have helped me so much today, son. Bless you!"

That's what's been going on for the past few weeks here.

Please send me your flight info so I can be at the airport to pick you up.

I'll sign off with a wish: I wish I were home with you right now, you beautiful woman. It's where I want to be. I love you in my bones.

Jake

Jake, my love,

Your email was like a dove perching in the tree outside the kitchen window. I feel like the last few months of email and phone calls have been the best talks we've ever had. I miss you terribly. But I also still feel hurt that you left so quickly.

I can't wait for vacation. The hospital's been unbelievably busy and we're very short staffed. I see more and more frowns every day when I walk past the nurse's station.

I got a letter from Alma. She says they've moved to a small town near her folks. Howie's got a job in the post office and has gone back to college for a teaching degree. Alma says he wants to teach high school history.

She also says that Pax recently wrote to Howie. He's finishing his tour in Afghanistan in two weeks and wants to visit them.

I saw Phyllis in the supermarket yesterday, and she looked pretty stressed. She said Pax doesn't send her email anymore, only letters. He told her that getting email from her was distracting, and that was dangerous. He also encouraged her to ask Shiloh for help. That was the one thing she felt good about.

On a happier note, Phyllis said that Pax and Nabi might be getting married when Pax gets out.

Back to you and me. I had such hope when I read your email. The phrase "moral dislocation" sounds right. I know you are such a good man at heart. Your ex-students call here almost every day wondering how you're doing.

Speaking of your ex-students, please call the principal's office, Mr. Finn. No, seriously! Mitchell called on Tuesday. He wants you to call him. He's working on next year's schedule and assigning classes. Sounds like he'd love to have you back after your "sabbatical."

Your friend Herb is right. If you didn't care about what happened in the war, or if you found some way to rationalize it, it would just come back, which is what it has kept doing.

The truth, my love, is that we all need to take responsibility for what our soldiers have done and continue doing for us. We need to lift our share instead of letting them carry the entire burden alone.

I just read that the Hebrew translation of "Thou shall not kill," is "Thou shall not murder." Did you know that? I take issue with this translation because I believe that you have never murdered. I know this in the depths of my heart.

Only four days left before I'm with you!  Be at the airport promptly at 12:05, mister, and ready to start a new chapter with me. I can't wait.

Naomi

# The End

# ABOUT THE AUTHOR

Since publishing <u>The Making and Unmaking of a Marine</u> seven years ago Larry took on a leadership role as physiotherapist at Four Winds Hospital where he was the Director of Veterans Treatment. In 2013 Larry retired from Four Winds Hospital, but continues as a Board Member of the Four Winds Foundation.

Larry's work with veterans has involved collaboration from 2010 to 2012 with Scott Thompson of Intersections International; together they developed the Veteran Civilian Dialogue (VCD). The VCD is a program that highlighted the necessity for communication to become part of the healing process for both veterans and civilians. Their program was presented to the Pentagon, and various universities throughout the country. When Scott left Intersections Larry invited Dr. Peter Pitzele, the founder of Bibliodrama, to take his place and together they continued the program for a year where they developed a cohort-training program. Over the years <u>The New York Times</u>, <u>Washing Post</u> and other national and local media have written about the effectiveness of the Veteran Civilian Dialogue.

Larry's second book <u>Brotherkeeper</u> is a novel that explores the relationships of veterans to their families and communities. This latest book arises from his concern for the welfare of veterans as they return to civilian life. That concern has also lead to a collaboration with Dr. Peter Pitzele, and Dr. William Tagale, Dean of Wisdom University. Together they are developing curriculum for a course that will address war's effect on morality. Their premise is that morality is a critical link in understanding Post Traumatic Stress Disorder. They are currently in consultation with Dr. Jonathan Shay author of <u>Odysseus in America</u> and other related books on Post Traumatic Stress Disorder.

Larry spent 1967 to 1971 in the Marines, a combat tour in Vietnam 1969 1970. Larry Winters: went to war, came home from war, and is at war with war!

I left Vietnam in 1970, returned in 1994 to ask for forgiveness from the Vietnamese people, and did not actually take my first full psychological steps home until

2013. At that time I read the expression moral injury in Jonathan Shay's books <u>Achilles in Vietnam: Combat Trauma and the Undoing of Character</u> and <u>Odysseus in America: Combat Trauma and the Trials of Homecoming</u> it was then I realized moral injury had been the reason my soul would not return home. I lost trust in God, American military leadership, political leadership, and my own ability to be able to behave morally in my life after what I had done and not done in the Vietnam War. My many years of working as a psychotherapist with veterans and trauma victims I developed the insight that almost all trauma is about moral injury and the loss of trust. The massive amounts of money spent by the Veterans Admiration for vets with PTSD has not emphasized moral injury, therefore the healing of PTSD is sporadic at best. It is my belief that PTSD and trauma can only be healed by conscious attention of the communities we live in.

If you have found truth within the pages of <u>Brotherkeeper</u>, Larry encourages you to read Dr. Shay's books and to visit Larry's websites **www.lawrencewinters.com** and **www.makingandunmaking.com** where the discussion continues and all are welcome.

Lawrence Winters

larry@lawrencewinters.com

# ABOUT DR. JONATHAN SHAY

Dr. Jonathan Shay is a doctor and clinical psychiatrist. He holds a B.A from Harvard and an M.D. and a Ph.D. from the University of Pennsylvania. He is the author of <u>Achilles in Vietnam</u> and <u>Odysseus in America</u>. Which compare the experiences of veterans with that of Homer's Iliad and Odyssey.

Dr. Shay's work with Posttraumatic Stress Disorder (PTSD) led to the concept of *Moral Injury* as a distinct syndrome from PTSD. In his books Shay describes both the concept of "Moral Injury" and what he believes should be done to help returning veterans make the transition to civilian life:

"I have appealed for renovation in our military institutions to protect service members from psychological and moral injury. In addition to political demands for such renovation, the American citizenry has other work to do. As a society we have found ourselves unable to offer purification to those who do the terrible acts of war on our behalf. I believe this is something to be done jointly by people from all our religions, from the arts, from the mental health professions, and from the ranks of combat veterans— not from the government. What I have in mind is a communal ritual with religious force that recognizes that everyone who has shed blood, no matter how blamelessly, is in need of purification. Those who have done something blameworthy require additional purification and penance, if their religious tradition provides for it. The community as a whole, which sent these young people to train in the profession of arms and to use those arms, is no less in need of purification. Such rituals must be communal for them before they return to civilian life. This new cultural creation also must stay free of the taint of sectarian, political, and ideological partisanship, which would willingly kidnap such a ritual. All modern soldiers go into battle under constraint — they have enough to carry without being blamed or credited with the political decision to fight that battle."

**<u>Odysseus in America: Combat Trauma and the Trials of Homecoming</u>**

**Jonathan Shay M.D.**

www.ingramcontent.com/pod-product-compliance
Lightning Source LLC
Chambersburg PA
CBHW070443030726
47503CB00004B/878